Mum's the Word

Lorraine Turnbull

Copyright

Fat Sheep Press, Le Bois Vert, Lescarpedie, 24220 Meyrals, France.

ISBN 978-1-9163890-7-6

Dedicated to my daughter.

*Love yourself, be yourself and shine like the brightest star
to light the path for others.*

About the author

Lorraine Turnbull wanted to be a farmer since she was five years old. In her mid-forties, she uprooted herself and her family and moved to a run-down bungalow with an acre of land and an Agricultural Occupancy Condition in Cornwall. She retrained as a teacher, worked as a Skills Co-ordinator for The Rural Business School, and started commercial cider making in 2010.

In 2014 she won the Cornwall Sustainability Awards Best Individual category, and successfully removed the Agricultural Occupancy Condition from her home. She moved to France in 2017 and her first book was published in May 2019.

Connect with Lorraine:
Facebook
www.facebook.com/LorraineTurnbullAuthor/
Twitter @Lorraineauthor
Instagram Lorraineauthor

Chapter 1

The head injuries should have been the hardest thing to disguise, but the pigs had done a first-class job. In their excitement, they'd already wrenched the head from the torso and Bull was now missing part of his nose, looking more bull-like now than he had in life.

Ann-Marie carefully removed her Marigolds, and took the other pair from Elaine. The boars were almost sated now and had made a grand job of her dear, departed husband, who now looked as ugly on the outside as he had been inside. The stench of blood, warm meat and pig shit filled her nostrils, and amidst her elation, she felt sick.

'Who would have thought the old man had so much blood in him?' she quoted from Macbeth and turned to her friend, 'Tea?'

They returned to the farmhouse, carrying the gloves and skillet, and she remembered suddenly it was time to give her mother her pills. Boots were carefully removed and placed in the sink alongside the stained Marigolds. Elaine brought in her carrier bag of clothes from her car and went to the downstairs bathroom to change, whilst Ann-Marie filled and boiled the kettle. As she waited, she scrubbed the boots, marigolds and the skillet clean, before setting the tea-tray with three cups and popped two teabags in the pot. She added the two bottles of tablets and a plate with some hobnobs.

***

'Elaine!' she called. 'Tea's out. I'll just take mum's up to her.'

There was a muffled acknowledgement, and Ann-Marie took a deep breath and carried the tray up the stairs. 'Here you go, mum', she said breezily, handing her the tea and the pills, 'I'll just see Elaine away, and come back up to help you dress'.

Isa was sitting up primly in bed with rosy cheeks and glittering eyes. She was looking much better this morning, Ann-Marie noted. This day was getting better and better.

'You've been busy already this morning, and I can wait. This bloody stroke! Take yer time – and say thanks to Elaine…for visiting.'

Ann-Marie fixed a smile on her face. 'Aye, I don't know what I'd do without her,' she said hurrying down the stairs.

'Never heard a thing,' she whispered to Elaine, who was sipping tea, and sat down. It was a perfectly normal morning and she was having a cup of tea with a friend. The only sign of any excitement were their flushed cheeks and bright eyes. Elaine finished her cup and carried it to the sink, ready to take her leave.

'I'll have to get back before Malky's home. He's at the Lodge tonight.'

Of course he was. Bull should have been there too. The most important part of his week.

'Did you wash your hands?'

'Yes.'

'And you'll put your clothes through the wash the minute you get home?'

'YES.'

They had been meticulous as they cleaned up after the event. Every single permutation and possibility had been pored over, examined and discussed for over a fortnight, and in the end, the whole business of killing Bull had been dead easy. Even persuading him to buy in three huge new boars that had helped cover up their crime had been easy. The boars that right now were feasting on his fat carcass.

'D'ye want me to come back later?'

'No, I need to act daft remember, and realise he hasnae come in to get washed and changed, and then *discover* him in the pens, and then make the phone call.'

The friends stared at each other for a few silent seconds.

'I'm glad he's dead. Ah don't know how you didnae kill him years ago!' Elaine spat, her accent having reverted to the original working-class Clydeside.

Ann-Marie shot her a cold stare.

'Quietly,' she hissed, pointing at the ceiling. 'We need to stick to the script and keep our heads. Don't you go drinking tonight and say anything.'

Elaine blushed and grabbed her handbag and car keys. Ann-Marie realised this last comment was unduly harsh and grabbed her friend's hands.

'I'll phone you tomorrow,' she said. 'I couldn't have done it without you. But we have to be careful.'

Their eyes met and they exchanged smiles, then Elaine caught sight of the clock. 'Need to go!' she barked. Yes - they needed to keep to the schedule.

Ann-Marie waved goodbye as her friend's old car left the yard, and returned the now pristine boots outside the farmhouse door. Everything had to be normal, she said to herself. In the kitchen, she changed her clothes and placed all her working clothes in the washer. Silly to take chances, but she was confident that there would be no suspicion; just a tragic farm accident. She just had to carry on as normal, she told herself as she had a quick but thorough shower, and then cleaned the shower afterwards.

She returned to her mum's bedroom, helped the frail woman out of her nightie, washed her gently, and then dressed her as the old woman chattered on about the farm TV programme they'd watch tonight.

'It'll be nice just to sit and relax the two of us together', Isa said, sending Ann-Marie's heart into overdrive, until she remembered it was Lodge night and *would* be just the two of them, like any other Lodge night. She smiled, as she tucked the duvet around her mother. Well, every night would be relaxing from now on, Ann-Marie thought, managing to smother a hysterical giggle.

'You'll be up and about in no time mum. The doctor said we should try and get you walking; at least to the bathroom. It's only been a *mild* stroke.'

Isa stared hard at her, 'No, hen, this is the start of a decline; and yes, maybe I'll recover enough to walk this time, but Ann-Marie; this might just be the *first* stroke. Bad enough you've had to put up with that burden of a man, but I don't want you to have to put up with me too, or *you'll* end up ill. We need to get some help in, just for a short time.'

Ann-Marie sat heavily on the bed and held her mother's hand. The hand that was now red and swollen from years of work on the farm, but still the hand of a loving and caring mother that Ann-Marie adored. She was suddenly exhausted and overwhelmed but mustered a smile from somewhere.

'Don't talk like that. You're not a burden, and you know right now that we can't afford a carer. Let's just see if you get a little stronger, and we'll take it from there. Now, green cardigan or pink?'

'The pink. The green one makes me look like a corpse and I need to feel cheerful to face poor Sadie's visit this afternoon.'

'Great. You can think about how you're going to convince her to divorce that waster of a husband of hers, although I don't think she's got the bottle. Right. I'm going to do some paperwork before I start dinner!' she said changing the subject and walking downstairs to the office.

'I'm working on an idea already!' her mother called though the door.

***

Ann-Marie turned on her computer and set her alarm clock for 2pm. Working on the month's accounts would keep her brain busy, she thought, then she'd take the premade sandwiches upstairs for a late lunch with mum, and somehow get through the rest of the afternoon. The blue screen stared at her, waiting for a command, but the events of earlier that morning kept replaying in her head.

She'd had no choice, she told herself firmly. She angrily recalled that life-changing conversation she'd overheard between Bull and Malky at the last Lodge Ladies Night dinner, before having to endure the forced sex that always followed a Lodge night. That night she finally realised that she had only been a means to an end for all those years. He'd only *ever* wanted the farm, and after everything she'd endured, she was *not* going to risk a divorce.

She exhaled, blowing the hate and the tension out with a long controlled breath. A single tear escaped and ran down her cheek, splashing on the keyboard. She angrily wiped it away, chiding herself for feeling sorry for herself. *Not for him.* She'd never shed a tear for him ever again.

The alarm suddenly rang loudly, wrenching her back to the present with her heart racing madly and the realisation that she'd sat and done nothing for over an hour! She switched the machine off, took a deep breath, collected the tray of sandwiches and juice and carried it upstairs. Her mother was watching some old black and white movie and switched it off.

'Very quiet, isn't it, hen?' Isa mentioned casually, picking up an egg sandwich.

'Bull's out with the pigs, looking at those new boars.' Ann-Marie answered, busying herself pushing straws into the two juice cartons, and avoiding her mother's eyes.

'Aye, well, you've got enough to do. Best not disturb a man whilst he's out with the animals,' her mother said, sipping the juice.

They heard a car pull into the yard, a door slam and a familiar voice call, 'It's just me!' from Sadie, as she climbed the stairs. Ann-Marie tidied the tray and stood up, telling her mother she'd pop down and put the kettle on.

As Sadie entered the bedroom, Ann-Marie gasped in horror as she and her mother looked at a swollen lip and bruised eye on the woman's face.

'Not again!' Isa bellowed.

'Oh, Auntie Sadie! Have you been to hospital?' Ann-Marie said sadly. This wasn't the first time she'd seen her mum's best friend sporting bruises from her husband.

Sadie shook her head and sat down on the bed, dabbing at her eyes, 'It's the drink again. He'd a skinful last night, after losin' £500 on the dogs, an' gave me a pastin'.'

Ann-Marie discreetly left to pop the kettle back on. Poor Sadie needed to pull herself together or retirement was going to be hell if Mark continued to batter her and gamble away all their savings. She cast an eye towards the pig barn. At least *she'd* finally come to her senses and ended Bull's abuse.

She took a fresh pot of tea upstairs and sat with the women for a few minutes.

'I was just saying to Sadie that this nonsense has to stop,' Isa said raising her eyes to her daughter. 'She's still young enough to live without that wastrel.'

Sadie was a good ten years younger than Isa and had just retired, but looked younger than her years, although the frequent bruising on her face was beginning to age her.

Ann-Marie smiled sadly at her, 'Yes, you really do need to divorce him.'

'A *divorce*? And lose half the house? No, we'll need to think of a better solution than that,' Isa frowned and stared hard at Ann-Marie.

Ann-Marie hated that look. A knowing, penetrating stare. Mothers know everything, she remembered with a flush of fear. The phone downstairs began to ring loudly, thankfully giving her an opportunity to escape.

***

The local butcher shop wanted to know if they were sending any pigs to the abattoir, and the phone call distracted her for a moment. She scribbled down the message and absently hung up, before quietly closing the office door, and leaning against it. After just battering her husband to death with a frying pan, the last thing she needed was hearing about Sadie's mess of a marriage. She ran her hand over her eyes, willing herself to keep it together for another few hours and wishing the day would just end.

It was four o'clock before Sadie left, and Ann-Marie began to prepare the supper for her and her mother. It was early, but she needed *something* to do as she watched the clock hands in the kitchen slowly, ever so slowly creep forwards. They wouldn't eat till five because of Isa's medication and the hour was dragging. She couldn't phone the police till five because that's when Bull would normally come in to wash and change. Five o'clock. Tick, tick, tick.

She threw oven chips and two chicken escallops into a tray and put it into the oven, willing herself to continue to act normal as the ticking of the clock seemed to grow louder. Too early! She turned the oven back off and raising her eyes to the ceiling took a deep breath to calm herself.

Tick, tick, tick. A tin of sweetcorn filled a saucepan and was placed on the stove. Ten more minutes before she could turn the oven on. Ten minutes to kill, she thought, going over the events of the day in her head.

Her daughter had phoned her father that morning, wheedling money from him again. Despite her recent separation, Lynda could do no wrong, and was *entitled* to a wee handout, according to her father. Ann-Marie suspected Lynda was having an affair, but had kept silent, preferring to keep her thoughts to herself rather than risk a slap. Oh, yes, she knew how to keep a secret, she sniggered to herself; her heart fluttering as she recalled the events of the past couple of hours.

***

It had all gone *perfectly*. Elaine had arrived mid-morning and patiently listened to him boasting about the new boars, puffing his chest out like a cock on a dung heap. Ann-Marie suggested Elaine should come to see them; how Bull had a real eye for quality stock. It was the opportunity they needed and he couldn't resist the chance to brag. *So* easy. The women donned their yellow Marigold's and followed him as he strode into the pig shed.

He clambered on top of the concrete wall of the pig pen, towering above them, bragging crudely. The in-heat sows were housed in the pen next-but-one to tease the boars, and they were frothing at the mouth in excitement.

'I'm telling you Elaine, those sows'll know they've been shagged by a champion! They'll be walkin' like John Wayne for a week.'

The women stood slightly behind him, looking up as he mouthed his final crude throwaway comment.

'Aye, Ann knows what its like to be shagged by a champion, don't you hen?' he laughed nastily.

She nodded to Elaine who sharply pulled Bull's ankles, sending him crashing head-first into the pig pen. Ann-Marie leapt forward; and pulling the cast-iron skillet from behind her back swung as hard as she could at his head, as he tried to push himself up on to all fours cursing. He turned his bloody face upwards to receive the final massive blow.

He'd hardly made a sound; not that you could hear anything over the noise made by the pigs squealing loudly at the sudden chaos. A pool of blood haloed around his head. The women stood breathing quickly, anxiously looking for any sign of life for what seemed like an age. Finally, after all those years she was free.

It was Elaine who spoke first. 'Definitely pan-breed,' she giggled hysterically.

Ann-Marie rolled her eyes, but determined to cover any sign of the attack, she picked up and threw a bucket of pig nuts over the carcass and let the boars in from the adjoining pen. Starved from the night before, they squealed with excitement as they rushed to feast, whilst the women stood and watched.

'Aye, definitely deid.'

***

She reflected on the final insult that had sealed his fate. He always called her Ann. Hated the Catholicism of the name Ann-Marie. Bad enough to have married a Catholic, he had told Elaine's husband Malky, but it was the only way to get the farm.

She'd overheard this at the last Lodge dinner; a ladies night, when the wives and girlfriends were invited. This and the customary rape at home afterwards filled her with a consuming cold rage. Rough justice, she thought. Perhaps her father would be looking down on her and understand the sin she had committed. He'd always hated Bull and their marriage.

Not that she'd be going to confession, she laughed, as she imagined the fantasy confession in her head. Forgive me Father for I have sinned. It's been 31 years since my last confession and I've just put my husband out of my misery...

Being a Catholic married to a Protestant was still, even these days, a bit of a taboo in Glasgow. She recalled the shouting from her father and the tears from her mother when she told them that she and Billy were getting married. And after the shouting, the shameful silence when she tearfully told them she *had* to get married. An abortion was out of the question, of course and her father told her she'd made her bed and had to lie on it now. She'd been too ashamed to tell her parents that he'd forced her and was a bully, even back then.

As the only child, she'd inherit the farm, but after her father died, Billy insisted on developing the pig side, and dominated the two women. As their profits increased so had Billy's girth, leading to the nickname of *Bull* he gained ten years ago when he started to balloon out. The increasingly frequent arguments over the running of the farm led to his shocking announcement a fortnight ago that he wanted to sell up.

Lynda; always *her father's daughter*, smelt a windfall and took his side against her mother and grandmother. Ann-Marie was convinced this is what had caused her mother's stroke and was the final straw.

Pushing the memory away angrily, she stood up and turned the oven on. 'Hell mend you Billy Ross! It's *my* farm and *I'll* decide what's happening to it!' she said aloud, her hands shaking and her heart racing.

'Calm,' she told herself taking a deep breath and expelling it slowly.

Tick, tick, tick. Her heart had picked up the rhythm of the clock and was banging in her chest. Would this day *never* end? She turned the oven on at a quarter past four.

***

Eventually, she took dinner upstairs for her and her mother, and forced down a couple of forkfuls, before taking a deep breath and saying, 'Billy should have been in by now to get changed.'

Isa looked at the clock on the wall and grunted, 'He'll be late then.'

'He's been in that barn with the pigs all day.' Ann-Marie said carefully. She *stupidly* hadn't rehearsed this bit and lying to her mother was harder than she imagined.

Her mother stopped eating and put her knife and fork down on the tray.

'Well, you'd better go and shout him I suppose,' she said grimly.

With a thumping heart, Ann-Marie escaped down the stairs, opened the door to the yard and called his name. 'Billy!'

So *stupid*, she said to herself. He'd *never* answer. She *knew* he'd never answer. But, technically, her mother was a witness and *had* to be able to hear her calling. She called a second time, louder. Part of the game.

'BILLY!'

She tried to imagine what she *should* do next. Well; go see if he was in the barn, she thought. That's what she would have done normally. She pulled on her wellingtons and walked over to the barn, knowing that he'd never respond to her calls, thank God; but going through the motions all the same. She hesitated at the door for a second before entering. The pigs were where she'd left them, and Bull was where she'd left him too. She tried not to look as she lifted a bucket with some feed nuts and coaxed the boars into the empty pen, and then headed back to the house to make the phone call.

Chapter 2

In a flustered voice she told the operator that she didn't know what service she needed; that she'd just found her husband in the pig pen and thought he was dead. She didn't need to fake the anxiety in her voice and her hands were shaking as she told the prepared story and then replaced the receiver.

Then, after a deep breath to steady herself, she went upstairs to tell her mother, who listened to the same story without interruption as Ann Marie's voice shook. There was an uncomfortably long silence before Isa spoke. 'You need to hold it together now Ann-Marie. I know you're upset and I cannae help you. What's happened has happened, and we need to deal with it. Keep your head and remember; you're in *shock.*'

Ann-Marie nodded woodenly and headed downstairs, whilst taking deep breaths to steady her jangling nerves. What a strange response, she wondered as she sat waiting for the emergency services to arrive.

***

A short time later, she led the paramedics and the police ashen-faced to the barn, whilst explaining she'd only just found him there, and had moved the pigs into the next pen. She realised he was dead when she saw him. The paramedic made a quick examination and turned to the policeman, shaking his head. Ann-Marie walked outside the barn, leaning on the door for support. Being there again; knowing he was lying just a few feet away, combined with the police, the pigs squealing, the smell, having to behave normally *and* act the grieving widow all endowed her with a white face, racing heart and the appearance of extreme shock. A policeman guided her into the kitchen and forced her to sit on a chair, whilst more police cars and a van arrived in the yard. Men appeared in white paper suits, she saw through the open kitchen door, and a couple of cops stood outside talking quietly but earnestly and darting occasional looks in her direction.

Bureaucracy took over, and through the open door she saw police tape appear across the barn doors. The ambulance drove away. Had they taken Bull? She wasn't sure. Questions. A policewoman appeared and made her a cup of tea. Disgustingly milky, she set it on the table untouched. She wasn't really taking it all in. She hoped they *saw* she was in shock. She'd never felt so scared in her life, but was fervently praying that she could pull it off. *A tragic accident*; she'd overheard from one of the cops.

She'd made a statement which was written down, and mentioned that Elaine had been there this morning, and her mother was ill upstairs, oh; and her mother's friend had visited this afternoon. Nothing unusual, and no, she hadn't heard anything unusual.

Meanwhile, her mind was in overdrive. Elaine would be waiting at home for the police to arrive. Then she'd have to tell Malky about the accident. She prayed that Elaine could manage without mucking it up, and she would *of course* phone her son, Calum, who was a DC based at London Road in Glasgow. The police woman had gone upstairs to take a statement from her mother and now returned to tell Ann-Marie that someone was on their way to inform Lynda. Ann-Marie realised her mother must have told her that. The well-oiled police machine was collecting all the information they needed for what appeared to be a tragic farm accident.

***

A few minutes later the phone rang and Ann-Marie had to endure Lynda wailing hysterically. She wanted to come and see her father but didn't want to bring the kids and couldn't get anyone to watch them.

Not one word asking how I am, Ann Marie thought clenching her teeth. She kept the call short, trying to fool her daughter that she was distraught was harder than she thought; she just felt matter-of-fact and detached, so was relieved when Lynda said, 'You're in shock mum; call the doctor. Get Elaine to come and stay the night.'

'No, I'm okay. I'm just tired… and I need to eat something. We'll talk in the morning.'

She replaced the receiver and then pulled the cord from the socket. The detective turned an inquiring look to her. 'It's a small world and I don't want to talk to anyone else,' she said squeezing another tear out, and poured herself a glass of water at the sink. She'd need to drink a couple of glasses to replace the tears she'd squeezed out today she thought, but they were far fewer than she'd shed in the past.

It seemed like a lifetime before they took the body away and left; well; all of them except an officer at the gate; *guarding the locus,* the detective told her. There would have to be a post-mortem and a Fatal Accident Enquiry because Billy had died at his place of work, and they would return the next day. Before leaving, he expressed his condolences as a matter of course, and asked if she wanted anyone there. Ann-Marie shook her head and said 'I really need something to eat! Oh – *the pigs*! I need to feed the pigs!'

The officer stared at her in horror, before realising that there were *other* livestock, not just the pigs that'd killed that poor sod in the barn. Livestock, of course needed fed and watered. 'Just tell me what they need and I'll get someone to feed them,' he said and barked an order to an officer at the door to find the food and feed the animals.

'Try and rest Mrs Ross. I know you'll probably not sleep, but I'll come back in the morning and we can see if we can contact some local farmers to help you out. You said there's no staff here, isn't that right?'

'Yes. We only have fruit pickers in from August till December. Bull…*Billy* liked to do everything himself regarding the pigs.'

'Well, I'll see you tomorrow' he said shaking her hand, 'and again - I'm sorry for your loss.'

It seemed like hours later when she finally shut the door. Silence filled the room and she sunk into a chair, going over the many conversations and questions since they had arrived. Who knew murder was so bloody tiring? she thought.

When she returned to her mother's bedroom, she was thankfully asleep. Ann-Marie turned the light off and crept downstairs to drink two large whiskies; she'd have no sleep tonight.

***

The next day everyone arrived early, starting with Lynda, who'd finally found someone to look after the kids. She arrived red-eyed and insisted on visiting the barn where the accident had happened; much to the annoyance of the cop who'd been posted all night to protect the scene and received a verbal foul-mouthed volley from her for his trouble. Ann-Marie pulled her back to the house and spent an uncomfortable hour with her until Elaine, Malky and their son Calum had turned up. Elaine had brought an overnight bag and was staying, thank God.

Lynda demanded to go to the mortuary, but Calum calmed her down and explained that she'd have to wait till after the post-mortem. A police car arrived to collect the police officer, and left shortly afterwards, leaving a card with the contact details of the DI who was in charge of the case. There were phone calls from the newspapers, which Calum dealt with, and he tried to explain the procedure that was unavoidable but now taking place. The post mortem would be done the following day but the investigation for the FAI would take months.

'FAI?' asked Ann-Marie.

'Fatal Accident Inquiry,' Calum explained. 'A sudden death report will be filed and sent to the Fiscal...the

Procurator Fiscal. If the PM is okay you'll get the death certificate and be able to plan the funeral.'

Elaine had insisted he come, and it added legitimacy to the situation, Ann-Marie thought as Calum repeated the procedure to Lynda for a second time.

A few local farmers had dropped off sympathy cards and offers of help, but she told them all that she was fine and would manage, and that she really wanted to be left alone. With her grief.

***

To Ann-Marie's relief, Lynda decided to take charge of phoning the relatives. She told Lynda she couldn't face it; but in reality she hated his family, and Lynda would ensure that the right *note* would be communicated. Malky told her the Lodge would be there for her if she needed anything. She almost laughed out loud but thanked him and said she really just needed time. At the end of the afternoon, after feeding and settling her mother, she and Elaine were finally alone and could talk.

She poured two large whiskies and they sat in front of the fire in the living room. Neither of them spoke for some time before Elaine lifted her glass in a toast,

'To the future.'

Ann-Marie downed the whisky in one. 'I think that went rather well, to be honest,' she said with a tired smile.

'It's in the Paisley 'papers',' said Elaine handing her a copy. The front page was explicit. 'LOCAL FARMER KILLED AND EATEN BY PIGS' it announced with a colour photo of the farmhouse with policemen outside. Ann-Marie folded it and placed it on the table.

'Calum said it's all just procedure, and apart from the accident hitting the 'papers you should be able to return to some sort of normality in a few weeks. The post-mortem'll be tomorrow, and then you'll get the death certificate and be able to plan the funeral. He's got a pal at Paisley CID who said it's just a formality.'

'They told me that. He's lying in a fridge apparently, and not roasting in hell; well, not yet.'

Elaine cackled quietly. 'I told them we were in the house the whole time, and that I only saw him when I arrived at half twelve. I said he'd had his dinner an' gone back to the barn to do the pigs; and that I left at half one. They thought it funny that everyone calls him 'Bull' and not Billy. Malky had to give them a statement too. I don't think we'll hear anything else till after the post-mortem. But they did say that there will be a Fatal Accident Enquiry as he died on the farm. That's normal Calum says.'

She got up and poured herself another whisky. 'Malky was very concerned about Lynda. He's gone over to see her as she's on her own as the kids are away to their father's for a couple of days,' Elaine confided.

'I'm surprised. I thought she'd have had her fancy-man in to *comfort* her.' Ann-Marie said crossly.

'Are you sure about that?'

'Och aye, - that's why her and David split up. He came to see me before Christmas, told me he was convinced there was someone else. You know – the phone rings and when you answer they hang up? And her always going out to see 'a friend' who's having problems? And have you no' noticed that she's started to doll herself up a bit?

26

Why is she doing all that if she's separated?'

At that moment the phone rang. 'Speak of the devil,' she said to Elaine as she saw Lynda's number on the caller display and picked up the receiver.

'Are you okay mum?'

'Aye, Elaine's here and going to stay the night. Have you told everyone now? Not that there is much we can tell them – about a funeral and all that…'

'Well, I've got most of them. It's been a terrible shock of course. Malky… popped by and asked if he could get me anything. He wanted to know if you wanted a Masonic funeral….I said probably not, but said I'd ask you.'

Ann-Marie rolled her eyes and shook her head, but said nothing, allowing Lynda to rabbit on.

'Uncle Bobby wanted to know if you were going to keep the farm on now?'

Ann Marie stiffened. Always looking to make a buck; but that was fast even for Bobby!

'Mum?'

'Lynda – it really is *far* too early for me to even think of that! Your father just died yesterday.' She shot a look at Elaine, who was listening intently, who almost choked on her whisky.

'Right now, I've got enough on my plate dealing with that. I'm not even thinking of what happens after today. Tell Bobby that I *don't* want to discuss the farm at all for the time being. Christ Almighty – he's not even cold yet!' This last comment finally managed to shut Lynda up.

'Right, well…Malky's still here so I'll pass on about the funeral. He wants to know if Elaine is staying at yours? If she is he'll get a take-away tonight.'

'Yeah, Elaine is going to cook something, then I'm having a bath and I'll try to get some sleep. It's been a long day.'

'Alright mum. I'll call you tomorrow. Try and rest.'

The phone went dead before Ann-Marie had even said goodbye and she replaced it with a bang. 'Well, that didn't take long did it?' Ann Marie exclaimed to Elaine, 'Bull's no' even cold and Bobby wants to know what I'm doing about the farm! I wonder if she was the one that put the idea in his head?'

'I heard. That's just not on. Well, ye can choose yer friends…but *family?* No. At least Malky's looking after her. So; what do you want to eat? Will *we* get a take-away? Indian? Chinese? I'm guessing you don't want pork?'

They stared at each other for a second and burst out laughing.

Chapter 3

Malky watched Lynda walk naked to the ensuite with a sly smile. Even after two kids she was still a good-looking woman and liked the 'attention' he was more than happy to give her. They had been seeing each other since December despite David's increasing suspicions. Unfortunately, Lynda had inherited her father's temper and a slanging match just after Christmas had ended with David shouting accusations and then packing a bag and walking out. Elaine had told him that the couple were *having problems*, but didn't elaborate, but then, she didn't have to.

After a week of enforced abstinence, Malky booked a room in a cheap motorway hotel, where they spent a few stolen hours before he had to shower off the smell of sex and perfume before furtively returning home to dowdy but dependable Elaine. He was enjoying the thrill of no-strings sex with a younger woman, but whilst Lynda's appetite excited him, he had to be careful. Jesus, Elaine would take him to the cleaners if she found out, and his name would be mud at the Lodge!

But Lynda was a determined sexy minx. She was always gagging for it and despite the risk, he just couldn't resist when she phoned dangling the bait in her husky voice. She was lucky to have him; a man in his prime who knew how to give women exactly what they wanted, he smiled. Anyhow, Elaine was away at Ann-Marie's tonight, and Lynda's kids were at David's, so he could enjoy her all night, he smiled.

***

Another raw sunny day dawned and Ann-Marie had a coffee with Elaine before she left, and then, after having a brief silent breakfast with her mother, headed out to feed the pigs. Apart from the boars, there were now just a dozen pregnant sows. She opened the barn doors wide to let in a cleansing breeze. The police had hosed out the bloody empty pen where Bull had died, but she avoided it all the same.

Might as well go the whole hog, she joked to herself, and started to clean a couple of the pens. She turned the radio on quietly and soon banter and catchy pop music was filling the silence. She worked briskly, cleaning and bedding up the pens before moving the sows into them.

Meanwhile, the boars watched her from the pen they'd been moved into after the accident. They stared at her, and she wondered what they were thinking? Pigs were too clever. She'd never liked them much, and their small knowing eyes followed her as she replaced the barrow and tools by the door. Bull had loved the pork. Big pork steaks or dry-cured rashers heaped on a plate with sausages. His huge appetite made quick work of any food, but how he loved his pork. She'd always told Bull that too much bacon would kill him, and yet again, she'd been proved right, she thought with a smile, and returned to the house for dinner.

Her mother was feeling a little better today, and managed to half-dress herself. They were both more cheerful, and Ann-Marie wondered if part of the reason was that her mother was pleased that Bull was no longer around. Since his death they had both avoided talking about him, which suited her fine. They ate quietly, until interrupted by the shrill ringing of the phone.

The Liaison Officer from the Police informed her that the post-mortem had been concluded, and she could now get the death registered and organise the funeral. Ann-Marie took a deep breath. Nothing had been flagged up by the post-mortem, and she was in the clear. Elated, she quickly rang Elaine, who agreed to come over so they could collect the paperwork together.

A squeal from the barn brought the boars sharply to mind again. She wanted them gone, and the horrible memories with them. She could hardly put them into the food chain; although the thought of selling pork to the Lodge for their next Lodge dinner made her giggle. No, they'd have to be destroyed. Terrible waste, but no matter; they had done her a wonderful service. She phoned the local abattoir to arrange their disposal.

They'd been expecting her to call, the foreman told her, 'Awful business Ann. I'm so sorry. If it's a help to you we can come out and collect them tomorrow, then you'll no' have them there at least. You don't need that right now.'

'That's very good of you Alan. There's three in total, a bit feisty - Obviously.' Talk about stating the bloody obvious, she thought, rolling her eyes.

'I'll get Ian and Davie to come and kill and remove them in the morning. About nine, ok?'

'That's great; I'll get the movement forms ready for you. Thank you Alan,' she said, hanging up.

Alan turned to the other man in the office, 'You owe me a tenner. I told you she'd have they pigs shot.' And he bellowed through the door to the cutting room, 'Davie! Tomorrow, first thing - take the gun and go to the Ross's to kill and bring those pigs!'

He got a thumbs-up from Davie who returned to his butchery.

Ann-Marie was thankful that she didn't have a stream of visitors calling to offer sympathy. A handful of cards had dropped through the letterbox, but she'd drawn the curtains against callers, and after lunch retreated to her living room and the friendly and comforting glow of the fire. She'd had a few nasty flashbacks to the events of yesterday, which she reasoned was probably to be expected for a while, but they crowded in when she was tired. And she *was* tired. She grabbed a blanket from the bedroom and returned to the sofa to close her eyes for a while. She hadn't slept the night before, and decided to sleep downstairs until she had cleared their bedroom of everything that reminded her of him. Her mother had agreed that getting life back to normal was important, but even she had seemed surprised at Ann-Marie's haste.

The next morning she woke stiff and sore and slowly began the routine chores. The abattoir truck arrived just before nine, and she showed Davie and his assistant where they were, handed over the paperwork and then returned to the house whilst they dispatched the boars and loaded them into the truck. Isa had managed to get to the toilet herself, delighting Ann-Marie and they enjoyed a coffee together, until Davie chapped the door about forty minutes later, telling her he'd hosed out the pens for her, and after handing her a sympathy card, returned to his truck.

With the boars gone she could relax a little more, and over lunch, she sounded her mother out on the possible way forward for the farm. Was it too soon, she asked? Rather than concentrate on commercial pork, she wanted to return to cider and juice production, with some farm-produced meat for sale. She'd have to take on some staff, she explained, but her mother enthusiastically approved.

After this, she spent a good hour upstairs emptying the bedroom of all Bull's personal things, before stripping the bed and putting on clean bedding. She was just making a pot of tea when a car drove into the yard. With a groan she recognised Bull's brother and sister.

'Who's that?' called her mother from upstairs.

'Bobby and Liz.'

'Tell them I'm sleeping,' Isa called down with derision.

Bobby and Liz had come to share her grief, they said coming into the house. The atmosphere was heavy with mutual dislike, but the ritual had to be endured, she thought, watching Liz brush dog hairs off the chair before she sat down. Ann-Marie wondered how long it would take before the real reason for the visit would come up, and she didn't have to wait long, because after the obligatory whisky Bobby asked how she was going to manage.

'Bobby, the farm will run as it has done for the next few months. Mum is on the mend, but I'll have to take someone on. Things just can't stop here, so I'll keep busy and in a few months see how I feel. But this is our *home*, and I don't see that changing.'

Liz started to say something, but Bobby shot her a dark look.

'Well, of course it is. It'll be hard to manage without him, but we're here if you need us. We're family, after all.'

She forced a small smile, and stood up, determined to end the charade.

'Anyway, thanks for coming over. I'll let you know about the funeral. It'll be the Crem, but I don't know the date yet. Elaine and I are going to the undertakers today.'

'Well…you know where we are…'

They reluctantly took the hint and got ready to leave. Liz picked her way over the muddy yard to their car and turned to Bobby once they were inside. '*You* could have been a bit more proactive!'

'What could I say!' he muttered under his breath as he waved goodbye to Ann-Marie, stood inside the farmhouse door, 'She'll need to sell up; she can't manage this place on her own. Smug cow.'

As the car swung out the gate Ann-Marie angrily pulled on her old brown cord jacket and pocketed the cider shed keys. Vultures. She knew they thought she couldn't manage the farm herself. Well, they were in for a shock. She had big plans for the farm. *Her* farm.

She crossed the yard and swung open the cider shed and inhaled deeply; enjoying the smell of fermenting apple juice. She'd loved making cider ever since she was a little girl, helping her dad, and although she missed him terribly, she was glad he hadn't been around to witness Bull's growing contempt for both her and the farm. She pushed the sad thoughts away and lifted down the pump hoses from their rack. The past was the past; dead and almost buried. Not that Bull was going to be buried. He'd always liked a good blaze and Ann-Marie was determined that his cremation would just be the start of his burning in hell.

****

The previous autumn produced 20,000 litres juice, with the pomace used to feed the pigs. The first batch, pressed in September had fermented into cider, and was ready to be racked off into maturation tanks so she spent a busy morning pumping cider from tank to tank before returning to the house for lunch.

The dogs were fractious and she ate quickly; glad for the excuse to escape from the house and took the dogs out to the orchard for some exercise. This was her favourite part of the day, and even in February, the orchard welcomed her, with bare dark twigs reaching upwards. The sky was a clear cold blue and the breeze cut through her jacket, but as she surveyed the rolling Renfrewshire countryside with its brown striped ploughed fields and the snow-dusted Campsie hills in the distance, she was content. The sun shone on the dark trees, turning every raindrop into a diamond. The carpet of snowdrops would replaced by primroses shortly, and when the orchard blossomed, bluebells would reflect the sky. She always felt happy here, and was looking forward to sharing the beauty of the orchard as part of her plan to put the cider once again at the heart of the farm.

The apples had all been pruned and the hedges flailed the previous month, so she could concentrate on getting last year's cider ready for labelling. New label designs sat on her desk, but they could wait till the evening, she thought, striding through the orchard and calling the dogs to heel.

It had been an interesting week to say the least, she reflected as she walked, but she had no regrets. She'd given the bedroom a good *bottoming out*, as her mother advised, and moved all Bull's clothes and personal things to the spare bedroom. Lynda might want to look through the stuff, she imagined. The coffin would be a closed casket, she had decided and no-one was going to see him, but clothes had to be given to the undertaker and she'd cheerfully put his Masonic suit into a carrier bag ready to go that afternoon. Dead, but not yet gone, she reflected. Perhaps she should print off a count-down calendar for the back of the office door; she chuckled as she returned to the yard with the filthy dogs.

Elaine was waiting for her upstairs, keeping Isa company, who was sitting up in the bedroom chair, looking better than she had for weeks.

'You'll need to change quick if we're to be at the undertakers for four,' Elaine said, shoo-ing Bracken away. Ann-Marie ordered the dogs to their baskets downstairs, grateful again for Elaine's friendship. Her insistence on going with Ann-Marie to the undertakers meant Lynda didn't have to; and everyone was relieved.

Pulling on her Sunday navy trousers and top she was

soon ready, looking respectable and dowdy. They were the same clothes she'd worn to her father's funeral five years ago. 'Will I do?' she said at the doorway.

'Aye, you look the part.' her friend sniggered, standing up. Fashion had never been Ann-Marie's thing. They picked up the bag with Bull's clothes, said goodbye to Isa, and got into the car.

'Showtime!' laughed Elaine, revving the engine as they drove out the gate.

'Holy Mary! This isn't a movie Elaine. You're name's not Thelma and I'm not Louise! Calm it. You don't know who's watching.'

***

They both admitted later, over yet more whisky, that it had been cathartic organising the funeral. The cheapest casket; not that she had asked for that, one car, family flowers only and a short service. Ann-Marie told the undertaker that Billy was not a religious man. He had been surprised, as a fellow Lodge member that it would not be a Masonic funeral.

'No. I don't want that. He never said he wanted that, and I don't. Short and simple.'

She played her trump card, 'After all, his death was a *horrible* and tragic accident. I just want closure now and to try and forget all this.'

The undertaker nodded sympathetically, 'Of course.'

Well, it was true. She *did* want to forget it all. *That* part was true. The date was set and the arrangements made. *My God, all sorts of questions!* Did she want entrance music? Exit music? Who was to say a few words? She hadn't thought of that.

Did she want a piper?

Oh Holy Mary!

'Of course!' she said brightly whilst Elaine looked at her in surprise. 'This is a celebration of Bull..*Billy's* life,' she said looking at Elaine pointedly. Elaine smiled at her and patted her hand sympathetically.

'Can I get back to you with the other details? I can't really think at the moment.'

The undertaker was kindness itself, 'Of course Mrs Ross. It's been a terrible experience for you. Just email me or phone. The details are on the card,' he said pushing a business card towards her.

'My daughter would like to come and see Billy if that's okay? And after that I want the casket sealed please.'

'Of course. All she needs to do is contact me to arrange to come to the chapel of rest.'

And it was done.

Back in the car Elaine turned to her, 'A *piper*? Why waste your money on a piper?'

'What could I say? Anyway, it makes it look better - as if I really care…'

Elaine rolled her eyes.

'It's one day Elaine. Actually - it's less than an hour. Let's just get it over with. Can Malky say a few words? He was Bull's best friend.'

'I'll ask him. I'm sure he'd be pleased to do it.'

'And I *don't* want folk back to the house. We'll have an afternoon tea thing at the Watermill Hotel. Then we can leave and that's it done and dusted.'

'Okay, let's go and book that now then we can go and

get a drink. All this skulduggery is geein' me a thirst.'

She'd need to stop drinking after the funeral, but Ann-Marie had to admit that whisky was helping her get through the days and nights at the moment. Luckily Bull had a stock of Lagavulin in; and when Elaine dropped her back at the farm, she made her wait until she'd returned to the car armed with two bottles.

'I'll never drink all of it, and I think I'll try and cut down the malt.'

***

She phoned Lynda that evening, told her the arrangements and that she could go see her father if she phoned the undertaker.

'I'm going to take Uncle Bobby with me,' Lynda announced.

'You don't have to go if you think it'll upset you... 'Ann-Marie began.

'No, it's not that. I just think as he's dad's brother... and him and Auntie Liz asked to go with me...as family.'

Bobby and Liz again. It was early days, but the death; instead of pulling them closer together was a wedge between them, and now Lynda was siding with *them*. Ann-Marie had never liked them. Apart from despising her because she was a Catholic, and had *forced* Bull into a shotgun wedding; they were weird. Unmarried and living together, she'd always wondered what exactly the 'relationship' was between them. She'd seen them coming out of a bedroom together at a family wedding reception years ago looking flushed and guilty. Her stomach had turned at the obvious conclusion. She'd mentioned it to

Bull at the time, and he'd angrily slapped her. She kept her suspicions to herself after that. Talk about keeping it in the family!

'…MUM!'

'What? – Sorry – just tuned out for a second love. It's been a very long day.'

'I *said* do you want the boys to come to the funeral? Do you think they're too young?'

'Well, it's up to you. It's a short service and maybe it'll give them closure too. Have a think about it.'

'Well, I'll need money to buy them both suits to wear…' Lynda wheedled.

'That's fine. I'll sort it tomorrow at the bank.'

She put the phone down and considered. She'd gone through the bank statements and seen the monthly payments to Lynda from her fathers account. That was going to stop. His account was frozen, of course, but she wasn't prepared to continue to fund Lynda's lifestyle from now on. It was time madam stood on her own two feet and got herself a job.

She poured herself another whisky and settled in the armchair by the fire, enjoying the peace. The dogs stretched out enjoying the heat and she sat staring into the embers. What a change from her and her mother uncomfortably enduring evenings filled with Bull's drunken tirades and demands to sell the farm. No more control, no more nastiness and no more pawing and forcing. No more Bull. How had she put up with it, with *him*, for all those years?

The phone rang and broke through the uncomfortable memories and she spoke to a cousin from Australia, apologizing that he couldn't come to the funeral. So; Lynda had been on the jungle drums and everyone had been informed. Good. It saved her repeating the same fake sadness and listening bored stiff to their sympathy.

She poured another whisky and went to her computer. In the last fortnight she'd secretly discussed new labels with the printer, and he'd come up with a fantastic new range, which had delighted her. A new look for a new start, she thought as she approved them and sent the email to the printer to go ahead with a print run. Then she climbed the stairs to check on her mother.

Isa was settled in bed, watching TV quietly. Perhaps they could try and see if she could manage the stairs tomorrow, she'd suggested, beaming a radiant smile, 'I'm feeling much more like my old self,' she said, 'And it would be nice to sit by the fire in the evenings again. Just the two of us. Just like old times.'

Ann-Marie started slightly, but her mother just smiled broadly.

She called the dogs for a final walk, and seeing the frost on the ground, pulled another log from the dwindling pile by the door. Tomorrow she'd need to move logs from the woodpile to the house, and organise cutting and stacking the logs laid up in the barn. Another *man's* job. With this thought, she called the dogs back in, settled another log on the fire and dozed in the chair.

Chapter 4

At the farm store the next day Ann-Marie pinned a job advert on the sales board and collected some sacks of pig pellets. She ignored the pitying looks from the counter staff and sighed to herself. She was; as her mother would have said, *the talk o' the steamie*, but she knew once the funeral was over everyone would find something or someone new to talk about.

She returned to the farm to find Lynda waiting in her car. Ann-Marie took a deep breath and braced herself for whatever was coming.

'I thought I'd come with you to the bank.' Lynda said, following her mother carrying feed sacks to the shed. Lynda was dressed to the nines and carrying animal feed was not on her agenda.

'You'll need to wait till I've stacked these and get changed.' Ann-Marie said, 'but you didn't need to bother Lynda. I've got all the paperwork ready.'

'I've decided to bring the boys to the funeral, so I'll need money to buy them new clothes.' Lynda announced, 'I thought I'd just get the money when you're there.'

Ann-Marie straightened up and wiped her hands on her jeans. 'Lynda, I think we need to talk about money.'

Two angry red spots appeared on Lynda's cheeks.

'I know your father was giving you money every month, but that has to stop. You need to start living within your means, and if that means getting a job, well, you'll just have to. I need to take on some staff and I'm not continuing these payments your dad started.' There, she'd said it. She faced Lynda's angry look. Surely she must have been expecting something of the sort; or perhaps she didn't think her mother knew about the regular monthly payments from their bank account?

'If dad was still alive he'd not be happy…'

'Well, he's not. And I have to hire someone to help and still have bills to pay. The boys are both at school. D'ye not *want* to go back to work? After all, what do you *do* all day? On your own?' she finished pointedly.

'Mum, I'm thirty-two now and don't need your advice!' Lynda retorted angrily and strode to her car, 'I'll wait for you in the car.'

Ann-Marie returned to the house to change and the journey to the bank was icily quiet. Business was concluded quickly, with the cancellation of Bull's cards and chequebooks, and ending the payments to the Lodge and to Lynda. She took out £300 cash and handed it over to Lynda. 'For the boys' clothes for the funeral.'

Lynda looked her squarely in the eye, 'Thank you. Do you want me to take you home now as I'm heading to Glasgow?'

'No, I'm meeting Elaine for lunch.'

'Thick as thieves, you two. Okay, I'll call you.' she said with a brief kiss of her mother's cheek.

She waited till Lynda had disappeared round the

corner and then walked to the solicitors. She needed to wrap up a final bit of business before meeting Elaine.

Paisley was not the bustling town it used to be. She remembered the thread mills, the jam and chocolate factories and the butcher's shop, where people queued out the door for sausages on a Saturday. All gone. With the advent of out-of-town shopping malls, the High Street was now full of empty shops, but as she walked the near-empty street, she admired the buildings built by the thread and cloth barons long ago, as she made her way towards the solicitors' office. She used the same family firm her parents had used, and was welcomed in by the familiar secretary to the office where Jim, her solicitor ushered her in to sit at the old wooden desk.

'Sad times,' he said briefly and passed her a glass of malt. She was pleasantly surprised and they drank an un-named toast. 'You've had a lot to endure recently. I was sorry to hear about your mother's stroke; and now you've suffered the cruel loss of your husband.'

He downed the malt, removed the empty glasses and popped his glasses on. 'So, what can I help you with?'

'I know what Billy's will said - that everything, barring a small bequest of £1000 to Lynda reverts to me. I'm not here about that. Lynda's never taken anything to do with the business and I need to look at protecting what I've built...what I'm building.' She noted the slight raising of eyebrows and carried on.

'Mum and I have discussed the future of the farm and agreed to run the pig side of the business down. There's no profit in pigs right now, and I'm going to stop commercial production. I'd like to expand the cider making, with a tap room and small shop and offer a small amount of pork. I think it'll be more profitable, but I want to protect the farm and see if we can find some way to run it as a company.'

She could hear the old wall clock ticking sluggishly as he considered.

'Well, to be frank I'm surprised. I have to tell you that you're in for a bit of a rough ride from both your daughter and from Billy's brother. It's a small town and I've heard …well…rumours.'

'What *sort* of rumours?' Ann-Marie stiffened in the chair. *Please God he doesn't mean…*

'That with your mum's stroke and Billy's death you were thinking of selling the farm.' he looked her square in the eye.

'Well, I can certainly squash that rumour. I'm *not* selling the farm!' She was furious. She knew he wouldn't share any details, but she could imagine Bobby mouthing off…or even Lynda. It was still a small town, and gossip travelled fast.

'When the funeral's over I'm applying for planning permission for a tap room/shop and work will be completed before summer. I'll be employing staff to do the orchard work, the pigs and man the tap room. I don't want Lynda involved in the running at all.'

If Jim was surprised he didn't show it. Instead, he sat back and considered.

'Very well. Let's get the funeral out of the way and I'll look at some ways to protect your business. We can set up a meeting in, say a month? Meantime, I'll start wrapping up Billy's estate and I'll see you at the funeral.'

They both stood up and as she headed to the door, Jim put his hand on her shoulder,

'Are *you* alright? Is there anything you need? You seem very …tense.'

She looked into his face. She'd met him frequently over many years, and they had always had a *rapport* of sorts, but as she returned his gaze, she wondered if she had been too candid and too cold.

'It's all been very unsettling, but I think I'm over it all now - the shock anyhow. Life goes on,' she smiled briefly, hoping she'd not been too quick in coming to see him. The last thing she needed was to make anyone suspicious; certainly not the family solicitor.

He stood watching her walk out the door for a second, his mind mulling over the conversation, and the fact that despite her loss, she was looking better than she had for years. He told his secretary to note when the funeral was and to pencil him out for that morning or afternoon.

Ann-Marie pulled her coat around her and walked down to Paisley Abbey where she'd arranged to meet Elaine. She sat waiting in the cloister, and her mind wandered.

She'd committed a mortal sin, but was unrepentant. If there really was a heaven and a hell, surely God wouldn't reject her when she died; after all, she had endured her own hell for the last thirty odd years.

Although Elaine was her confidante, Ann-Marie had not told her everything. There had only been one child of the marriage because she had ensured that there could never be more. He'd rewarded her continued failure to become pregnant with drunken slaps or worse.

She became almost as good hiding her bruises as she was hiding her contraceptives. Isa had heard her cry out one night, perhaps a year or more ago, and had angrily confronted him in the morning. Bull had been more careful after that, but it didn't stop; and recently, she'd also had to endure his bad-tempered demands to sell the farm.

Elaine arrived at last, bursting in on her reverie, breathless and flustered with complaints about Malky. He'd arrived home late last night and she thought she'd smelt perfume off him. They'd had a *huge* argument, she said, and she'd not slept well. She was out of sorts and Ann-Marie bought her lunch to cheer her up, after which they wandered round the shops before she dropped Ann-Marie back at the farm.

She changed and headed into the office to complete some paperwork until late afternoon, when she threw the pen down and gathered the dogs for a walk. She headed through the meadow alongside the swollen burn, hoping to see if there were any deer feeding in the margins. The light was going and the sky threatening, with huge battleship grey clouds masking the surrounding hills. Rain was due and was probably going to last at least overnight. The dogs were soon filthy, and as they turned back towards the farm in the encroaching gloom, she noted her neighbour out in the next field with his gun. Ewan waved and she waved back. He held up a brace of rabbits and she raised her hands in farewell as she made her way up the track to the house. Smoke curled from the chimney and a welcoming light in the kitchen beckoned her. She was looking forward to lamb stew and sitting with her mother in front of the fire. It was a good life, she reflected and then corrected herself; would *now* be a good life. Perhaps it was also the time to start spending a bit on the house as well as the farm; even spend a wee bit on herself for a change? After all, there would be more money in the bank now that there were no Lodge dues or money going to Lynda. This was *her* time now.

'Come on girls,' she called cheerily and led them into the kitchen. The answering machine was winking and had three messages; two in response to her job advert and one from the printer, telling her the labels would be ready in a week. She kicked off her boots, hung up her jacket and started to ladle out two bowls of stew. Yes, it was a good life.

After dinner, she arranged interviews for the next morning. Duncan lived at the neighbouring farm and was coming at nine. She knew he'd just finished agricultural college and had known him all his life. A sensible lad, Isa agreed when told. The other applicant; Roddy McKenzie, she didn't know. She had to give him directions, so knew he wasn't local, and expected him at eleven. She went upstairs to the spare bedroom and gathered all the bin bags full of Bull's clothes, took them downstairs and popped them in the back of the pickup, ready to go to the dump the next day. Then she and Isa watched a television programme about vets, before she helped her mother up to bed, and fell into her own bed with a book, ready to face another restless and nightmare filled night.

Malky arrived with Elaine at nine, just as Duncan turned up for his interview. She asked him to take a seat whilst she quickly read over the eulogy Malky had written. It was brief and heartfelt and she passed it back with a smile.

'That's lovely Malky. It really does hit the right sort of note. D'you miss him?'

'Well, aye, of course. He was a pal and we had the Lodge in common,' he said, and after the tiniest of pauses added 'Of course, I don't think he'd be the easiest person to live with…'

He must have seen her surprise because he added quickly, 'I know he'd been a bit…well, a bit of a bully; aboot the farm. And now it's yours again.' He took her hand gently. 'If there is *anything* I can do to help you Ann-Marie, I'm always here.'

Ann-Marie saw the look of surprise on Elaine's face too. Poor Malky always fancied himself as a bit of a ladies man, the sad old sod. She withdrew her hand quickly and thanked him, changing the subject brusquely to hide the pitying look on her face. 'Now, I'm really sorry, but I must have a wee chat with this lad, who has been waiting so patiently…'

'Of course!' Malky said brightly. 'Come on Elaine, Ann-Marie needs to get on and we need to be away. We'll see you soon,' he said again and propelled Elaine to the door.

She closed the door behind them and took a deep breath, seating herself opposite the quiet young man and started to ask about his hopes and dreams. That was a good way into the interview she hoped. A few minutes later she told him to get his jacket on and she'd give him a tour and tell him about *her* dreams for the future. An hour later, drenched with cold rain, they both warmed themselves in front of the fire in the living room. Her mother was delighted, and she thought they'd make a good team. He wasn't so young that he couldn't talk to her, nor too old to resent a woman as his boss. He'd start on Monday, and if they were both happy in a month they would make it permanent. When she waved him away, she picked up the phone and called his father to confirm the arrangement.

At five minutes to eleven a landrover arrived with a strapping red-haired young man who could only be Roddy McKenzie, she thought. It was still raining and she beckoned him in.

'I've just made fresh tea,' she said shaking his hand, and signalling him to go through to the living room, where her mother smiled a huge grin, and beckoned him to sit.

'Fab. Black, three sugars,' he told Ann-Marie whilst fussing the two dogs playing round his feet. 'Cockers?' he asked Isa, whilst rubbing Bracken's ears.

'Yes, Bracken is the oldest and that's Bramble. D'you have a dog yourself?'

'Not right now,' he said, taking a seat by the fire, 'But I like dogs. My parents had a farm tenancy near Stirling, but when they both died, well; I had to find somewhere else. I'm renting a flat in Erskine now, so no dogs right now.'

'I'm sorry for your loss,' Ann-Marie said and broached her own situation to clear the air. 'You probably read about my late husband's…accident? Well…farms have to go on and I need help to run and develop the farm.

Shall we take a walk round and I'll tell you my plans and we'll come back here for a chat after?'

He downed his tea in one and stood at the door, whilst she donned a jacket. Isa grinned enthusiastically and gave her two thumbs-up to let her know that Roddy would do very nicely, much to Ann-Marie's embarrassment. She rolled her eyes and they headed out to the yard.

An hour later and they sat back in front of the fire. He'd picked up a log and placed it on himself, seeing the fire had died down and Bracken jumped up to nestle in beside him. If he was as proactive around the farm he'd fit in fine, she thought.

'Well, Roddy, what d'you think? Do you want the job?' she asked, settling down to find out more about him and what he thought about the farm and the job.

'Well, I don't know much about cider making, but I'm keen to learn. I want an interesting job, but I want to put down some roots too, an' I don't see why my roots can't be here. I'm tidy, responsible with good references and have bills to pay, so yes, I'm keen if you are?'

Ann-Marie looked over to her mother, who took the hint.

'When can you start?' Isa grinned.

Ann-Marie laughed, 'I think you've got the job.'

They sat a while longer talking about his family home, and the more they talked; the more Ann-Marie warmed to him. It was a good fit, she smiled, as he finally pushed the dog to the floor and stood up.

'Well, I need to get back. I told my boss I'd be back before the end of lunch. Thanks Ann-Marie, Isa,' he said shaking their hands, 'Keep me in the loop. You've got my mobile number.'

'Thanks Roddy. I'll get my solicitor to draw up a proper contract and get him to post that to you. Shall we say 6th April? That's the beginning of the tax year and will make it easier for accounting?'

'You're the boss!' he grinned. He ran through the sheets of rain and leapt into the landrover and with a cheery wave was gone.

'Well, he's a breath a fresh air and a bonnie lad!' Isa said beaming.

'Far too young for you, mother' Ann-Marie chided.

'Och, I'm not too old to look. Oh, be still my beating heart!' she laughed, fanning her face dramatically with the newspaper. 'At least he wisnae makin' sheep's eyes at you like that great pillock Malky wis earlier!'

Despite the heavy rain washing the farm muck and dead leaves into the yard, Ann-Marie was in a good mood when she went to clean out and feed the pigs at lunchtime. The radio kept her company until 2pm when hunger drove her to the house for a bite to eat. 'No walks today.' she told the crestfallen dogs, looking at the endless sheets of rain falling outside. They curled up on the sofa instead, content with the warmth and the company.

Chapter 5

The funeral went off without any drama, with Ann-Marie sitting dry-eyed with Isa, Lynda and the boys opposite Bull's coffin. She half-listened to Malky's eulogy, and waited impatiently until Bull's coffin slide behind the curtains to the furnace.

Soon he'd be basting in his own fat and sizzling away, she thought and tried very hard not to smile.

At the end of the service she thanked those not going on to the wake; a few neighbouring farmers, and the Police Inspector in charge of the investigation, who had slid in unobserved at the back of the room. Afterwards at the hotel, she wondered if she detected some coldness between Malky and Lynda, but the moment passed, and she had to focus on yet another farmer paying their respects. By five o'clock it was over and she was exhausted. She had just pulled her coat on when her solicitor appeared and kissed her on the cheek.

'How're you doing?' Jim asked.

'Fine, I just want to go home and have a bath,' she answered, a little shortly.

'I've put some things in the post to you, but I'm not talking shop here. Is there anything *you* need?'

'Just sleep. Tomorrow's just another day.'

She looked shattered, but not heartbroken and he wondered, not for the first time, if the marriage hadn't been a particularly happy one. In his years as a family solicitor he had developed an ability to recognise the signs. Feeling uncomfortable under his scrutiny, Ann-Marie mumbled an excuse about getting back for the animals, before turning to Lynda, who was waiting with the boys.

'Come for tea with the boys tomorrow,' she said impulsively, 'there are some new chicks that one of the hens has hatched.' She waved goodbye to Jim, and turned from his gaze to collect Isa.

'We'll come round after school,' Lynda said briefly, trying to herd the boys towards David who was waiting to take them home. Ann-Marie and Isa walked towards her pick-up, accompanied by Malky and Elaine.

'Do you want us to come back with you?' Malky asked, helping Isa into the car.

'No, I'm fine. The eulogy was perfect Malky, thank you.'

He walked back to his own car, tactfully leaving the two friends together for a moment.

'Nice of Calum to come,' Ann-Marie said, hugging Elaine, 'God, I'm glad that's over.'

'Remember, we've still got the Enquiry. *Then*, we can put all this behind us.'

'You're a true friend. I'll never forget this Elaine. Never.'

'We're away for a couple of days next week. Malky's had some notion to keep us young and fit, and suggested we walk a bit o' the West Highland Way, believe it or not. I'm no' keen; but we're stayin' at a swanky B&B to make a romantic break of it. I'll phone you when we're back.'

She drove home silently, mulling the day over in her head. Bobby and Liz had turned up unexpectedly before the funeral to collect Bull's Masonic case and some photographs. He'd stupidly mentioned the future of the farm again, but Isa had angrily told him to mind his own business. Avoiding them would now be easy. As she drove into the yard, she was pleased to see Duncan had been busy. The woodshed was full, and the yard was clean, and he'd stuck a note into a milk bottle on the doorstep which she read with a smile. 'Pigs cleaned & fed. HUGE box delivered and inside barn.'

'I'm going straight to bed,' Isa said, climbing the stairs, followed by her daughter. Ann-Marie changed into worn denims, a thick lamb's wool sweater, and then pulling her coat and boots on, took the dogs for a quick walk in the gloom. Tomorrow is a new start, she thought to herself, and returned to the house to quietly celebrate.

***

Duncan appeared early, and after coffee, hesitantly suggested rearranging the bottling shed layout, to improve efficiency. It was a good idea, she agreed, and took them all day, and they had just finished when Lynda arrived with the boys. Keen to avoid Lynda's prying eyes, Ann-Marie closed over the shed door, but realised immediately that she needn't have bothered. Lynda was busy appraising Duncan. Ann-Marie politely introduced him as the next-door neighbour's son and her new farm worker, but Lynda's fleeting interest had already vanished.

Duncan took the boys to see the hen and her chicks, whilst the women went into the house. Ann-Marie set the table, whilst Lynda sat and chatted with Isa about everything and nothing; the weather, how the boys were outgrowing their shoes, the sorry state of the shops and the price of groceries, and then the afternoon tea was set on the table. By tactfully avoided talking about the farm, Lynda's marriage or Billy, the women conversed pleasantly for over forty minutes.

Duncan returned the boys and escaped back to the yard, whilst the kitchen was filled with the noise of children flinging boots and coats into the corner and pulling the wooden chairs along the slate floor. They ate ravenously as growing lads do, and as they chattered about chickens and school, Ann-Marie complemented Lynda. They were good lads and a credit to her, she remarked.

'Even if Neil *is* sneaking meat under the table to Bramble', she said with a knowing smile to the younger boy. 'You can give them some scraps in their bowls after we eat,' she conceded.

The boy grinned triumphantly, and if Lynda was surprised at the warmth of her mother's interest, she didn't show it; and as soon as they had all eaten explained that it was a school night and they needed to return home to do homework. The boys hugged Ann-Marie and Isa and promised to come back soon because Duncan had offered to show them the new piglets when they arrived.

Ann-Marie told them in a stage whisper that she was

thinking of buying some lambs.

'Would that be nice?' she asked two eager little faces.

'Granny that would be magic!' said Alex whilst Neil, the younger, nodded grinning and showing the gap in his teeth.

'Can we give them names?' he lisped.

'Of course you can!' she ruffled their hair fondly.

'Sheep?' Lynda asked with a raised eyebrow, 'I thought you were struggling with the pigs?'

'Well, Duncan is helping me, and I've always liked sheep. There'll only be a few and they can go in the orchard.'

Lynda rolled her eyes and herded the boys through the rain and into the car. She hated the muck and smell, and the tiny, old fashioned house. If she was in charge she'd have sold it in a heartbeat, like her father had wanted, but she knew better and kept her mouth shut.

Ann-Marie waved them off, pleased that Lynda had accepted Duncan's new appointment and also pleased to hear that Lynda and David were at last talking, although he had not yet returned to live in the house. Lynda needed something to focus on rather than Billy's death and the farm. Maybe in time she'd see the value in the farm, but the main thing was that the farm had reverted back to Ann-Marie's control.

She looked online for the next livestock auction and pencilled the date on her calendar above the computer. Lambs she wanted and lambs she would have, she thought, thinking they'd look good in the home orchard. She pulled her boots and waxed jacket on and calling the dogs, went to check that the fencing would be secure enough.

Duncan had just finished cleaning down the yard and they fell in-step together, walking to the orchard. She mentioned the lambs and he grinned. 'It'll be like a pettin' farm soon!' he said. 'One of the sows is due to farrow soon and then it'll be like spring has *finally* arrived in Scotland.'

'Oh, I don't know about spring, but a few lambs will be nice for the boys *and* me! And an orchard will look lovely with sheep in it. We'll both go to the auction, and you can impress me with your stock choosing skills,' she grinned back.

The fencing was good, and ending the day on a positive note, she sent him home. Another small step forward, she thought happily, calling two bedraggled spaniels back and headed for home.

***

The next morning, they made a start on the labelling. They worked well together and soon there was a large stack of sealed and marked boxes of cider neatly stacked on pallets, ready for delivery. She'd hear what Roddy thought of Duncan's ideas later when they discuss the refurbishment of one of the stone sheds as a tap-room and sales area. Her solicitor had left a message with Isa that he'd drop in on his way home so she prepared some sandwiches and a chocolate cake was already cooling on a rack above the range; out of reach but not out of sight of the dogs, who sat underneath, guarding it against any unknown and invisible thieves.

'Tea-time!' she announced, arriving in the shed with a

pot of tea, some mugs and large slices of chocolate cake on a tray.

'This is so good.' Duncan mumbled, stuffing a whole slice in his mouth and smearing his cheeks with chocolate crumbs and icing.

'You eat like a pig,' she laughed, as a vehicle pulled up outside, and through the open door she saw the ginger-headed Roddy get out of his Landrover. 'In here!' she called, 'Your timing's perfect – we're having a tea-break.'

He came in grinning and introduced himself to Duncan before settling into a chair at the table and pouring himself a mug of black tea. 'You've been busy' he said indicating the pile of cardboard boxes.

'Yeah, broken the back of the first batch,' she said with a smile, 'it's been a good day.'

Jim arrived shortly after, and after all the introductions had been made, they demolished the cake and took a tour of the sheds. Jim was quiet and it didn't go unnoticed.

'What?' she demanded.

'Without appearing crass or insensitive', he began, 'this is all very quick after Billy's death.'

Ann-Marie's heart thumped. She *had* moved too quickly. She tried to read his face for an emotion, but like all lawyers he had a poker face. Was he suspicious or just concerned she was making a hasty decision?

She decided to brazen it out, 'Well, we'd already been planning some changes, but Billy's death has been a wake-up call. I'm not getting any younger, so it makes sense to scale down the livestock and to take on some staff.'

'Yes, I understand that, and that makes sense.' Jim

answered, placing his hand on her arm. 'However, I think you may want to consider moving a little slower to allow your …family to get used to the idea of change.'

Ann-Marie frowned, and tried unsuccessfully to shake his hand off.

'I'm just suggesting you perhaps hold back a bit, until after the Accident Enquiry. That'll give everyone time to get used to gradual change,' he said in a gentler tone.

Roddy put his mug down. 'It's no' my place to say, but the cider won't be in the shops till Easter so we can carry on with the refurbishing of the shed and stuff. We don't need to put signage up or advertise until after the Enquiry if that makes things easier.'

Jim nodded. 'That's sensible,' he continued, and moved his hand to touch her clenched hand, 'I wasn't *having a go* at you – I'm playing Devil's Advocate and trying to view these changes as others might view them.'

'But it's *my* farm!' she cried, pulling her hand away.

'Yes, but don't throw *all* Billy's involvement out the window the week after the funeral Ann-Marie! You don't want people to talk.'

She sat angrily considering what he said, whilst he and Roddy helped themselves to more cake. He had a point. The last thing she needed was to stir up family resentment or questions from family or anyone else. That could make things awkward if people started to think Billy's death had been *convenient*. She met his eyes and nodded silently.

Duncan dragged Roddy to look at some ideas he had for a cider garden next to the proposed tap room, leaving Jim and Ann-Marie alone, before he diffused the atmosphere by insisting on visiting her mother. She was delighted to see him but failed to persuade him to stay. Heavy rain began to thunder down, and Jim wanted to get home before the light was gone completely.

'Well, ladies, I need to be on my way. Great to see you on the mend Isa, but don't overdo it.' He walked to the door and refusing Ann-Marie's handshake, kissed her lightly on the cheek, bringing a furious blush to her face and making him grin like a boy, before running to the car to avoid becoming soaked. 'And if cake is going to be a regular thing, can I ask for a lemon drizzle next time?' he called cheekily.

Roddy and Duncan were running back to the house in the icy deluge and overheard his parting comment.

'A *bigger* cake,' called Duncan, 'or maybe *two* cakes!'

Ann-Marie waved goodbye and they all crowded back into the kitchen out of the rain.

'Okay, slowly, slowly,' she said to them both. 'I get it - but we can crack on with the background stuff meanwhile. You two disappear – it's after five and this rain is on for the night. Let's call it a day.'

Duncan grabbed his jacket and the final slice of cake, before accepting a lift home in Roddy's car, leaving her alone. She looked upwards at the solid grey sky and then retreated into the warmth of the house. The smell of lamb hotpot filled the kitchen and she had to shoo the dogs away from the table, as her and Isa sat to eat.

'Jim seems to be going out of his way to call,' Isa mentioned casually.

'And what is that meant to mean?' Ann-Marie answered with the spoon half-way to her mouth.

'Well, he's never paid us social calls before,' Isa retorted.

Ann-Marie didn't reply, but she had also wondered at the increase in interest. Ignoring the possibility of attraction, she instead wondered if Jim was perhaps suspicious or just warning her. One thing was certain; she had been trying to move too fast and now realised the danger. The last thing she needed was tongues wagging. A sharp tongue could cut your head right off.

Chapter 6

When she collected Bull's ashes from the undertaker's she wondered what to do with them. The undertaker had sensed her discomfort, and suggested that most people scattered them in the Garden of Remembrance at the crematorium; but she shook her head silently. Her father's ashes were there, and her mother's would in time join his; and she didn't want to contaminate that place with *his* remains. Most of all, she didn't want him to be *at rest*.

She took the large purple tub out to the pickup and hesitated. She felt guilty about putting it; *him*, in the back of the pick-up, like a sack of feed or bale of hay; and what if he *bounced* out if she hit a bump or took a corner too quickly? An indiscreet snigger escaped her as she pictured this and then pulled herself together. He'd need to go in the passenger seat; she realised unhappily, and spent a few minutes strapping the tub with the seat belt.

'What am I going to do with you, *darling* husband of mine?' she asked the purple plastic tub as she started the car. For the first time, since she'd killed him, she was at a loss to know what to *do* with him. She could almost hear him laughing at her discomfort, which annoyed her considerably.

Then suddenly; the most amusing and wicked idea just popped into her head and she had to smother a joyous laugh; aware that parked as she was in the undertaker's car park, just off the main road, she could be seen, and that would never do. Her heart raced as the idea took hold and grew in her mind, freeing her from indecision. She patted the purple tub with a smile. *Now*, she knew exactly where to dispose of him, and he'd be so angry, so deliciously upset that it pleased her enormously. Oh revenge really *was* a dish best served cold! God! It was perfect. *Perfect*!

***

In the restaurant, Lynda accepted another glass of chardonnay with a smile. David was trying so hard, she thought. This restaurant had been one of their favourites before the boys were born, and was exclusive and expensive. She'd like him to "wine and dine" her at least one more time, before accepting that he'd move back home, and she'd have to resume her mundane existence. She just couldn't understand *why* she couldn't have all the nice meals out, all the nice clothes she liked. Her mother had existed for years, making do and wearing clothes until they fell apart, and her father had despised her, ignored her; and had started to funnel little gifts of money to Lynda, to enjoy herself. He'd always called her his *little princess*, and she didn't want the praise, the admiring looks and the attention she attracted to stop. She realised, looking at David that their relationship had changed. They were no longer lovers, but somehow had slid into a steady, if mundane existence that revolved around the children, his job and keeping house. She was desperate for the excitement of their early relationship, but David, didn't appear to share her craving. Too clever to complain outright that boring and infrequent sex and money were the main issues; she had cited his long working hours and a lack of romantic gestures on his part, and he seemed to accept this. She could hardly tell him about her bedroom fantasies and her desire for a bottomless bank account. Poor David would have been mortified and convinced that his suspicions of an affair were true.

She remembered how, at the start of winter, she'd ordered herself a little toy from a discreet ladies-only website, and had spent secret afternoons in bed, going through batteries faster than a teenager with a Gameboy. Still, it wasn't the real thing, and the cost of batteries was *ridiculous*!

A chance meeting one evening in the West End had changed all that. She'd bumped into Malky in a trendy bar off Byres Road. Oh, if his fat old wife had known he was there, dressed to the nines and flirting with office girls half his age, she'd have been furious. Lynda had felt his eyes on her the whole time at the bar and drunkenly flirted with him after he'd bought her a drink or two and offered to take her home. She'd dumped her friends and agreed, because she'd at least avoid having to pay for a taxi, and he *was* paying her lots of attention and made her feel sexy again. In the car, she'd allowed her short dress to *accidentally* ride up her thighs, showing the tops of her stockings, and he'd been unable to hide his interest. They'd found themselves parked in a deserted car park, where they spent some time steaming up the windows of his car.

For the next few weeks the affair continued. He was no Daniel Craig, and was getting on a bit, but was *very* willing, *and* took her for a couple of expensive meals too. That was, until the funeral. When she finally managed to get him alone for a minute and challenged him, he'd coldly told her it was finished. Elaine was becoming suspicious, *she* was too expensive for him to maintain, and he'd had enough, he said casually. Lynda was furious. How dare *he* finish with her!

But the spectre of suspicion took root, and she decided it was time for her and David to get back together, at least for appearances sake. She'd called him to talk, reminding him how much she missed him, playing on his blind love for her and, true to form; ever predictable David suggested they go for a meal. She spent the afternoon preparing, and dressed to impress in her little black dress, arranging her hair the way he liked, and basked in his admiration as they sat in the restaurant. It was just like old times, she sighed. As if on cue he grazed the inside of her wrist with his fingers and she met his gaze.

'You look fantastic tonight,' he whispered.

She returned his gaze with a slow smile and slipped her stocking clad foot from her shoe, sliding it up his shin slowly, 'You look pretty good yourself David. I miss you. I miss …us.' She dangled the bait, lifting her glass to her lips and took a delicate sip, running her tongue over her bottom lip.

'Shall we get the bill?' he grinned.

She reeled him in like a fish on a hook.

'Why not?' she smiled back.

They drove back to the flat with an air of excitement, and hurriedly sent the babysitter home. As soon as she was out the door, David pulled Lynda into his arms, kissing her hungrily. She delightedly took his hand and led him to the bedroom, locking the door. This was one night they definitely didn't want the children barging in. But, not for the first time, David was excited and couldn't wait, and he pushed her urgently onto the bottom of the bed, pulling her towards him.

'Slowly!' she growled. She needed him to last until she could get the sweet release she needed, and wriggled in delighted abandon. So good, so…

'Too late…' he shuddered.

'NO! Not yet!'

But it was over, almost before it had started, and she was furious. 'Couldn't you *wait*?'

'I couldn't help it! It's been months… and you dressed like that? What were you expecting? I'm sorry.'

'I was expectin' a night of passion! I was *expecting* the earth to move and the waves come crashing around me! Move!' she said angrily, and strode to the ensuite leaving him lying on the bed.

'It'll be better next time.' he called sheepishly but got no reply as he heard the shower run.

Nothing had changed then. It really was just like old times, old, boring and leaving very much to be desired. She'd have him back for the money and the security, but would be disappointed in the bedroom, *again*. Meantime, she needed to calm down, persuade David that she still loved him and that all was well between them.

Forcing a smile onto her face, she returned to the bedroom and kissed him. 'Next time,' she said, 'I'm calling the shots!'

He flicked the quilt back and welcomed her back to bed with a grin. 'Better get back in the saddle then.'

***

Elaine sat in the bath examining her blisters. The things you do for love, she thought, reminiscing about the nice weekend they'd just returned from. She'd been aghast when Malky had suggested a weekend walking; but it had been a laugh and they *were* spending more time together. She'd had her hair cut and coloured a light blonde, just like Joanna Lumley's; and they had indeed had a romantic time in the B&B, and she found she was actually enjoying the walking, and the chance to spend time with the man she loved.

She eased herself out of the bath and into the new silky pyjamas she'd bought for the trip. They weren't as warm as her flannelette ones, but Malky had certainly responded to her new image this weekend, she thought with a chuckle. Perhaps she'd been ridiculous, suspecting him of playing away. After all, *who* would he be having an affair with? She blushed as she recalled checking his phone, but there were just the contacts she knew – men from the Lodge, Ann Marie, Lynda, Calum and a few of his friends from work that he went golfing with. She really had been a stupid woman, suspicious for no reason!

He'd even suggested a trip to Cornwall in the summer with a meal at the famous Seafood Restaurant if they could get a booking. She'd been thrilled, after watching TV programs set in the Duchy, and setting her heart on one day visiting the locations in person; and dinner at the posh restaurant was a dream. Fancy Malky being willing to stretch to that, and all because he loved her she thought, giving herself a last puff of perfume before joining him downstairs.

'How are the feet?' he asked passing her a tumbler of Lagavulin and patting the sofa.

'Not too bad considering, but next time, can we walk when the weather is a better?' she smiled, sitting besides him.

'Of course, my angel,' he answered, kissing her hand, 'I'm already planning our wee trip to Cornwall like we talked about. But we'll need to keep walking meantime to make sure your feet harden up a bit. Sun, sea and romance,' he wiggled his eyebrows saucily.

She smiled. Marriage was about compromise she conceded. Growing older needn't mean looking like a saggy auld bag-lady. After all, if Joanna Lumley could look great at her age, so could she. A shopping trip was on the cards, she decided, and she might even persuade Ann-Marie to have a long look at *her* wardrobe too.

Her mind drifted as she shifted in the uncomfortable new underwear, and she idly wondered if she could order lubricating jelly online, instead of buying it at the chemist from silly wee lassies who sniggered between themselves at her. It wasn't as if women in their fifties didn't have sex, she thought, crossly, and sex she was certainly having. It was great to have the old Malky back, and she was going to make the most of this second honeymoon, even if she was risking a flare up of thrush with all the sex and nylon underwear she was now wearing.

Malky settled himself beside her. It had been easy to persuade her to agree to the weekend away, and better than he'd expected. He'd realised after dumping Lynda that he'd had a lucky escape. He wasn't ready for acrimony or an expensive divorce, and the affair with Lynda had been too close to home. She'd confronted him at the wake with venom, threatening to tell her mother and Elaine that he'd seduced her while she was grieving for her dad, and he'd angrily hissed that this would just confirm her as a trollop to her mother and Elaine, who already suspected she was having an affair.

Damage limitation was the new game, and he was papering over the cracks in his marriage. He'd arranged seats at the Easter dinner dance at the golf club and told Elaine to buy something nice. She'd been delighted; and he'd impulsively booked a weekend at a nice B&B. He was being the perfect, romantic gentleman, and at night; after a drink or two in front of the log fire she had responded enthusiastically in bed. Her feet might be hurting but she wasn't too tired for *that*, he noted with a smile; and she *was* looking trim, having ditched her usual shapeless clothes for more flattering ones. A few more walking trips and she'd start to lose that fat she'd been carrying around for the last few years. Oh yes, he was working hard to be a model husband and looking forward to the summer trip to Cornwall. It would give Elaine something to brag about at the golf club, and add to the illusion of the perfectly happy contented couple. It was a shame about Lynda, he thought with a smile, but there were other bored ladies out there, who'd welcome him with open arms, he reasoned as his fingers played idly over Elaine's silky pyjamas.

Chapter 7

Lynda was scrolling through her phone, whilst David and the boys were watching television. Almost immediately after moving back home, David had suggested she look for a part-time job, and Lynda was gradually coming round to the idea herself. She'd have extra cash and a reintroduction to the business world, where bored professional men were abundant. A couple of large firms in the West End were advertising and she considered both adverts. She'd need to brush up on her office skills, but could easily manage the role of Personal Assistant. She handed her phone to David to let him look at the details.

'I'm going to apply for this one,' she said. 'It looks interesting and the money's pretty good for part-time.'

He was delighted, and poured her another glass of white wine as he handed the phone back. At last she seemed to be getting over her father's death, and a new job and more money would give her something positive to focus on. How she could sit at home day after day was beyond him, and a new job meant she'd be bringing money in and not spending it. He'd kept quiet so far about the new clothes, the expensive hair and beauty appointments. After two kids and the death of her dad she was entitled to have some fun, but she just didn't understand that his job wasn't paying the kind of wages to support a luxury lifestyle. But, if she managed to land a good job he wouldn't have to face another argument about money, and she'd be too busy to go on these too frequent nights out with friends he didn't really know. He pushed his suspicions away, telling himself that he'd been ridiculous imagining she'd been carrying on with someone else, that he'd just been a bit jealous of her freedom whilst he was working.

Lynda was day-dreaming about working in a plush office with a Daniel Craig look-a-like. She smiled at the thought of those professional, bored married executives who could take her for an expensive lunch, and possibly more, before going back to their none-the-wiser spouses. But she had to land the job first, and that meant brushing up on her IT skills after the weekend. She could get good references from her old employers and create a false one to fill the gap for the years after having the children. David spoilt her mood by mentioning her mother.

'Mmm?' she said, dragging her eyes from her phone.

'You said something earlier about your mum wanted to arrange scattering your dad's ashes. What does she have in mind?'

'Oh, some memorial tree she wants to plant. She doesn't want to keep the ashes in the house.'

'No, I wouldn't either. Yuk. She seems to be getting on with it all though. D'you think she's depressed?'

'*Depressed*? No. In fact I think she's relieved he's not around to badger her about selling up. I'd have jumped at the chance, but she's determined to run the place. Anyway, she wants to plant a *special* apple tree and bury his ashes there. It's nicer than chucking them on the grass at the Garden of Remembrance, I suppose.'

'So, when's this happening? I suppose we'll have to all go as family?'

'Yeah. She suggested Sunday. Morbid and pointless. He's dead and I'd rather we just moved on, but it's one of these things, isn't it? Families – who needs them?'

The movie finished and she chased the boys to their room, 'I'll just be glad when the whole business is done - the ashes, the Enquiry – everything. I just don't want to think about it any more.'

As she watched the boys brush their teeth she knew that wasn't true, and she'd been thinking about it a *lot*. She was furious that her mother refused to sell the farm; they'd have all been set up for life. Well, technically it would have been her gran's money, but after buying a wee bungalow for her and mum, surely there'd be loads left over? What did old people *need* with all that money? Her mother dressed like a tinker and Lynda despised her frugal and frumpy lifestyle. Making ends meet, working from dawn till dusk for a pittance, in all that mud and poo. Some life; she thought; but no-one lives forever, and then it'll *all* come to me.

***

Ann-Marie was changing into her pyjamas. It had been a long day again, with one of the sows farrowing and produced 10 piglets. Duncan had taken photographs of the new arrivals for the new website that was slowly coming together. He was impatiently waiting for the apple blossom and some sunshine, and the Renfrewshire climate was holding him back.

The large purple plastic tub was now sitting in the woodshed, but not for long. Tomorrow, she was meeting Elaine for lunch, and she'd reveal her surprise. She chuckled to herself again. Sunday was the official day the family would say their last goodbye's to Bull; but tomorrow Ann-Marie would dispose of the last physical remains of her dear departed husband in the most fitting way possible. After that, she just had to sit through the Enquiry, which she had been assured was just a formality.

Elaine was full of chatter as she and Ann-Marie ate their lunch in the quiet old fashioned pub in Johnstone. Ann-Marie listened patiently whilst Elaine nattered about the romantic weekend. She'd never really liked Malky, who was too much of a ladies-man, staring at other women; but according to Elaine, he'd been turning on the charm big-time this weekend. 'I'm surprised you had such a good time,' she managed to say, when Elaine finally drew breath.

'Oh the walking was murder!' Elaine laughed, 'and ma feet'll never be the same again, but Malky was on good form and we had fun, day *and* night!'

Ann-Marie rolled her eyes at this revelation, but Elaine happily chattered on,

'We're going to Cornwall in the summer to see a bit of the coast. Malky's booked a table at The Seafood Restaurant in Padstow so I cannae wait! I need to buy clothes, so will you come with me to Glasgow? You might pick up somethin' new yersel,' she said, looking pointedly at Ann-Marie's worn corduroy jacket that had seen more outings than a Scottish umbrella.

Ann-Marie was taken aback. 'What's *wrong* with my clothes?' she retorted.

'Och, they're fine for round the farm, but don't you want to buy some new things? For your *new* life now?' Elaine said a little pointedly.

Ann-Marie scowled.

'Just saying.' Elaine remarked meekly, 'Anyway – today's mystery outing; what's the scoop then?'

Ann-Marie leaned forward excitedly, 'I've had a fantastic idea; you'll love it! You know the family are scattering Billy's ashes on Sunday? Well, they *won't* be. I don't want any part of him there on *my* farm. So, we'll be scattering ashes *from the fire* under the new apple tree. I've already emptied the plastic tub and refilled it.'

She took a sip from her white wine, watching Elaine's eyes open wider and wider. She was waiting for the punch line, but Ann-Marie casually slipped her old jacket on, enjoying the suspense.

'I'm not saying anything else till we get in the car, but this afternoon, *we're* scattering Billy's ashes, his *real* ashes! It's a *surprise*,' she grinned, and called the waitress for the bill.

'I love surprises!' laughed Elaine, pulling on her coat.

Once they were in the car and driving towards Glasgow, Ann-Marie explained.

'I'd been thinking about what to do with them for a while. A man like that needs to have something *special*. I did consider scattering him at Celtic Park, but you need special permission and that would just cause talk.'

She looked over quickly at Elaine's face to see the look of astonishment replaced by delight. 'Celtic Park!' she squealed, 'Oh my God! For a bigot like him that would have been genius!'

'So, *then* I thought, where else can I scatter him so he'll never feel at peace and be birlin' in his grave, so to speak.'

'*And?*' Elaine could be barely contain her excitement as they turned onto the motorway.

'Well; if you were a real dyed-in-the-wool Orangeman, where would you never, *ever* go?'

Elaine knew Ann-Marie would answer her own question, but the suspense was killing her, '*Well?*' she demanded impatiently.

Ann-Marie was enjoying herself, 'I've split the ashes into two carrier bags, as there's just so much of the stuff. Even for such a big man I was surprised at the size of the tub; so, half of it we'll scatter at St Bernadette's in Erskine...'

Elaine howled with laughter at the thought of Bull resting for ever in the grounds of a Catholic church.

'...and the rest is going to the Sarry Heid pub.'

Elaine stared at her with stunned admiration.

'*That* is pure genius! *The Sarry Heid!* How're we goin' tae manage that?' she finally gasped in her excited Clydeside accent.

'I have a plan...' Ann-Marie said. 'You'll just have to wait and see.'

They parked off the Gallowgate and walked to the pub carrying one of the bags. The Saracen's Head pub; the hallowed ground where Celtic fans thronged on a match day, was today almost empty. They found a small table and Ann-Marie ordered two halves of lager at the bar, whilst looking around to check the clientele. One old man was sitting nursing the usual Scottish refreshment – a half of beer and a small whisky, known colloquially as a "hauf and a hauf". He looked like he'd been there since opening time, probably a jakey, she thought. She returned with the drinks to the table and caught Elaine fiddling with her rings, which she always did when her nerves got the better of her.

'Okay, tell me the plan; although how we're goin' tae scatter ashes in here without anyone noticing is beyond me!' Elaine whispered, gulping the lager.

'In the bag I'd put some old ciggie douts that I picked up in the car park in Johnstone. I was going to fill the ashtrays; but they just fling their douts on the street here. So part of dear Billy will just have to be dumped outside the door.'

'But someone'll *see* you!'

'We're not in a hurry are we? Don't fret – I'll manage.' She slipped one of the lunch napkins into the bag and filled it with a handful of ashes, then waited till the barman busied himself restocking under the bar. Then she walked towards the door, passing the smouldering fire place where she casually threw in the full napkin before walking outside, leaving Elaine looking aghast.

The street was empty, so quickly tipping some of the bag onto the pavement right outside the door of the pub, she then returned inside, carefully spilling some onto the floor, grinding it in with her foot.

'Is there a ladies here?' she asked the barman, as he

rose from the shelves and bottles under the bar.

'Oh *aye*, hen. Wur a *tourist* attraction now you know!' he said proudly, pointing the direction and Ann-Marie headed to the toilets. First the gents. She would act the confused woman in the unlikely event she got caught, and flushed half the contents down the toilet. A quick visit next door to the ladies, and she emptied the bag. 'In you go, Billy! Rest in peace!' she said flushing Billy's mortal remains away.

When she returned to the table, Elaine had finished her lager and Ann-Marie downed hers in silence, and crooked her head to Elaine, standing up, and taking the empty glasses to the bar.

The barman took them with a smile and watched the women leaving, 'No' their kinda place John,' he called to the barely conscious man slumped in the corner.

Outside Elaine was jubilant, 'If ah didnae see it with ma own eyes, I'd never have believed you'd get away with it! You've some brassneck!'

They walked back to the car and sat inside in silence for a moment. Ann-Marie sat watching the street taking slow deep breaths. Old men, housewives and delivery men preoccupied with their business, getting on with their day and ignoring two slightly flushed women sitting in a car.

'Did you *really* flush him down the pan?' Elaine finally demanded.

'In the gents *and* in the ladies!' Ann-Marie said, putting her hands on the steering wheel, 'Oh my God, I'm shaking!' she laughed.

They drove back towards Erskine, laughing together

at the sheer audacity of the plan.

They parked in the car park at St Bernadette's, took the second bag and simply walked along the path to the church door, scattering ashes like confetti.

'Why here?' Elaine asked as they walked.

'No reason except it's Catholic, and I never come here. I don't want any reminders of him at all. It's bad enough we had to kill him on the farm, but I'm not having him there in any form now.'

The bag was empty and Ann-Marie folded it up and pushed it into the hedge. She didn't want to take that home. Her conscience had enough to keep her awake in the wee small hours. They returned to the car, and Ann-Marie drove Elaine home.

'So – shopping? Will you come with me on Monday? Get the train and I'll meet you in Glasgow.'

'Yes, alright; maybe I could do with some new things. I'll talk to you on Sunday night.'

'I've had a great day!' Elaine said with a grin, 'Thanks for lunch and…everything!'

Chapter 8

Sunday arrived with sunshine and a fresh breeze chasing billowing white clouds across the vast sky above the farm. Ann-Marie took the dogs out for a long run to clear her head before the arrival of The Family. Today she had to endure the ridiculous charade of laying Billy's ashes to rest under the new memorial tree that was to be planted next to the soon-to-be taproom and shop. Of course, none of the family knew about that project yet, she smiled to herself, but today was the day the family bid Billy a final farewell. Ann-Marie swilled away the bad taste in her mouth with a third cup of coffee on her return to the house. She'd had another sleepless night despite the sleeping pills the doctor had supplied her, but accepted this as divine punishment for her sin. The Enquiry had been set for mid-May, and she could survive on four hours oblivion nightly until she got through the whole sorry episode.

Not that she was sorry at all. After the mental and physical abuse she'd endured for all those years she had finally worked up the courage and hate to end it, and had no regrets. Divorce would have meant a messy splitting of the assets, and she wasn't going to risk losing her family home and everything she and her parents had worked so hard to create.

And she was *fine* whilst working and getting through the days. It was at night that she was punished. Even with a whisky chaser, the sleeping tablets only afforded her dreamless sleep for a few hours. This morning a vivid sneering apparition with a half-detached nose and open laughing eyes had woken her with a jolt. She'd had to strip the bed and have a shower at five am. She dreaded to imagine what her mother thought.

After doing the morning rounds, she'd returned to the house for breakfast and Isa, seeing her exhausted face, ordered her to rest for a few minutes on the saggy sofa.

Too soon, a soft growl from Bracken alerted her to noise in the yard and she stiffly rose to see who had arrived. Catching a glimpse of the clock she groaned; she'd been asleep for over an hour and Duncan was hosing down the yard. He was settling in well, she thought as she put the kettle on, and it was kind of him to offer to come round to spruce up before the family arrived. The tree was sitting in a hessian sack with a spade next to it. *Red Devil.* Perfect choice she thought wryly, but it would look pretty next to the seating area, with pretty spring blossom followed by cherry red fruits. And of course the apples would just join the millions of others in the cider or juice in future.

She called out to him and he agreed immediately to a roll and bacon and a mug of tea and she started to prepare a snack for them both. Sunday on a farm is like every other day with animals to be fed, watered and cleaned out and the two of them worked till lunchtime ensuring all the farm jobs were done before the Big Event of the day. He waved goodbye as David and Lynda drove into the yard. To Ann-Marie's annoyance Bobby and Liz followed them in. She realised that this must have been Lynda's idea, and swallowed a knot of anger as she went to greet them all.

David took the boys to see the animals, leaving Bobby and Liz looking a little out of place in the yard.

'I see you've hired some help then.' Bobby said as his eyes followed Duncan off down the lane.

'Well, as you said yourself, I couldn't manage to run the place on my own,' Ann-Marie forced a smile. 'He's the neighbour's lad and he's working out fine.'

'You could have saved yourself all this if you'd taken my advice...' Bobby began.

'*Not* today Bobby. Today is going to be difficult enough without you interfering in *my* business,' she said with just the tiniest emphasise, before turning brightly to Lynda, 'I thought we'd have lunch first. It's just a cold buffet, and I'm sure it'll stretch to an extra two.'

If Lynda felt uncomfortable at her mother's obvious annoyance at the unwanted arrivals she didn't show it, and took the opportunity to change the subject;

'I've got that job I applied for! David's so pleased for me.'

Whilst Bobby and Liz congratulated her, Ann-Marie smiled. David must indeed be relieved at extra money coming in rather than going out of the household, although she noted Lynda was wearing a new tailored trouser suit. Now, even more, she'd have to dress to impress, she thought to herself as she them inside and began making a large pot of tea.

Lynda followed her and sat down at the long wooden table. Her idea to invite Uncle Bobby & Auntie Liz had been a disaster, she acknowledged. David had warned her, but after the phone call offering her the job, she'd rashly phoned and invited them. They were family, she explained to an exasperated David, but he'd correctly anticipated Ann-Marie's distaste.

'She doesn't *like* them,' he'd argued that morning, as he knotted his tie.

'I don't care! They're my dad's brother and sister.'

'You should have just left it alone. The pair of them make me uncomfortable and your mum hates them.'

Sitting across the table from them, she watched their unease. Liz sitting rigid and white and Bobby with that stupid smile of his. Were they *actually* holding hands under the table? Liz caught her staring, and her hands quickly returned to the table top. Lynda quashed her distaste and passed the sandwiches to the boys sitting next to their grandmother. Only another hour of this nonsense and she could go home.

Outside, David took charge of planting the tree, and they gathered round the chosen spot. Ann-Marie took the purple canister and tipped the contents slowly into the deep hole that she had dug the previous day. A small layer of soil on top and the tree was ready to go in, and no-one had even noticed, Ann-Marie thought with satisfaction. The boys held the trunk as David back-filled the hole, firming it in with his boot. Ann-Marie smiled and agreed he'd done a fair job of planting it. The boys watered it with the cans provided, and then with a melodramatic tear, Lynda spoke quietly.

'Rest easy daddy.'

If only they knew, Ann-Marie thought silently. He'd *not* be resting easy as countless catholics' ground his ashes underfoot at the doorway of the Sarry Heid, or visited the toilets there, or even walked over him on their way to mass at St Bernadette's. I hope he rots in hell. I hope he suffers as much as he's made me suffer all those years, she said to herself.

David put his hand on her shoulder, 'Are you alright? You're very flushed.'

She patted his hand with a forced smile, 'I'm fine. The whole thing has been quite hard. But this has been … helpful. I think I'll be able to move on now.'

David took charge, ushering the boys into the car and telling Lynda to leave her mother to rest that afternoon. Liz and Bobby hovered around like an unwelcome smell before Bobby finally spoke his mind.

'Ann-Marie; today isn't the time, but Liz and I were thinking that maybe you should still think on selling up. There are a couple of land developers at the lodge who would give you good money for this place. I'm happy to …'

Ann-Marie turned on him with icy contempt, 'Out.'

***

Work on transforming the farm gathered pace as the weather improved. The yard was resurfaced, and the grass corner next to the new taproom was mown, with some rustic post and rail fencing quickly erected. The orchard was starting to bloom with pink and white blossom dancing in the breeze, and Duncan had uploaded some incredible photos to the new website. Cider was being delivered to local shops, pubs and restaurants and an advert was placed in the local and national newspapers.

Ann-Marie had agreed to Roddy's suggestion of having an opening evening, with some local restaurant and bar owners, and the press. The date was set for just before Easter weekend.

One of the pigs was to be kept for a spit roast, and a local chef friend had agreed to do some buffet food. All the necessary legal paperwork had arrived for them to serve alcohol and everything was on track. She'd even succumbed to Elaine's suggestion of a shopping trip and bought a new outfit for the event.

A well-tailored trouser suit with a pink blouse that would look business-like and yet fun; or so the sales woman at the department store had said. Ann-Marie felt out of her comfort zone, but she agreed to buy both the suit and the dreaded magic knickers that would; according to the saleswoman, give her a sleek look. Elaine had put it more directly, she recalled.

'They hold your belly in and lift your bum back to where it was twenty years ago.'

The saleswoman rolled her eyes and forced a smile, 'Madam makes the point *perfectly*,' she agreed.

She wore the outfit to welcome the press from the local paper, and had to admit she felt good. She impulsively also chose polo shirts and sweatshirts with logos for herself and the lads. In for a penny, she sighed as she emailed the order.

Elaine and Malky had visited with offers to help; but

she refused with a smile. Her staff were were to help now, and together they made a good team, so she led them inside for coffee, whilst Malky's eyes were everywhere, taking in the transformation of the farm. 'You really have done a fantastic job, Ann-Marie. I can't believe it's the same place!' he gushed, suddenly aware of the increased value of the small farm.

Ann-Marie sipped her coffee. It was a bit of a backhanded compliment, but he hadn't meant it that way, she knew. The under investment in the farm had finally been rectified, and everything was running like clockwork, and in line with her plan to relaunch the cider commercially.

'Well, she's not *just* a pretty face,' Elaine snorted. Getting away with murder *and* regaining control of an increasingly valuable business was purely down to Ann-Marie's determination and brains, she thought, smiling broadly to her friend.

'No,' Malky said, looking directly into Ann-Marie's eyes, 'she has a pretty face and brains too.'

It was an undisguised attempt to flirt and Elaine's face darkened, but Ann-Marie immediately made light of the comment. 'Men always try and soft-soap us, Elaine. Malky thinks all his sweet-talk will get him some cake!' she said turning to her friend, 'I wouldn't have been able to do *any* of this without your help.' She hugged Elaine fiercely; wanting to ensure that she understood that she'd absolutely no interest in her idiot of a husband. The last thing she needed was her friend; *her accomplice*; being even the tiniest bit jealous.

She pushed a plate of cake towards Malky, and smiled at Elaine.

'Men only want what they cannae have. Look at him with that cake! I might have to move with the times to run this place, but I've no desire to have another man in my life. No matter how pretty they talk.'

Elaine laughed, but she hadn't missed the point. Ann-Marie valued her friendship more than all the idle compliments in the world. She shot Malky a disgusted stare.

Malky swallowed his cake, and his huge mistake quietly. Elaine would probably give him hell in the car on the way home and he'd have to make a joke about it; but he'd realised that Ann-Marie would never jeopardise her friendship with Elaine. If he was to be the next man in her life, he'd need to make sure Elaine was out of the picture permanently.

He redeemed himself when the farm workers appeared for coffee. Ann-Marie was telling Elaine all about the new corporate polo shirts, when Malky suggested finishing off the look by having the lads in kilts. Ann-Marie and the two lads were delighted.

'It would be a fabulous talking point.' Roddy agreed.

'And the women would *love it*,' Duncan laughed, 'even with *my* legs!'

Elaine laughed and joined in, 'Aye, all men look great in a kilt! One of the places we stayed had the men behind the bar in kilts. The customers loved it, *especially* the ladies!'

Ann-Marie laughed, 'Well, it's a great idea. Well done Malky.'

'Aye, it's not often he has great ideas, but that's a belter!' Elaine laughed; her annoyance gone, and Malky out of the dog-house.

Ann-Marie turned to her staff, 'Ok, you two. If you can sort a couple of matching kilts for yourselves before the big night…at a budget, mind; then go ahead.'

Roddy grabbed Duncan, 'Come on, there's a place in Greenock that sells kilts cheap and I know the manager from rugby. Let's go see him.'

They disappeared quickly, laughing and joking, and the pickup left the yard with the radio almost drowning out the sound of the new gravel flying.

Ann-Marie turned to her friends, 'They've both been great. They're so enthusiastic and the farm has had a great transformation.'

Pleased that the earlier awkwardness had passed, Malky picked up Elaine's jacket and held it for her with a smile. 'Time to let this woman get on with her day. Let's go home. I don't want you waiting to see young lads in kilts; the excitement'll go to your head.'

She laughed and slipped the jacket on.

'Remember and come to the opening,' Ann-Marie reminded.

'Wouldn't miss it for the world,' Malky said, kissing her chastely on the cheek.

Chapter 9

Spring arrived early with gentle sunshine and a soft breeze. On the hills surrounding the farm the grass was turning a pale light green, scattered with golden dandelions. The hedges began to green up, and the apple trees were a frothy confection of pink and white blooms filled with honeybees and a gentle happy hum.

As Ann-Marie returned to the yard she tried to view it professionally. Clean and tidy with a new layer of gravel, it looked cared for and welcoming. The new gate sign sported a new logo and opening times. She was content that everything was going well. The new sheep in the paddock were due to lamb any day now. They would make a nice addition to the farm, bringing visitors to see the lambs and providing meat for the small shop they were opening. The Suffolk crosses were easier on the eye than traditional Scottish blackface sheep, and her grandsons would perhaps see their first lambing, she smiled to herself. Maybe one or both of them might be interested in taking up the reins when she was ready to let go.

***

With her own thoughts as far from the farm as possible, Lynda was settling into her new job, and had impressed her boss with her efficiency and knowledge. It was, however, taking her longer to get to know the existing women in the office, who were a little stand-offish. She reasoned this was not only because she was new, but also younger and prettier than any of them. The boss waited till she had been there a week before inviting her to his office for a brief chat.

'How are you settling in Lynda?'

'Great, thank you. The work's interesting and I'm happy to be part of it amongst so many interesting folk.'

'Well, I'm pleased.' he said, 'My wife didn't think I needed a P.A., but I've got some personal projects coming along and needed someone to assist with these in addition to the usual office work. How would you and your husband feel about you working the occasional night away? I've got some business to take care of in London and I need to have someone discreet to take to the meetings.'

He watched her face intently to gauge her reaction. This hadn't been mentioned in the interview, and Lynda's heart raced as she considered. Noting her hesitation he added, 'Of course, you would be paid more, and accommodation and meals will be picked up by the firm.'

He was good-looking in a hard way, about ten years her senior and she understood from the guarded office talk that he ran a tight ship. Shame he was married, she thought before accepting the proposal, 'I'm sure occasional trips to London will be fine,' she smiled brightly.

'That's great', he said, 'I'll give you a few days notice to get things in place at home, but most of the meetings will be short and we'll be back in Glasgow the next morning.' He raised his eyes and stared at her directly, 'I need you to be discreet. My London business is completely separate and private to my business here. If it doesn't work out then we will have a parting of the ways.'

She felt a tremor of excitement, but answered him confidently, 'I understand completely, Mr Walker. And I'm *always* discreet.'

She returned to her desk, aware of the covert looks from the other women. As she completed the half-finished report, she replayed the brief conversation in her head. The extra money would be great, and the odd trip to London was exciting; but she'd recognised the look in his face; the predatory look that vanished almost as soon as it had appeared. That look, and the bait of extra money were the reasons she'd agreed.

As she typed, she considered the little that she knew about him. He'd started Walker Associates ten years ago and now it was a bastion of legal respectability in the professional West End of Glasgow. She now knew he was married, but Mrs Walker never visited the office, and he absented himself once a week, when he visited a prestigious country club. She found herself wondering what he looked like naked. 'Get a grip, Lynda', she said angrily to herself, hoping her excitement wasn't detected by the sharp little eyes in the office, and tried to concentrate on the report she was completing.

***

Two sheep had lambed overnight, each producing a perfect and pretty set of twins. In a day or so, she'd let them out into the small paddock next to the cider garden, where the small Red Devil apple tree was growing strongly in the decent soil enriched with ashes from Ann-Marie's hearth. She barely gave it a thought now; just another apple tree with no significance or meaning.

As the nightmares and bad dreams dwindled, and her excitement with the farm grew, she had to constantly remind herself to avoid careless words. Only Elaine and Isa were aware of the inner tension that she hid; until, on the morning of the launch, her solicitor arrived unexpectedly.

Jim Muir had decided it was the time to grab the bull by the horns and tackle her head-on regarding how she was coping after Billy's death. His unfortunate use of the phrase "possibly seeing a professional" particularly enraged her; and Isa made herself scarce as Ann-Marie visibly bristled at his direct questioning.

'Do you mean see a *shrink*?' she'd replied with disgust, 'I'm not mental.'

'Bereavement counselling,' he'd clarified quietly, 'I went for some after Jill died years ago. I found it... helpful.'

'Oh, I see. I don't know Jim; I think I'm getting through it. I don't really want to talk about myself or Billy to a stranger; in fact I don't really want to talk to *anyone* about it.'

He placed his hand on top of hers, and she felt with surprise the rough dryness of his skin. As a farmer, with hands constantly wet or dirty, Ann-Marie kept the dryness away with regular applications of Udder Cream. It really did work, and she failed to suppress a smile at the thought of suggesting Udder Cream to a solicitor.

'What?'

'Your hands are always so dry. You really should use some cream on them or you'll start to look old.'

He laughed out loud. 'I never knew you cared or even *noticed* my appearance,' he said full of mischief, making her blush furiously as she pulled her hand away.

'That's not what I meant! I was just concerned. *As a friend!*'

'Oh, that's alright then. I don't need to preserve my honour!' he laughed and stood up, 'I must away,' he said theatrically, holding the back of his hand to his forehead like a tragic Pre-Raphaelite subject; 'Alas, clients beckon.'

'Fool!' she muttered quietly, following him to the door. As he stepped through he suddenly stopped and turned and his face was uncomfortably close to hers. She noticed for the first time that his eyes were a startling china blue.

'I *am* your friend, and I care about you. Have a think about what I said. I'll see you this evening.'

And then he was gone; with his car ambling out the gate and him waving out the car.

Well, what was *that* all about? She asked herself as she returned inside and deliberately ignored her mother's questioning look.

Isa was biding her time. After tonight's launch and before the Inquiry, there was plenty of time for an interrogation. On more than *one* subject.

***

Thankfully, the big day had dawned bright and sunny. Renfrewshire had washed her face and was looking like a bride on her wedding day with fluffy white clouds set in an azure sky. Ann-Marie sent a silent prayer that the weather would last till the end of the evening.

The animals were all fed, cleaned and watered early and the pigs and sheep turned out to keep their sheds pristine. She reminded Roddy and Duncan that no matter how good everything looked, it was still a farm with a farm smell and the townies who were due that evening would not appreciate the *fresh country smell* that farmers had long accepted as normal.

They grinned and went back to preparing and primping. Parking had been extended by cutting the small paddock to cope with large numbers of cars as there had been nearly 100 invitations sent out. Fairy lights had been hung around the barn and trees and solar markers to light up paths and parking areas. Ann-Marie groaned at the expense but Roddy explained that they would be necessary for Christmas sales too, and so she grudgingly accepted the wisdom of it.

'Speculate to accumulate you said!' he'd shouted from over the yard, moving the lambs and their mothers.

'Aye, but don't speculate so much with *my* money!' she'd shouted back good naturedly.

It was mid-afternoon when the reporter and photographer from the newspapers arrived, wanting to capture some photos in the sun before the crowds arrived. Ann-Marie and the boys changed into their corporate finery, and she felt a surge of pride as they had their photos taken in front of the new tap room. It had been the right decision to go with the kilts, and the photographer was keen to take a few in front of the orchard too. Dad would have loved to see this, she said silently to herself, blinking back a sudden tear. Cars began to arrive and Roddy and Duncan's rugby club friends helped with parking the guests, and manning the bar. Ann-Marie was busy working the crowd and pressing the flesh of the councillors and local worthies who seemed delighted with the refurbishment. Jim had appeared from nowhere, guiding Isa to a chair near to one of the temporary heaters, and then shaking hands with someone, before coming over to her.

'I didn't know you'd arrived!' she exclaimed.

'I've been watching you from over there, and enjoying seeing you smile. I'll go and make sure the reporter gets the right information; *you* enjoy your success,' he said and headed away through the crowd. Before she had time to think, Roddy was introducing her to the manager of one of the city's off-sales chains and she had to switch on the sales pitch.

It seemed like no time at all when Jim announced from the door that the hog roast was ready, and that as soon as they had raised their glasses to Ann-Marie and the continued success of High Glen Farm, they could all collect some delicious home-produced artisan hog roast rolls.

There was a loud cry of approval and the crowd stampeded for the door to claim their food. In the general crowd Ann-Marie spotted Roddy chatting to a pretty blonde whilst collecting dirty glasses. He gave her a "thumbs up" sign and continued to dart around the barn, clearing and tidying as we went.

Jim appeared again at her side, grinning.

'You're like the cat that's had the cream,' she said smiling, 'What have you been up to?'

He presented her with a glass of champagne. 'I've been saving this for you. It's not cider, but I thought you'd appreciate it now that we know the launch has been a resounding success.'

She took the glass with a smile. Demi-sec rosé champagne; impressive, she thought.

'Has it been a resounding success then?' she asked sipping appreciatively.

Jim's eyes twinkled, 'I've been eavesdropping on conversations everywhere. The taproom, shop and the cider are going down well. I overheard the manager of one of the top hotels saying he's putting in an order for bottles tomorrow. *All* the price-lists have been taken and I've directed people to the website until you get some more printed. You're a success woman! Now relax and enjoy the rest of the evening.' He left her with the glass of champagne and darted off to talk to a knot of potential customers returning from the hog roast with laden plates.

She mingled with the crowd, many of whom were personal friends or business acquaintances, and noted with relief that no-one had mentioned Billy, the accident or anything that would spoil her mood, and she started to relax.

As folk started to drift off into the night, she walked outside to see what Duncan was up to, but she needn't have worried, as he and a couple of friends were sitting round stuffing themselves with rolls and pork and more than a few empty cider bottles lay at the back of the serving table.

'You go easy on that cider,' she warned him, 'I want you here bright and early without a sore head.'

He grinned and laughed and she left him to his friends, taking the opportunity to walk to the gate and look back. The fairy lights she'd moaned about looked great. The yard and taproom looked great. The gamble had paid off.

Jim was walking towards her, smiling.

'I need to go,' he said. 'If I stay, I'll help you finish that champagne; and I can neither drive home drunk nor stay with the prettiest girl at the party. I have a reputation to keep.'

Blushing furiously, Ann-Marie didn't know whether to walk away or slap him.

'I think you've *already* had too much! Such nonsense! Do you want one of the boys to drive you home?'

'Nope,' he grinned and waltzed off to his car. She watched him drive away; raising her hands to feel the heat from her face, and then returned to the barn, the party, and the all-seeing eyes of her smiling mother.

As the night finally ended, Roddy and Duncan and a couple of friends piled into Roddy's car, and she turned off the lights and headed into the house. Her mother had gone to bed, but couldn't have failed to see the large bouquet of pink roses and another bottle of champagne on the kitchen table. A scribbled note thanked her for a lovely evening. She could barely read the solicitors scrawl but knew it was from Jim.

She eased her feet out of the court shoes and popped the cork of the champagne. She'd have a little glass now, then change out of her dress and walk the dogs in her pyjamas before bed.

Chapter 10

Suddenly, the dogs were barking, and milky sunshine streaming in the window. Her eyes flew open and she realised with a start that she'd slept in. Outside she heard familiar voices and the sound of bottles clinking. She padded upstairs quickly to change, shooting the clock a venomous stare, as she took a second or two to focus on it. When she finally emerged, feeling a little the worse for wear and allowing the two very desperate dogs to relieve themselves; Duncan and Roddy joked about how much she'd drunk the night before.

'Don't you be mixing your drinks now!' Duncan mimicked.

'I want you here sharp in the morning!' Roddy added with a smirk.

'Alright, alright. I get it,' she laughed. 'Now, for the love of God, someone make a big pot of coffee. I've got the most ferocious head.'

They spent an hour filling the pickup with empty bottles and bags full of waste ready to go to the refuse centre, and then sat soothing sore heads with more coffee. Isa spent the morning washing glasses and plates, complaining loudly that they needed to buy a dishwasher.

Lunch was of course, left-over roast pork and stuffing rolls. Roddy had sensibly stripped the remains of the hog roast into containers for her freezer and the rest was refrigerated ready to take to the rugby club that night. Wasting food was a sin. She remembered her father long ago telling the story of how his Irish great-grandparents starved during the Famine before immigrating to Scotland. Only through hard work and saving every penny had they managed to scrape enough money together to buy what was then a derelict farmhouse and a few acres. Although it was many years ago; a different era really, family values never changed, and Ann-Marie accepted the logic of a by-gone age.

At the table they ate quietly, and she realised with a smile that she wasn't the only one nursing a sore head. By mid afternoon, the taproom was spic and span and the farm was back to normal. The computer was full of messages and orders for both cider and meat, forcing Ann-Marie to sit patiently to answer them all, and the day passed until Roddy popped his read round the office door to say he and Duncan were off home, and that Isa was asleep on the sofa.

Farm life returned to a new normal, with the usual routine punctuated by deliveries going out and new arrivals in the form of lambs, piglets and chicks adding to the chores. Dandelions were joined by wild daffodils nodding their heads near the stream, and the home paddock filled with snowy white sheep and lambs playing with each other.

Isa had felt well enough to resume her Tuesday evening outings to Sadie's for their knit and natter sessions, and

Lynda seemed happy in her new job. Standing at the fence enjoying the warm sunshine and blue sky, Ann-Marie watched the sheep snickering to their lambs. She should be rejoicing that everything was going so well. But as surely as dark clouds were gathering on the horizon, the spectre of the Enquiry was looming; and she needed to lay that particular ghost before she could rest easy.

They had a team meeting in the kitchen to discuss the hiring of seasonal staff and it was agreed that instead of hiring foreign pickers, they would approach the Scottish Agricultural College for students. Harvest was many months away, but Roddy also suggested mopping up the end of the picking season with a rugby club picking party and barbeque, and this was added into the work schedule.

A phone call from Jim ended the meeting, and his news dampened the atmosphere. The Enquiry was set for the following Tuesday at Paisley Sheriff Court, and he'd asked to see her the day before to run through the procedure. Ann-Marie's stress level rocketed and she sent the boys away whilst she phoned Elaine, who immediately agreed to meet her for lunch on the Monday.

Elaine was nervous. Ann-Marie could hear it in the fast volley of words tumbling out, and tried to calm her.

'It's just a formality remember.'

'But it's at the *court*.' Elaine wailed loudly, forcing Ann-Marie to move the receiver away from her ear.

'It's *alright* Elaine. I'm meeting Jim before I meet you, and he'll go over it. Just this last hurdle. Don't lose your head now! I need you to keep *calm*.'

'But, what if they start asking questions?'

'They *won't* ask you questions. You made a statement *remember*? If there had been questions, they'd have asked you before now. They know you'll be nervous. Look, I'll need to go, but I'll see you Monday at twelve at the pub. Don't be late.'

She hung up, twisting her hands anxiously; and then out of the corner of her eye, saw her mother standing watching her. Her breath caught in her throat and her heart began to thump in her chest, but she was unable to move, unable to drop her eyes from her mother's fixed and penetrating stare. How much had she heard? How much did she *know*?

'I think its time for a little chat Ann-Marie', Isa said and locked the front door with a loud click.

Isa returned to the sofa and picked up her knitting, waiting for Ann-Marie to join her. She casually rolled the excess yarn back onto the ball and placed it beside her before looking up. 'There's no point beating about the bush, so just tell me straight how Billy had his *little accident*. And Ann-Marie; I want the truth; *not* that story you gave to the police.'

In a way it was a relief to finally be able to talk about it, and the details began to spill out. Isa sat impassive, whilst Ann-Marie, white-faced and tearful told her everything. In a few short minutes she had completed her confession and sat awaiting her mother's reaction. The clock ticked sluggishly, stretching every painful second into a lifetime.

Isa sighed and finally spoke.

'You're my daughter and I love you; but why oh why

did you put up with that bullying, that *abuse* for all those years? I knew *years* ago that you were miserable, but it wasn't *my* marriage. Wasn't *my* place to say anything; and you never uttered a word. And now this.'

She paused and raised her cold blue eyes, searching Ann-Marie's face for an answer, but Ann-Marie had told all; and had nothing to add. She felt that she had, in fact, said quite enough.

Her mother sat quietly. She didn't appear to be shocked or horrified, but just said nothing. Meanwhile, Ann-Marie's brain was in overdrive, going over all the possibilities that this admission might have raised, and whether the confession would result in another stroke.

'Aren't you *angry* at me mum? Disgusted at what I've done?'

Eventually, her mother took a deep breath and looked her straight in the eyes,

'I'm angry that you didn't do it *sooner* you stupid girl! Barring the Enquiry, it appears that you've got away with it; and I'm *glad*. You didn't deserve that and now you're free from that…*creature*', she spat crossly. Ann-Marie's eyes widened, but Isa wasn't finished. She got up and went to fill the kettle before returning to the sofa.

'Can you trust Elaine to keep her mouth shut?' she asked. Ann-Marie nodded silently.

'Well then, you can also trust that what *I* know will go with me to my grave.'

Ann-Marie stood to go and make the tea. Isa pulled her knitting needles back to her and began to knit, 'Mum's the word, Ann-Marie. Mum's the word.'

The morning of the Enquiry dawned with Ann-Marie pacing her bedroom floor. She'd been reassured by her solicitor that it was just a formality, a final summing up of the circumstances of the accident. She'd coached Elaine over and over until she was word perfect in the remote possibility of there being any questions; and her mother was maintaining her complete lack of knowledge due to her recent stroke. Nothing could possibly go wrong. And still she paced; her head full of disjointed thoughts and flashbacks of that awful day.

Billy was getting his own back, she imagined. Coming back to haunt her with her crime; filling her head with the squeals of pigs, the disfigured face dancing in front of her eyes in the wee small hours. Her brain, like a videotape; replaying the events of Billy's death, over and over. The sound of him hitting the concrete mixed with the excited screams of the pigs. Pounding and pounding the skillet into his skull. Small black piggy eyes staring at her. Feasting, feasting.

Oh, how he would be enjoying this! There was nothing he liked better than hurting her, whether physically or mentally, and she could easily imagine his gloating. She tried to push the thought from her mind, because *realistically*, she told herself, she was in the clear. It was just a formality. She pulled the bedroom curtains open to let in the first faint glimmers of daylight. Night terrors; skulking in the dark corners of her room as well as in her mind, feeding on the darkness. The sunlight finally banished them, and she felt marginally more at ease.

She quietly made her way downstairs and put the

lights on in the kitchen as she drew water for the kettle. There was no way it could come back to her, not now. Not after all this time. Surely this had to be the end of it? After all this time with no suspicion, no more questions, no investigation she could put the whole thing behind her. Then it was only her conscience, and her mother, and Elaine that she had to mind. That; and the final reckoning when she would have to plead her case to the highest Judge of all.

***

Lynda had reluctantly taken the day off work for the Enquiry, and was dressed in sombre black, which at least looked good on her she admitted as she took a last look in the mirror before leaving the apartment. Her uncle and aunt had insisted on attending and were collecting her. She knew this would be the formal conclusion of the circumstances of her father's death, and was only attending because it was expected. Her mother and Elaine were the nearest thing to witnesses, and Lynda was praying that her mother didn't choose today to become emotional; not that she'd shown much emotion since the accident itself. She'd read the glowing article in the Glasgow Herald about the relaunching of the cider, and aside from a slight resentment at not being invited, she acknowledged that her mother was making a go of the farm.

In the car, Lynda was keenly aware of Bobby and Liz's bitching resentment. The sooner she could distance herself from them the better. She'd regretted taking their side in the half-baked plan to persuade her mother and grandmother to sell up, which had backfired, causing resentment and distance between them, and now she had to endure their barbed comments in the car.

The sooner today was all over with, she could get on with her life, and focus on herself, and the excitement of the first business trip to London the following week. She didn't need this rehash of her father's accident or her aunt or uncle spoiling her day; and so when they parked, told them that she would get the train back to work afterwards. 'It's not necessary for me to be here, so if it goes on and on I'm leaving early,' she said crisply.

'You're *here* to find out how this accident happened!' Bobby snarled.

'We *know* how he died! It was gruesome and I want to get on with my life. I don't know what you think coming here'll achieve,' she snarled back. 'It's not like *you'll* gain anything by it!'

Liz was visibly flustered, 'Don't speak to your uncle like that Lynda. He was *our* brother and we've a right to be here.'

'Oh for God's sake, let's get on with it!' Lynda marched towards the court building, leaving them trailing behind.

'Don't say a word Liz!' Bobby growled at his sister.

Inside Ann Marie, Elaine, Jim and Calum were already waiting. Calum, Elaine's son was attempting to sooth his anxious mother, 'You probably won't even be called and if you do it'll be just to confirm what you said in the statement. I'll call you tonight; I need to get to work.'

Jim was explaining to Ann-Marie the order of the proceedings. He'd seen Bobby, Liz and Lynda arrive and directed them to the public gallery, preventing any conversation with Elaine or Ann-Marie, who were both deathly white. After all that had happened Ann-Marie finally looked as if it was all too much to bear, and he was trying to make the whole necessary process as stress-free as possible. Then he spotted the Procurator Fiscal, and approached him for a private word. With a glance at the pale woman, he nodded, turned and entered the court room. Jim led Ann-Marie and Elaine to the witness room and they huddled in a corner.

'Any time now', he said quietly, 'I'm expecting your part to be very short just to confirm the statements you made. It'll all be very quick, and there really is nothing to worry about.' He smiled at Elaine, who beamed back. Ann-Marie was silent and pale and clenching her hands together, trying to keep it all together. And then her name was called.

Chapter 11

She left the Enquiry and stood with unsteady legs on the steps outside the Court, breathing deeply. People were milling around her, and although she was aware of them, she felt light-headed and remote. Elaine was still gripping her hand tightly, but Ann-Marie felt as if she was floating or falling. She looked up; briefly saw seagulls wheeling in the sunlight and then was consumed by the roar of traffic and darkness.

When she opened her eyes, her mother was sitting beside her bed, watching her.

'You've returned then,' she said quietly and reached to stroke the hair from her forehead.

Ann-Marie tried to speak, but the words wouldn't come; and exhausted by the effort she lay quietly, as her mother told her she'd fainted outside the Court. After a minute or two, she managed to wriggle slowly so she was sitting up, as Isa told her that everything was alright, that she was home, that everyone had left except Duncan, who was out feeding the livestock.

'Water?' she asked, handing her daughter a glass, which she took and sipped readily.

'It's all over,' Isa said. 'Multiple injuries due to, or as a consequence of a fall and or attack by pigs. End of story. Closed book. You're in the clear.'

Ann-Marie stared at her and sipped some more water. Isa stood up and opening the bedroom door, looked back at her daughter, 'You always told the fat pig that too much bacon would kill him,' she said with a smile, before leaving her to rest.

Ann-Marie sunk down into the duvet and closed her eyes. It was over. Tears came silently and she allowed herself the luxury of feeling sorry for herself; feeling racking sobs hurt her ribs and throat as the relief flowed through her. When she was exhausted and had no more tears to cry, she turned over and surrendered herself to a dreamless sleep.

***

It was a week before she felt able to talk to anyone, and Isa answered the phone, dealt with the family, staff and friends, turning everyone away and allowing her the space she needed to recover. She roamed the farm and the surrounding hills, accompanied only by the dogs. Bracken and Bramble were exhausted by the long daily walks and comforted her as she sat on the sofa in the evenings, listening to her mother's knitting needles clicking away, and the hiss of the kettle boiling. Isa had caught her searching for the bottle of malt one evening and calmly told her she'd got rid of it all.

'Drink is the root of all evil,' she preached, 'Just look at the trouble Sadie has with that wastrel Mark. I'm not saying you can't have *one*, but you need to stop relying on that stuff Ann-Marie, it'll not solve anything.'

She smiled at her mother, 'Aye, I've been drinking too much,' she agreed, closing the cupboard door, 'It'll not do me any harm being teetotal for a while, I suppose.'

***

She was sitting doing the accounts one afternoon when she heard a familiar car pull into the yard. A minute or so later, Isa opened the office door and beamed at her, with Elaine standing looking sheepish and concerned at her shoulder.

'Look who's come to see you,' Isa said, leaving them together whilst she tactfully took the laundry to hang on the washing line in the garden.

'How are ye feeling?' Elaine asked, following Ann-Marie into the living room.

'Much better,' Ann-Marie managed to summon a smile.

'God, you gave me an awful turn.' Elaine whispered and hugged her, 'I've tried to phone you *loads* of times, but your mother kept saying you weren't ready to talk yet.'

'She knows,' Ann-Marie said quietly. 'Everything.'

Elaine's mouth formed a silent O whilst her eyes opened wide.

'She guessed most of it; I just told her the details. But it's ok. She won't say anything, and we're not to talk about it. *Any* of it. Ever again.'

Elaine sat quietly. She was, for once, lost for words.

After the longest minute ever, Ann-Marie got up and put the kettle on, and a few minutes later made a pot of tea in time for Isa returning with the empty washing basket.

'Ah! You made some tea!' Isa said brightly, 'Just the job.' She pulled a packet of hobnob biscuits from a cupboard and joined the two friends in the living room, talking about the farm, a new cardigan Isa was knitting and nothing of any consequence.

Some time later Ann-Marie walked Elaine to her car.

'That was really surreal,' Elaine said as she got in the drivers seat, 'I can't believe we just sat and had tea and biscuits with your mother who knows you bumped off your husband and is totally okay with it!'

'We're not talking about it, remember? Never again.'

'I know, but…'

Ann-Marie silenced her with a glare, and Elaine started the car, 'Alright. I get it. But ahm gonna have to get this right in my head before I come back here. Your mother *knows*! Jesus! That's jist *mental*! I'll call you soon,' she waved and drove away.

***

Lynda was congratulating herself on landing the perfect job. She was making good money, the work was easy and this evening she was flying down to London with her handsome boss. They met at the airport, and as they waited to board the flight, he wanted to change the meetings he'd arranged for the following week, so whilst he made some business calls, she had to email or telephone various clients to rearrange meetings.

Outside the terminal building, a car met them and took them to the hotel, where they checked into their rooms.

'I'll see you downstairs at the desk in ten minutes,' he'd said curtly.

Lynda dumped her bag on the bedroom floor, and checked out the bathroom; not luxury, but not cheap, with some mid-range toiletries provided. She looked at her watch, wondering where they were going to a meeting at nine at night, but slipped her black wool coat on, patted her hair in place and headed downstairs quickly. Ian Walker wasn't a man who liked to be kept waiting.

Again, a car was waiting for them, and they drove for about twenty minutes, heading into Chinatown, before stopping abruptly in front of a restaurant.

'Don't speak unless I speak to you, and remember what I said about discretion,' Ian Walker said, opening the door and striding out. She slid out beside him and followed him into a restaurant, but to her surprise they walked straight through to the back, and after entering a corridor, climbed some stairs. A stocky man was waiting and opened a door into a smoky room. Her heart racing, Lynda realised that they were in some sort of gambling den. The room was small with one central table, around which sat several men. A fug of smoke floated like a low cloud in the shadows, and a thin, hard-faced blonde was draped over a fat middle-aged Chinaman who was pushing gambling chips into the centre of the table. One of the men got up and led them to a small separate table on the far side of the room. Large tumblers of whisky arrived for the men, and they sat talking quietly but quickly. She sat slightly back from the table, unsure how to react, but listening for any cue from her boss.

The conversation continued for a few minutes; punctuated by some swear words and at one time, a thump on the table, which made Lynda jump. Ian Walker threw her a smile and returned to the animated conversation. Her eyes darted around the room, realising no-one knew where she was, except this man whom she barely knew. This *meeting* was very likely underhand if not totally illegal, and she wished for dear life that it would all be over soon, and that she could return home and hand her notice in. In that split second she realised he'd spoken to her.

'*Lynda*,' he repeated, 'Please write out a receipt for Mr Li for £20,000, and then write that up in the black cash book please. Purchase of the motor vessel *Serenity*. This is Mr Li's card with his address.'

She took the card, and pulled the cash book and receipt book from her bag and began to complete them. The two men sat and drunk their whisky, and she was conscious that the Chinaman was staring at her. He made some comment in Chinese to her boss, who laughed and replied, surprising her that he spoke the language. She passed the receipt to her boss, who checked it before passing it to the other man. They stood and Ian Walker shook the man's hand, and turned ushering her towards the door.

Back in the car they drove a short distance in silence before stopping a second time. Again, they waked through another Chinese restaurant, this time emerging into a lane lined with warehouses. She carefully followed him in the near total darkness, into a grimy shed with a circular pit around which many men were watching cocks fighting. The din was incredible with everyone calling and shouting for their chosen bird, and the sour smell filled her nostrils. Lynda was revolted, but he hadn't come to watch, and she followed him into a quiet room filled with potted palms and a table with a fat white envelope lying on top. Walker lifted the envelope and opened it, checking the contents.

'Shouldn't we wait…' she asked nervously, when he turned and raised his eyes to the ceiling at the corner of the room, where a security camera was positioned, 'Receipt for £25,000 made out to Mr Wang please, and again, mark up the cash book Lynda. Consultation for staffing and other policies, today's date.'

She wrote as instructed and they left the receipt on the same table before retracing their steps.

Back in the car, he turned to her, 'One last call, then we'll go eat.'

Lynda was a bag of nerves, her mind working through all sorts of scenarios. Was this just dodgy business deals, money-lending or drugs? Was she being totally ridiculous, or could he only reach these kind of men at night? The car sped through leafy London suburbs and drove through electric gates to a large detached house. Again, she nervously followed Ian Walker inside, only to be delighted at the plush and expensive decor. This was the kind of house she dreamed of; huge airy rooms, thick white carpets and expensive white leather furniture. A short stocky man appeared in a navy dressing gown and beckoned them to a table, smiling. The men had a brief but friendly conversation which made little sense to Lynda, and then Walker instructed her to make out another receipt for consultation services.

Back in the car, he turned to her,

'You did well tonight. Let's grab some food before its too late; George knows my favourite place', he said tapping the driver on the shoulder.

George deposited them outside a West End restaurant, where they ordered steak and champagne, as the only other diners left the restaurant.

After he had taken a sip, he sat back and watched her looking around the restaurant.

'So, you like the finer things in life, then?' he asked with the smallest of smiles.

'How did…?' she began stunned at this almost instant reading of her character.

'Oh, I do a little research on all my new starts,' he smiled, 'I like to know what I'm paying for.'

She didn't know if she liked the tone of that comment, and sipped her champagne rather than answer. Their steaks arrived and they ate ravenously.

'I know it's London, but I never knew you could get a meal at midnight,' she ventured.

'Oh you can get almost anything at any time if you know the right people, and are prepared to pay well,' he answered. 'I used to work in London before returning to Glasgow, so I know it well.'

She took another sip of champagne and looked at him. His cheeks and chin had a blue stubble shadow now, but he still looked good; and she was pleased to notice that he was looking at her with interest.

He paid the bill and the waiting car took them back to the hotel.

'We'll leave at 7am, and be back in the office for a normal day,' he said outside her bedroom door, and held his hand out. Confused, she put her hand in his, only for him to drop it, 'The receipt book and cash book Lynda,' he said patiently.

Blushing furiously, she handed them over, mumbled a goodnight and rushed into her room. Ian Walker walked to his own door, smiling.

Chapter 12

High Glen Farm basked in the sunshine of the Scottish high summer, but not everyone was content. Roddy was waiting for a run of perfectly dry days to start the first cut of hay in the meadow and was anxious. The window of opportunity was short, and he needed at least three hot dry days to cut, turn and dry the hay before baling, and he was checking and rechecking the weather reports, because in the central belt of Scotland, dry weather, even in June, was not a certainty.

Duncan had taken charge of the livestock, and was competently managing the day-to-day chores on the farm, leaving Ann-Marie to manage the cider and juice, and the business side of things, and they were busy with increasing sales of cider and farm produced meat. A gentle and companionable routine had established itself and Ann-Marie had decided, now that her mother was back on her feet, to have a new bathroom installed in the house, and the plumbers were busy getting underfoot.

Tuesday evenings had been the regular Ladies Night for Sadie and Isa, and Ann-Marie had begun to stay for the evenings, instead of just dropping Isa off and collecting her later. Whilst the two friends sat and knitted, she read a paperback or listened to the gossip, fending off suggestions that she find herself a good-looking friend who would be much better company than two old women. The banter and old stories were almost the same every week, and the good natured camaraderie lasted until Mark returned later in the evenings, always drunk and usually in a foul temper, heralding the time for Isa and Ann-Marie to reluctantly leave their friend alone with him.

Tonight though, Sadie was upset; and so nervous that she almost dropped the plate of sausage rolls she'd heated up for their supper. Ever to the point, Isa demanded to know what the problem was, and Sadie dissolved into tears, explaining that yet again, Mark had been gambling and lost, and had been drinking even before he left the house that evening.

'I'm frightened,' she admitted quietly, blowing her nose into a wad of toilet tissue.

Isa let her ramble on, her face set grim with anger.

'He's jist so *angry* all the time now. Yesterday there wis a letter from the bank saying we were overdrawn…I went this morning and sorted it out, but he's been drinking all day today, sayin' it's all my fault, and its *not*. It's the gambling, well - and the drinking. He won't see he's got a problem and I don't know what to do.'

Isa and Ann-Marie exchanged looks. Over the last few weeks he had been getting worse, and although they'd both begged Sadie to leave him, they knew they were wasting their breath; that she wasn't brave enough to make that big decision.

Sadie gulped her sherry and tried to hold back

the tears.

'He had a big fight with the downstairs neighbour yesterday, because he's been shoutin' at their kids when he's been full of the drink. I jist wish…'

'What? Wish what?' Isa prompted as Sadie started blubbering again.

'Oh, I jist…well…' she cast an embarrassed look at Ann-Marie, 'I jist wish Mark wis dead too. I'm *so* sorry, Ann-Marie, I don't mean to remind you about Billy… but you really are better without him, and I wish…' she snivelled as the unspoken wish died on her lips.

Ann-Marie flushed, and tried to cover her embarrassment by furtively looking in her handbag for a packet of tissues, which she passed to Sadie.

'Aunt Sadie, it's fine, don't worry. Now, the main thing is to make sure *you're* okay? Can we arrange for you to see a solicitor, to at least get some advice?' she pleaded.

'Oh, no! If he found out, he'd be so *angry!*' Sadie blanched.

She suddenly grabbed Ann-Marie's wrist, 'Shhh!'

There was a loud thump coming from downstairs and the sound of breaking glass.

'Christ! He's home!' Sadie cried, and sobbed into her tissue.

'Ann-Marie, go and put the stair light on for that fool,' Isa said sharply.

Ann-Marie stared at her mother with annoyance, 'I don't really…' she began, but then stopped as the women could hear Mark clumsily trying to mount the stairs, swearing profusely. Isa dragged Sadie into the bathroom to wash her face, and turned to Ann-Marie, 'I'll deal with

120

her if you deal with him,' she hissed under her breath.

Ann-Marie's eyebrows raised, Well, what does she expect *me* to do, she thought crossly, opening the door to the stairway, and flicking on the light.

He was already halfway up the stair and flailing his arms trying to grab the banister, and as the light flooded the stairwell, he looked up and she saw he was almost unconscious with alcohol. At the bottom of the stair near the slightly ajar door lay a smashed whisky bottle. He tried to focus, obviously expecting to see Sadie, and his frown darkened when he recognised Ann-Marie and then Isa, who had come out to see just how drunk Sadie's husband was.

'The three witches are in residence then?' he half slurred and half snarled.

'How drunk *is* he?' she asked Ann-Marie, looking down at the man who now resembled a typical Glasgow alcoholic.

'Hammered. I'm surprised he can manage the stairs,' Ann-Marie answered with disgust.

He half-crawled up to the top as they watched him. His flies open, shirt stained and hanging-out, and the smell of stale whisky hanging around him like flies round a bin. Then he finally stood in front of them, attempting to draw himself up to his full height of five foot six, eyes angry and red and face flushed with alcohol. Ann-Marie wrinkled her nose at the smell.

'*Sadie*…I wanna talk tae ye on yer own!' he snarled, raising a fist, 'Get this pair oot ma hoose!' he spat at them.

He staggered slightly, his anger unbalancing him. Isa's hand suddenly shot out, as if to grab his shirt, and then

121

a very strange thing happened. Ann-Marie was acutely aware of her mother pressing her hand firmly on Mark's head and *pushing*.

For a split second he teetered on his heels with a look of surprise on his face, and then he was cart-wheeling silently down the stairs to the bottom. He lurched and rolled from one wall to another on his way, tumbling as he fell. Ann-Marie stared in horror as he landed at the bottom with a sickening crack and lay still.

There was a moment of absolute silence as her mind processed what had just happened, and she slowly turned to look at her mother in horror, 'What have ye *done*?' eventually came from her dry lips.

'What was necessary,' her mother answered grimly, and turned and walked back into the living room, pulling Ann-Marie with her, away from the scene, and closing the door to the hallway very quietly.

Sadie chose the moment to reappear from the bathroom, her face stained with mascara streaks and her eyes swollen and red. She looked from Isa to Ann-Marie to the closed door, an unspoken question in her troubled eyes.

'Sit down.' Isa ordered. Sadie sat, bewildered. She looked to the door again, and then to Isa and Ann-Marie, and back to Isa.

'Where…?'

'*Quiet* Sadie, I'm trying to think,' Isa interrupted sharply.

The three women sat in silence with Ann-Marie's eyes fixed to her mother's face. Cold-bloodedly, deliberately and without any remorse, she had just pushed Sadie's tormentor down the stairs to his death. Of course, *she* couldn't say anything, couldn't judge, because she wasn't without sin. What was the saying, *those of you who are without sin, cast the first stone?* Then her eyes opened wide as the thought suddenly occurred to her that Mark might not actually be dead! Just because he fell…

'Mum,' she began.

'*Mum.*' Again, but more insistently.

'Be quiet, Ann-Marie,' her mother shot her a look and turned to Sadie, 'Sadie, dear, could you get me a glass of water please? And run the tap a bit and make sure it's really cold, would you?'

Sadie hesitated and then headed to the kitchen.

'What if he's not dead?' Ann-Marie hissed when they were alone.

'I know, I've been thinking we need to go and check. But he's no' made a sound. If he was still alive he'd be roaring and swearing, sure.'

'Well, he was so pissed maybe he's fallen asleep?'

Ann-Marie withered under the scornful look her mother gave her.

'*You'll* need to go and check,' Isa hissed at her.

Ann-Marie shook her head, '*I'm* no' having anything to do with this,' she whispered back crossly. '*I* can't get involved!'

'*I* can't go down with my legs!' Isa hissed back, 'Anyway, I need to deal with *her*,' she motioned to the kitchen.

Ann-Marie waved her hands at her mother, 'Evidence?'

'Wear gloves,' her mother said shrugging her shoulders, 'It's not as if you're *new* to this, is it?' she said tartly.

'Well, since I'm the expert here, I'll tell you that *me* being here compromises my...*Billy's* accident. We'll have to phone an ambulance, and if he *is* dead, then there'll be another enquiry, and if *I'm* here, they'll put two and two together. Holy Mary, what the *hell* did you push him for?'

'To help Sadie. She'd never have left him, and you seen the state o' him tonight. He'd ha' battered her good and proper. Mebbe even kil't *her*!'

Sadie returned with the glass of water and sat it in front of Isa.

'It's no for me, hen,' Isa said, gently handing her the glass, 'It's for you.'

Sadie took a sip and put the glass down.

'Mark's had a fall down the stairs, Sadie. Ann-Marie's going to check if he's alright, and then we'll phone an ambulance. But Sadie, Ann-Marie cannae *be* here, d'you understand?'

Sadie stared at Isa with huge eyes, and Ann-Marie wasn't sure she understood, but time was of the essence now and she shook Sadie's shoulder.

'Aunt Sadie, I'm going to get a pair of Marigolds, are they under the sink?'

Sadie turned and vacantly stared at her and then nodded slowly.

Ann-Marie went to search under the sink, found a pair of gloves and then headed past the women and out to the top of the stairs. Mark still lay in a crumpled heap at the bottom. The door was still slightly ajar and his back was leaning against it. She stood for a moment, thinking. *No neighbours.* They either hadn't heard it or were ignoring it. She carefully walked down the stairs and bent down to look at him. His head lay at a twisted angle to his shoulders and his eyes were wide open. She waved a hand in front of them, but got no response. She took a deep breath, and tried to think clearly; it looked as if he'd broken his neck, either in the fall or on landing. There was no sign of breathing and no noise coming from him, so she carefully stood up and walked slowly up the stairs, and back to the living room.

Isa met her eyes with raised eyebrows, to which Ann-Marie shook her head.

Isa took Sadie's hands with a deep breath, 'It looks like Mark is *dead* Sadie. Now, I'll phone the ambulance, but Ann-Marie is gonnae have to leave now, before the ambulance comes. She wasn't *here*, alright? So you take the cup that Ann-Marie used and her plate and go to the kitchen and wash them and put them away, alright?'

Sadie nodded silently and carried the cup and the plate away.

'How am I going to get *out*? He's lying hard against the door, and this maisonette doesn't have another way out.'

'You'll need to squeeze out, whilst I hold the door open. You go home and I'll get a taxi back…after.'

'Jesus, mum. Just when things were getting back to normal…'she began.

'That's enough! You'll go home, you weren't *here*, and *I'll* deal with Sadie and all *this*!'

Ann-Marie pulled her coat on and lifted her bag.

'You dropped me here at seven, *like normal*. I was to get a taxi back tonight, *like normal*,' Isa lied. 'I'll make sure Sadie understands that it was just her and me here.

You best be off now,' she said standing up.

Ann-Marie walked down the stairs first, avoiding touching the banister. At the bottom she carefully climbed over Mark's twisted body and pulled the door towards her. Her mother pulled the edge of the door open further and Ann-Marie managed to squeeze through the small gap. Their eyes met for a second and then she was gone.

Isa glanced at Mark for a second and then headed slowly back up the stairs and into the living room to ensure Sadie was word-perfect before she phoned the ambulance.

Chapter 13

The days passed and mother and daughter sought refuge in their own private worlds. Isa spent every morning at mass at St Columba's and nearly every afternoon with Sadie, whilst Ann-Marie managed to contrive being at the local Food Fair almost daily selling cider and meat at the farm stall, leaving the men to run the farm. In the evenings Ann-Marie stayed as long as possible in her office, whilst her mother kept to her room.

Duncan and Roddy both felt uneasy and speculated if there had been an argument or falling out between the two women, but neither came to any conclusions. The women were civil, but something had changed, and despite the soaring summer temperatures a brooding chill hung over the farm.

At lunchtime one day, Roddy stirred three sugars into his black coffee and explained about women to the much younger Duncan, who was mooching in the cupboards, looking for cake or biscuits. He returned to the table armed with some custard creams.

'It's not what they say,' Roddy explained, 'It's what they *don't* say. You need to be a mind-reader to understand them. And some of the things they say mean the exact opposite. So, if you ask them if they're fine and they just say '*yes*', then you're in *big* trouble. If they ask you to tell them if they need to go on a diet, or if their boobs are too small, or anything like that, you need to be *really* careful, because you jist *cannae* say the right thing. They'll always turn it and twist it, so you sound like an eejit, and then they go off on one, and of course, *everything* is your fault.'

Duncan munched another biscuit, as he thought on this. He'd just opened the packet a few minutes previously, but because no one was there to check, he'd almost single-handedly finished the packet, thoughtfully leaving one or two broken ones for his co-worker.

'So, basically, there's no point in me asking Shona Keenan out then? I'd jist be lettin' myself in for loads of trouble.'

'No, I didn't *say* that. And Shona Keenan is a nice lassie, by the way. I'm just saying its all lovely at the beginning, and then, after a couple of months it changes, and jist when ye think you're beginning to understand them, something happens and you're in trouble. Every single thing you do, or *don't* do is wrong.'

'So, d'you think *you* kinda know how they think, then?'

'No. I don't think any man *really* knows how they think.'

They finished off the packet of biscuits in silence and looked at the clock.

'Isa'll be back from church soon,' Roddy said, 'we'd better crack on. I don't want to be in here when she comes back. At least we can disappear somewhere on the farm, out of the way. Can you help me with the hay tomorrow? I want to get the machine ready before seven and ready to start cutting straight off. If this weather holds and we get it ready to bale by Thursday, I'll need a clear space in the barn, and to borrow your dad's flatbed trailer.'

The conversation veered into tractor-speak as they headed outside into the sun just in time to see Isa's car draw in. Eager to get on, and keen to avoid any turbulence, they both waved hello and quickly went back to work.

Isa clambered from the car and went straight into the house and sat down heavily on the sofa. Tiredness overwhelmed her for a few minutes, but she felt satisfied. She'd done her penance now, she felt; a whole week of offering up masses and saying prayers for Mark settled her mind. No confession, of course; that would have been *ridiculous*! She didn't *regret* for one moment what she'd done, and certainly didn't need forgiveness.

Sadie was a dear friend, if a little naïve, and had now accepted that the terrible accident that had killed him was brought on by his own drinking, which, in a way was true. This afternoon she and Sadie would arrange the funeral, now that the post-mortem had confirmed the cause of death as accidental death from a broken neck, after a fall whilst inebriated. No need for any enquiry, thank God. They had all been spared the intrusive questioning, and she and Ann-Marie could rest easy. *Rest easy*, she snorted to herself. They were both needlessly avoiding each other, and considering the secret they already shared, this little matter of Mark's death was making a mountain out of a molehill. You didn't stand and watch the slugs eating the hearts out of your best cabbages; you just went in there and picked them off for a fast death in a bucket with some salt in it. Not that Sadie was a cabbage, she reminded herself with a smile, although, she wasn't *always* the sharpest knife in the block. But she *was* her friend, and she liked to think that Sadie would do the same for her, if need be.

Outside in the yard, she could hear the machinery being moved ready for the big hay cut. She knew Roddy and Duncan would be working all hours to have it completed this week, but they'd have to resume doing the sales afterwards. Ann-Marie couldn't spend all those long days on her feet when she was paying staff.

Meanwhile, she'd talk to her daughter this evening and clear the air between them. The boil that was festering needed lanced, she said to herself. After all, if Sadie could be persuaded to accept the fact that it was an accident, then Ann-Marie needed to accept that too.

But Ann-Marie had *seen* her. The tiniest of pushes and he was gone. And the *look* she had given her! She was a little cross at that; after all, what *she'd* done was hardly comparable to beating her husband's head in with a skillet! Not that she blamed her one bit, with what that monster had done, and how he'd treated her all those years. Women *always* had the worst jobs in life. She remembered as a teenager having to look after her younger brother who was still in nappies. A late gift to the marriage, she'd overheard her father say once, but her mother, in her forties hadn't been pleased to fall pregnant again. A difficult birth and her mother bedridden for a couple of weeks meant Isa had to feed, bathe and look after Eamon. Sadly, he hadn't thrived, and died before he was two, and her mother had returned to work in the thread mills. Her father, worked all-hours at a nearby foundry, and Isa was used to preparing potatoes for the meagre evening meal after walking home from school. As the years went by and she grew into a young woman, she watched her parents grow prematurely old, tired out by life's struggle.

She'd vowed that her children would have a better start in life, and ignoring the offers from the handsome, loud young men she knew, she married the quiet man with the small ruined farm, and began married life working in the fields alongside her husband, from sun-up till sunset, and when the baby arrived, took Ann-Marie into the fields carried in a shawl on her back.

But mothers couldn't protect their children from the world forever, and Ann-Marie had fallen for the persuasive, loud Billy. Isa wanted better for her daughter, but the die was cast when Ann-Marie announced their engagement and pregnancy in the same evening. She was devastated. *Such* a man!

Finally, *finally*, Ann-Marie had come to her senses and dealt with Billy. Isa had *heard* the strange commotion as she lay in bed, recovering from the small stroke. She'd *heard* the squealing and the excitement and panic in the pigs, and turned the TV off in her room, straining to hear what was going on. She recalled struggling to push the window next to her bed open further. She couldn't *see* anything, but could hear Ann-Marie and Elaine eventually returning to the house. She strained to hear hushed whispering and taps running, and wondered. It wasn't until later that evening when Ann-Marie mentioned that Billy had not come in to get changed; and then when she'd *found* him dead in the pig pen, that she started to piece things together. And it was weeks before she finally overheard that illuminating phone call between Ann-Marie and Elaine, and the penny dropped.

Dirty work. That's all it was. Dirty work. The men made the mess and the women cleaned it up. It was as plain as that. Ann-Marie wasn't a *bad* person; she was just a person that bad things happened to. Like Sadie. Life was hard, and let's face it; she said to herself, it wasn't as if the world was a worse place for either of those two *animals* being removed from it! In fact, she was rather *proud* of herself, and of Ann-Marie. They'd been careful and no-one was any the wiser. Sadie had never been the brightest of women and had completely accepted her version of Mark's accident. In fact, she'd even come to believe that it *was* just her and Isa there that night. And now she could enjoy her retirement stress-free.

Of course, *Elaine* was the wild card in Ann-Marie's situation, but Isa had been assured that Elaine would never say a word about it. They just needed to avoid talking about it and eventually it would be forgotten. However, Isa decided that she and Ann-Marie needed to talk out this Mark *thing*, this problem between them, and get it resolved before it ruined their closeness. Stiff and tired, she hauled herself off the sofa and back to the car to collect Sadie and sort Mark's funeral.

When Ann-Marie finally pulled into the yard in

late afternoon, Roddy was waiting for her. She guessed immediately what it was about, after all, he'd been twitchy for days watching the weather. He briefly explained that they would start the hay early the next morning, and then helped her to remove the empty cider crates from the pickup to the shed.

She sent him on his way and stared at the house. No smoke from the chimney, because it was just *so* hot, but home was a welcome sight after a long day selling to the public. However, she hesitated before going inside; because she'd decided that afternoon that this was the evening she was going to confront her mother about the accident on the stairs.

Dinner was a cold ham salad and a baked potato, and she finally pushed the empty plate away and met her mother's eyes.

'We need to talk,' they both said at the same time, and then laughed. The tension broken, Isa walked to the sideboard in the living room and pulled two tumblers and a bottle of Lagavulin out.

'I kept it just in case,' she said, placing them on the table. 'How was Paisley?'

'Busy. Lots of folk buying meat, and a few buying cider; but it's just not a traditional drink here, and lets face it, Paisley isn't exactly a Mecca for tourists. We'd do better down the coast, I think.'

She took a large sip of the golden fiery liquid, and smiled at her mother, 'Now, if we sold *malt*, we'd be millionaires', she said appreciatively. 'Sláinte.'

Her mother raised her own glass and sipped appreciatively. She'd never really been a whisky drinker

133

but this slightly smoky and peaty one from the Isle of Islay was her favourite and a short tipple once in a while didn't hurt anyone.

Bracken and Bramble took the opportunity to slide up invisibly onto the sofa. Although the fire was not lit, they knew the comfiest place in the house, and as their owners were preoccupied, they made the most of the saggy warm cushions.

Meanwhile, Ann-Marie stretched and twisted her neck to relieve the tension there.

'You should have a hot bath,' Isa said, 'the lads doing the bathroom have done a lovely job, and it looks so much bigger than before.

'Aye, I will, in a while. Mum, I need to talk to you. About that thing. That…'

'You mean me giving Mark a push to help him on his way?' her mother said smoothly, filling her glass again.

'Yes.'

'Well,' her mother got up and carried her glass through to the living room and shooed the dogs from their seats, 'the way I see it is that Sadie needed a wee helping hand, so to speak. And he might've just fallen all by himself anyhow.'

'But he *didn't*.'

'Well the ambulance-men and the police thought he did, and Sadie did, and that's all that matters. Only you and me know what *really* happened and its no' as if either of us is likely to tell, is it?'

Ann-Marie sipped thoughtfully.

'And its no' as if we're going to make a habit of it, is it?' Isa asked reasonably.

'No.'

'So, let's just put it behind us, eh? No harm done. No-one any the wiser. Our secret. *Again*. Remember what I said before, Ann-Marie? Mum's the word.'

Chapter 14

Haymaking was completed with urgency and relief, and the barn was gradually stuffed to the rafters with bales of sweet-smelling hay. Ann-Marie drove the tractor and trailer, and the boys stacked the small bales high, strapping them against any movement. Isa laid-on picnics in the field and everyone ate hungrily. The long June days meant that everyone was in the fields before seven and they worked until ten at night. The machines stopped and started with emergency repairs or refuelling and clothes were changed regularly as they became wet with sweat or full of annoying, irritating dust. The capricious weather behaved, but the temperatures soared again, and all over Renfrewshire farmers worked through the nights, and the long Scottish evenings hummed with the far-off sounds of tractors and trailers moving to and fro with well-planned urgency to house the precious crop.

Roddy suffered, with his red hair and fair complexion, and in a fit of temper one afternoon, tore off his stained and sweat plastered tee-shirt, to reveal his Scottish farmer suntan - a milky white torso and brown burned forearms, 'Taps *aff!*' he cried, tired and sunburnt.

Isa tutted and handed him a tube of Factor 50 sunblock, which he sneered at and refused, and Isa made a mental note to buy some after-sun cream.

Dramatic sunsets filled the skies with red, violet and finally indigo, and the men had short nights to sleep and recover their strength under huge black skies peppered with stars.

When they finally completed the task, they lent a hand to bring in Ewan's crop next door, and at the end of the week, with the hay harvest at both farms safely brought in and under cover, and the air heavy with the sweet smell of hay and full of dust, the weather finally broke. Large drops of warm rain began to thump onto the yard as Duncan rushed to roll up the windows of the cars, and Isa traipsed upstairs to close the windows that had been lying open for days. The skies darkened and the air became heavier and suffused with the sharp ozone smell of the approaching storm.

Bramble and Bracken hid under the kitchen table and Ann-Marie turned the lights and the radio on to calm them and drown out the first peals of thunder.

A few minutes later, Roddy and Duncan burst in through the door to escape the deluge, dripping profusely onto the kitchen floor.

The storm lasted an hour, whilst everyone drank icy-cold homemade elderflower cordial and stuffed slices of Victoria sponge into hungry mouths, watching the torrential rain and flashes of lightning from the safety of the house. The noise and frequency of the thunder increased, letting them all know that the storm was directly overhead, and life just seemed to stop, with everyone holding their breath as they sat silently round the table. Roddy took the terrified Bramble into his arms and stuffed her under his shirt to Ann-Marie's amusement. Isa slapped Duncan's hand as he tried, unsuccessfully to steal the last slice of cake whilst everyone else was watching Roddy and the squirming dog. The rain thundered a tattoo on the roof, drowning out any attempts of conversation.

And then quite suddenly, like someone turning off a tap, the rain stopped. The oppressive heat dispersed along with the dark clouds and Ann-Marie opened the farmhouse door to see steam arising from the concrete yard, and patches of welcome blue sky overhead. The air was scented with warm damp earth and grass and the swallows, which'd hidden in the barn during the storm swooped to and fro to catch the insects revived by the rain.

'I think we could all have a lie-in tomorrow', she said, breaking the silence, 'It's not as if we haven't earned it. So, me and mum can do the animals in the morning, you guys can catch up on your sleep.'

Isa nodded, 'Yes, that's a good idea. And then, perhaps, now that the panic's over and the hay's in, I wonder if we can go and look at that wee bothy on the edge of the home orchard and see if anything can be done with it. Now that the farm has been updated and ticking over, it'd be daft not to invest in that sad wee place, and see if we can't make good use of it.'

Ann-Marie remembered playing in the tiny cottage when she was much younger, but years of neglect and life getting in the way had meant that she couldn't actually remember the last time she'd been down there.

'I'd forgotten all about that place. It must be in a right sorry state now', she said to Isa. 'Well, tomorrow after lunch we'll take a wee walk down and see how bad it actually is. Meanwhile, you two go home, and Roddy; put that dog down before you spoil it completely.'

Bramble was deposited on the floor and crept to her basket, as Roddy communicated his apologies to her and headed towards his car.

The house returned to a quiet companionable silence and both women snoozed for a couple of hours, easing sore backs and tired legs, until a car driving in woke the dogs and of course, the sleepers.

Sadie, who had avoided visiting since Mark's death, arrived, and with her usual 'It's just me', burst in on the living room. Ann-Marie stiffly got out of her chair and went to fill the kettle.

'I knew you'd be doing hay, so I didn't want to come earlier' she explained,' but I wanted to let you know the funeral's on Tuesday at ten. It'll be very small, but well, I'd like you both to come'.

Isa looked at Ann-Marie's face and answered for them both, 'Of *course* we'll come, sit down and have some tea. We've just been resting our eyes, after the storm.'

Sadie brightly chattered about the unusually long spell of fine and hot weather, as Ann-Marie prepared the teapot, cups and biscuits, watching her out of the corner of her eye. What a difference in the woman! From a sad, nervous wreck just a few weeks ago, she was bright eyed, relaxed and happy, despite the fact that she still had to bury her husband. She carried the tea-tray in and put it on the table before the friends and left them to it, taking the dogs for a run around the shorn hay field.

She revelled in the fresh breeze and looked fondly at the rolling green hills. Here and there oilseed rape was blooming a bright yellow, bright enough to try the eyes if you stared too long at it, and fields of spring barley, still green but moving in the breeze like a sunlit sea. She sighed and sat on the rock outcrop near the old drovers' road in the far orchard.

Everything was going well, and yet she felt unsatisfied. Maybe she needed a break away from the farm, she wondered; although just that morning her mother had suggested going on a date. A *date*! Ann-Marie was horrified at the idea. The company would be fine, and it would be nice to have someone to go to things like concerts or the movies, as she had avoided going to things like that on her own, but she baulked at the thought of anything *romantic*. After her own experience of married life she wasn't keen to embark on that sort of thing again. And *anyway*, she was no spring chicken now, and the idea of a deepening romance with the expected physical side of things made her feel quite ill. It was one thing undressing in the dark and getting into bed with someone who *knew* you; your fat bits, your saggy bits and all; but to undress in front of someone *new*; to bare your no-longer-young body and your sensitive soul? No, she didn't need a date *that* much.

She knew Isa was keen for her to take up Jim Muir's offer of dinner; that she'd stupidly recounted after he'd phoned a few days ago, to *catch up*, he'd said. Yes, Jim was nice, and a respectable solicitor and widower, but nerves and fear got the better of her, and she made all sorts of excuses, both to him on the phone and afterwards to her mother. She pushed the idea of dating to the back of her mind, called the dogs and headed home. Sadie's car had disappeared, and as Ann-Marie quickly prepared dinner for two, her mother filled the silence by telling her how Sadie was having a new carpet fitted and was considering joining a health club.

'She's embracing life without Mark then?' Ann-Marie commented with a raised eyebrow, eating the ham and potato salad in front of her.

'That's unkind', Isa answered shortly. 'You know she didn't have spare money before he died, with him drinking and betting it all away, and she's quite right getting out and about again. *She* sees that she's young enough to start again.'

Ann-Marie could see what was coming, and turned to her mother, 'No,' she said emphatically.

'What? I never said a thing.'

'Drop it mum. I'm not interested in getting *out and about* as you put it. Stop trying to push me and Jim together. The answer's no.'

'You could do a lot worse, and consider, just for the *company*…'

'I'm going for a bath and then bed. This subject is closed. Goodnight.' Ann-Marie pushed the chair under the table and walked upstairs, leaving Isa sitting crossly with the dogs.

'Well, I was only trying to help,' she said to Bracken, rubbing her ears.

***

The bothy was indeed in a terrible state, what they could actually see of it, through the jungle of brambles and elderflower bushes that concealed it. Although the walls were standing, the roof had collapsed at one end and the chimney stack looks perilous.

Roddy had filled the pick-up with loppers and heavy duty brush-cutters and the lads quickly cleared the undergrowth from around the building and piled it nearby for burning.

Bramble and Bracken ran to and fro chasing the disturbed wildlife that had long considered the ruin home, and then, as the sun came out from behind a cloud, it became again the building that Ann-Marie recognised from her childhood.

'It's smaller than I remember', she said to Isa, 'not really big enough to be a proper cottage.'

'It *was* a proper cottage when we came here at first, and with a lot of work and some money, could be again.'

'Oh mum, have we not enough to do without taking on a big project like this?' Ann-Marie despaired.

Roddy, who had been quietly walking around the building, finally spoke.

'I've a proposal. If Duncan and me could get water and electricity to this, and I spent my spare time here, rebuilding it, it would make a great wee holiday let, but I could live here whilst doing it up inside, for a year, rent free, in exchange for my pay. What d'you think?'

The two women exchanged looks, silently. This was a novel solution to the problem of what to do with a derelict building that could become an asset to the farm. He seized the moment, and continued,

'I can move in here once it's watertight, and work away on it. It would save me paying rent in Erskine and I'd be on-site too. You could just pay for the materials.'

'We'd need to draw something up legally,' Isa said to Ann-Marie, 'but, it's actually a great idea, and Roddy and Duncan could work on it when our cider season is slack. The hay's in now and harvest for the apples isn't for a few months – they could get the water, electricity and the roof sorted by then. What d'you think?'

Three expectant faces looked at her, waiting for an answer.

'Alright, but *only* if it's not going to cost a fortune. We can lay the water and cables ourselves and do most of the work, but I'll need to check with planning first what the situation is about reinstating it. So, no decision till I get the okay from them.'

'Well, you'll need to speak to Jim Muir as your first port of call, he'll be able to see from the deeds what you could do and maybe suggest someone at planning, if you need to tell them at all. He knows a lot of people there, you know.', said her mother triumphantly, walking back to the pickup with a jaunty air and a grin like the cat who has just found the cream, much to Ann-Marie's annoyance.

Chapter 15

After tidying her desk and generally messing around, Ann-Marie accepted the logic of what her mother had said, and finally phoned Jim Muir's office. Thankfully his secretary answered the phone, and after a brief explanation, she ended the call and picked up her handbag and car keys. She was meeting Elaine for a walk and tea in Largs, a small seaside town just a short drive away from the farm and needed to get her skates on if she wasn't going to be late.

Largs lay just over a few rolling hills in Inverclyde, and as she topped the last hill, the sea lay before her, shimmering in the sun, with the islands of Cumbrae and Little Cumbrae in front of her. She instantly felt her spirits lift and enjoyed the drive down the hill and into the familiar small seaside town. Unsurprisingly, for a June day, it was busy with older couples and after driving around for a few minutes, she finally found a parking space, and walked along the promenade to meet Elaine at the town's famous café. They had been visiting the place regularly over many years, and after tea and cake, they bought their traditional vanilla ice-cream cones, Elaine's with a flake and Ann-Marie's with raspberry sauce, and crossed the road to walk near the pier. The Cumbrae ferry had just disgorged a few cars and foot passengers and she and Elaine sat on one of the benches to watch the comings and goings.

Elaine gossiped about Calum and the boys, and about the next weekend's trip away with Malky. They were heading to Loch Lomond to do a medium walk around Balloch in preparation for their big week away walking in Cornwall, which had been brought forward unexpectedly by Malky.

'Why are you going earlier?' Ann-Marie asked.

'Oh, he couldn't get a table booked at The Seafood Restaurant, which was to be the big treat, but they had a space at the end of the month, so we're going then. It's only a few weeks away and the weather will be lovely. I'm so excited.' She popped the end of the ice-cream cone into her mouth and sat back on the bench, 'I've always liked Largs' she sighed. 'I thought when Malky retired we'd move down here and buy a bungalow, but he's no' keen.'

Ann-Marie closed her eyes momentarily and enjoyed the sun on her face. Even though she loved and would never change her way of life, it was so nice to escape from the farm and just sit and do nothing for a change. Bull had never liked the seaside and even when Ann-Marie had brought Lynda when she was a child; it had always been her mother who had come with them for the occasional day trip, never him. When Lynda had grown up, it became the place where she and Elaine had come for a short escape, an ice-cream and to let Elaine look at all the bungalows along the seafront. The gulls wheeled overhead and their cries and the sunshine were lulling her into drowsiness. If only whoever was leaning on their car horn would stop that infernal racket, she thought crossly.

'Och, ma hands are all sticky,' Elaine moaned. Ann-Marie tried to ignore her, intent on enjoying the sea breeze and the sunshine, but she could hear Elaine scrabbling around inside her handbag for something, and that, together with the gulls, and the infernal distracting noises forced her from her reverie. The moment she opened her eyes she was aware of someone leaning over her, blocking out the sun. She started a little, and the intruder, realising he'd given her a fright, crouched down in front of her.

'Hello!' cried Jim Muir, 'Didn't you hear me peeping the horn?'

Ann-Marie was dumbfounded, but Elaine recognised him and chirruped a hello in return.

'What are *you* doing here?' Ann-Marie stammered, a little rudely.

'Well, I was out at a meeting in Beith when I got the message that you'd called, so I called back and your mother said you were here with Elaine, so I just thought I'd go home this way.'

She stared at him in surprise, 'You were going home from Beith and stopped at Largs? Hardly on your way, is it?'

'Oh, I thought you'd be pleased to see me! I was just driving past when I saw you both sitting watching the ferry. How about an ice-cream from Nardini's ladies?' he said with a broad grin to Elaine.

'Oh, yes please!' Elaine grinned

'We've already *had* ice-cream, thanks', Ann-Marie said tartly, and with a dirty look to Elaine added, 'and *you'll* not be able to get into that new outfit this weekend if you eat another!'

Jim sat beside them on the bench, ignoring her less-than-friendly welcome. He stretched his long legs out in front of him, totally at ease.

'Oh, I love Largs,' he said with a sigh.

'Oh, so do I!' Elaine enthused.

'It's just lovely to sit by the sea sometimes, you know?' he said conversationally to Elaine, who nodded. Ann-Marie pointedly ignored him, so he just chatted to Elaine instead.

'I really must think about getting a wee dog, I think,' he added, 'then I'd have a bit of company and a reason to walk about here.'

'You don't need a reason surely,' Ann-Marie said, interested in spite of herself.

'Yes, but its *easier*. It's hard sometimes walking on your own. People just look at you, probably wondering if I'm looking at their children or casing their house, or whatever. At least if I had a dog then it'd look like I was just out walking the dog.'

'You're at work all day. It wouldn't be fair on a dog at home alone.' Ann-Marie retorted.

'Ah, but it's *my* office, remember and my rules. The dog could come to work with me.'

She didn't have an answer to that, so she sat and stared at the sea. What was he *doing* here? And why did her mother tell him where she was, for God' sake!

She stared at Elaine very pointedly, 'Well, we should be going,' she said when Elaine failed to take the hint.

'Oh, I could just take five minutes of your time to talk about this bothy project, if you have five minutes?' Jim said quickly, eyes twinkling.

Elaine patted his hand as she stood up, 'Oh, that's fine, we came in our own cars, so I'll be off. I need to get back anyhow.'

Ann-Marie looked at her in horror, '*Elaine!*'

'I'll call you when we get back after the weekend' she said primly to Ann-Marie, 'Bye, Jim, nice to see you again.'

She walked towards where her car was parked, and with a final wave of her hand, was gone, leaving her best friend sitting on a bench in the sunshine with a handsome man. Ann-Marie turned to stare resolutely at the sea again, watching the ferry pull out and head towards the island. She was furious at her mother *and* at Elaine, and was momentarily at a loss for words

'You're being a bit silly, you know.' Jim ventured quietly.

'I feel as if I've been manoeuvred,' she said briefly.

'I'm your friend as well as your solicitor, you know. We're not doing anything wrong. We're just *talking*. That's what friends do.'

'Look, I'm not being rude, but, well, this is all…well, I'm not *sure* what it is, but remember, I've just been widowed a couple of months, and I'm really *not* looking for any sort of relationship. *At all*. I mean, I'm *flattered*, but I'd just feel more comfortable if we can keep our … well, if we can just stay as a client and solicitor.'

He stared at the sea for a long moment before finally answering her.

'Ann-Marie, look. I'm respectable, house-trained and just a bit lonely. I'm *not* asking for a relationship. I don't really know what I want either, but I'd hoped, I *hope* we can maybe catch a movie or a glass of wine sometime. I *like* you, and I think we've maybe got a bit in common. Let's just see where this goes, eh? And I really would like a bit of company sometimes. No strings. No pressure. Now, I've got an architect friend who can have a look at this building and give you some ideas. Here's his card – I've talked to him and said you'd set up a meeting with him. I need to be getting back as I've got a meeting later, so shall we say we'll maybe talk over a glass of wine once you've talked to him? Even if it's just about the bothy.'

He stood up and pushed his hands deep into his pockets, looking very young and uncertain for a moment, 'It's just as hard for me to ask someone out, you know?'

And then he walked away towards his car, leaving her suddenly alone and bereft, to stare some more at the sea with plenty to reflect on.

***

She arrived back home just after tea-time, with her mother calling down from her bedroom, 'Your dinner's in the fridge.'

Glad not be under scrutiny, she took the plate out and sat at the table eating alone.

Maybe, he was right. She *was* a little lonely, and when her mother passed, well, it would just be her and the dogs, and she *was* a little young to look forward to another thirty or forty years on her own. She was also embarrassed at how she'd reacted too, so *rude* when he was just being friendly. She pushed the plate away half eaten and sat miserably at the table.

A few minutes later and her mother came down and into the kitchen in her pink twin-set and plum slacks.

'Where are *you* going all dolled up?' Ann-Marie asked.

'It's Monday night. Tomorrow is that eejit Mark's funeral, daftie! I'm off to Sadie's! Are ye coming or staying in?'

'Christ, you have a better social life than me!' Ann-Marie muttered, 'Alright – give me two minutes to change and I'll take you.'

***

They arrived at Sadie's to see her neighbour finishing mowing her lawn. He smiled and said hello, and she opened the door to them both with a big grin.

'Come and see my new carpet!' she said breezily, ushering them into the living room.

The old suite had gone and in their place two two-seaters in tan and cream check sat comfortably on a new oatmeal carpet.

'Jim next door's got a pal, and the two of them got rid of the old stuff, and his mate fitted the new carpet. They've been lovely since Mark died, really helpful.'

Ann-Marie was astounded. The place was transformed and Sadie herself looked fantastic.

'Are you all set for tomorrow then?' she asked, taking a seat on one of the new sofas.

'Yes, the car is coming at ten and I'll see you both

there shortly afterwards. I don't think there'll be much more than a few folk paying their respects – he'd lost so many friends with the drink, you see. I've decided just to come back here after. Ann-Marie would you like a glass of wine? I've stopped drinking sherry since Jim's wife bought me some Chardonnay and it's *lovely*.'

Ann-Marie nodded dumbly and took a proffered glass. This calm, assured and obviously happy woman was a totally different creature than the one of a month ago.

'So, are you managing alright then, Auntie Sadie?' she asked politely.

'Och, yes. Jim's cuttin' the grass once a fortnight and Ellen, his wife has been taking me to the supermarket. But, I've decided that after the funeral, I need to stand on ma own two feet again, so I'll manage; but since he died, the neighbours have been so lovely!'

Ann-Marie and Isa both smiled and settled in the new furniture, marvelling at the new lease of life Sadie was so obviously embracing. The evening passed delightfully, and it was much later that Ann-Marie dragged her mother away, bidding goodnight to Sadie and that they'd see her at the crematorium the next morning.

In the car, Isa was the first to speak,

'*What* a transformation!'

'Indeed.' Ann-Marie replied.

'The house looks lovely, but *my God*, Sadie looks twenty years younger!'

Ann-Marie focussed on the road ahead, but listening to Sadie's plans for the future had been enlightening, and she wondered what her mother thought.

'Interesting to hear that she's already joined the gym. She's not wasting any time, is she?' she said cattily.

Her mother looked at her sideways, 'Have *any of us* got so much time left to waste?'

Chapter 16

The architect arrived on the following Monday, and after measuring the building and making many, many notes, had a brief chat with Ann-Marie, Isa and Roddy. He'd been to see the original documents at Renfrewshire Planning Department, and then had a brief chat with Jim Muir, and suggested a small extension to the building to make it more comfortable.

'Originally there wasn't a toilet at all, so you'll need to provide a septic tank as well as water and electricity, but a small extension shouldn't be an issue. Reinstating residential status won't be an issue either, as it was previously used as a cottage, so I'll draw up some plans at the office, but I'd suggest keeping the same sort of cottage look, with a new slate roof, one bedroom, bathroom and a lounge/dining/kitchen. It's pretty basic, but you might want to think of some sustainability features, like solar hot water and lots of insulation – the planners like all that and it'll smooth the process. I'll draw up something and get back to you in a week or so.'

Roddy took charge and was soon directing Duncan to peg out the proposed trench for water and electricity cables, and apart from feeding animals and delivering and selling cider, the long summer days were spent pricing materials and selling cider to the increasing amount of visitors to the farm.

Elaine and Malky returned from Loch Lomond with a suntan and more than a few midge bites, and as she had reacted badly to the bites, Elaine made an appointment to see her doctor. She confided in Ann-Marie that lunchtime, thankfully, after they had finished eating.

'I wanted to see her anyhow. I've had a horrible rash and a bit of trouble with the waterworks, and it's not looking very good, *down there*', she said pointing below her waist. Ann-Marie was horrified, but Elaine kept on, 'I thought it was thrush wi' all this new nylon underwear, and me and Malky being a little more romantic…'

'*Please!*' Ann-Marie exclaimed putting her hands over her ears, horrified at such a graphic and intimate admission, 'No more!'

Elaine sat crestfallen, 'Whatever. I'm sure a week of antibiotics'll sort it before we go to Cornwall.'

Ann-Marie grabbed her bag and began to make ready to leave, keen to end the conversation, 'I'm off to Lynda's for tea with the boys after school, so I'll need to go. I hope it goes okay at the…erm, doctors, but I'll talk to you before you go. It's Tuesday morning you're away, yes?'

Elaine glumly got her jacket, 'Aye, Tuesday. I'm seeing the doctor this afternoon, so I'll give you a phone, alright?'

'Yes, well, I hope you get sorted out, and I'll talk to you tomorrow maybe.'

She couldn't wait to escape back to her car, glad that going to see Lynda had stopped the disturbing conversation in its tracks. Best friends or not, there were still some things that you just didn't discuss; especially at lunchtime, she thought. Soon, she was pulling into the parking area at her daughter's apartment and was pleased to see the boys run out to meet her, and for the next hour or so, her mind was preoccupied with school and news of Lynda's new job.

Lynda was chatty and delighted with her new job, and the increased income had obviously been helpful, Ann-Marie noted, seeing the new, huge wall-mounted TV screen, and the new dining set.

'Well, that's *why* I'm working', Lynda explained airily to her mother's surprise.

'I'm just surprised that a part-time job can be paying so much', her mother commented, 'You *are* putting some of it away for a rainy day?'

Lynda's face fell, 'Well, I will do, once I've replaced all our old stuff. It's not as if I'm going to leave such a plum job,' she snorted.

Ann-Marie held her tongue; after all, it wasn't her business, and Lynda was old enough to know how to run her own house. Different generations had different priorities, she told herself, as she helped Alex to do his maths homework.

'I *hate* maths, it's so useless!' he cried, throwing his pencil down.

'Now, you need to be able to count up all the money you make selling cider and juice, if you're going to be a farmer, you know,' his grandmother said, 'try turning the numbers into *things,* that always helps me. I hated maths too, but it's really handy when you're ordering feed and buying animals.'

Alex smiled a wobbly smile and tried again.

'Are you sitting with them to do their homework?' she mentioned casually to Lynda, only to receive a withering look.

'Yes mum.' Lynda could have frozen a bonfire with the look she threw her mother, and Ann-Marie decided that any discussion regarding education, childcare or household management were best avoided. What topics of conversation did that leave, she wondered, and of course, the farm popped into her head.

'Do you remember the old bothy down at the old orchard on the farm? We've decided to do it up, possibly as a holiday let.'

'Who on *earth* would want to stay in a wee cottage on a farm in Renfrewshire?' Lynda laughed, 'Most folks want a week away in the sun with a pool. I know I would.'

'Well, you never know. Maybe couples just wanting a wee quiet getaway…' Ann-Marie said sadly, realising the farm came way down in Lynda's interest.

'Is the cider doing so well that you can afford to pour good money into something like that?' Lynda added archly.

'Well, mum and I think so. If nothing else, it'll add to the value of the farm, and we could let it as a tenancy.'

Lynda couldn't think of any value other than money, Ann-Marie reflected sadly. She'd never be interested in taking on the business, which meant Alex and Neil would be the likely successors. They were very young yet, but there was time. Meantime, she turned the conversation back to one that Lynda was happy to talk about; namely herself and her new job.

'So, tell me more about your job. What's your boss like?'

Lynda brightened and immediately became more animated, 'The job is easy. Basically I do some typing, make up reports and make appointments. Ian's a bit moody, but terribly professional in the office, and his staff all seem a bit in awe of him, and I do some private work about one evening monthly with him in London and I get paid cash in hand for that, which is great,' she said waving her hand round the apartment to indicate just what the extra cash had paid for.

'Cash in hand?' Ann-Marie repeated, 'that sounds very odd for a legal firm.'

'Oh, it's *fine* mum! I think he knows what he's doing. It's for his more discreet clients.' Two spots of colour appeared on her cheeks, as she thought of the kind of people his discreet clients were, and of the next trip away, which was to be next weekend, and she busied herself popping the dishes into the new dishwasher to avoid her mother's prying eyes.

'As long as you're happy,' Ann-Marie said with a sigh. The subject was obviously now closed, and although she'd like to ask more questions about her boss and his *cash in hand payments*, she knew better than stir a hornet's nest. 'Well boys, I'll need to go home. I've got piggies to feed and eggs to collect. Maybe you can come for Sunday lunch and stay and help me?'

Alex grinned and Neil threw his arms round her legs as she rose from the sofa, 'I can come and stay and help you every day!'

'That's just because you want to avoid school!' she

answered, with a rub of his head, 'And that's no good – you'd miss your friends and not learn enough to help me.'

She turned to Lynda with an easy smile, 'Talk to David and if you're free come for lunch on Sunday.'

She kissed the boys, gave her daughter a peck on the cheek and left, taking the scenic route back to the farm via Houston's pretty village. The three pubs in the tiny village were making the most of the unusually long spell of sunshine and couples sat outside as she drove slowly through the narrow roads and out towards the farm. Mid June was when Renfrewshire looked it best; and sadly the summer days were flying past. The apples were starting to swell and would soon be colouring up and before she knew it, September would arrive with the busy harvest season and the new student pickers coming to begin pressing season. Was it a sign that she was getting older, that the seasons just rushed past nowadays, or simply because everything was going well? What a difference since last year, she thought and instantly regretted it, as a now rare apparition of Bull jumped into her head. She almost missed the turn into the farm lane and had to brake violently as a result. No more living in the past, she vowed; *that* life was done.

As she drove into the farm, her mother was talking to a silver-haired older man outside the small taproom cum shop. He had a beautiful black and white cocker spaniel on a lead and he and Isa were laughing about something. She was pleased to see he was carrying a box of cider back to his car, and said hello as she got out of the old pickup.

'This is Bob Anderson, and Archie', Isa said,

indicating the dog who was wagging his tiny tail as if his life depended on it. Ann-Marie bent to fondle the dog's head, noting the perfect markings, 'He's stunning!' she said appreciatively.

'Aye, he's a bonny dog, but obedient too', replied Bob, 'well, we best let you girls get on with your day,' he said with a wink to Isa, who coloured prettily. 'Come on Archie,' and when he held his car door opened, Archie jumped nicely into the passenger seat and sat still.

'See you again, I hope?' Isa twittered. Ann-Marie groaned, but Bob, the silver haired stranger answered immediately, 'Very soon!', and with a wave, drove out the gate, leaving Isa sighing.

'You shameless hussy,' Ann-Marie said tutting.

'If you've got it, flaunt it, that's what I say,' Isa said with a grin, 'Anyway, the dog was lovely too. So, how was Lynda? Still spending money like water?' she asked, as they went inside.

'New huge wall-mounted telly, new dishwasher…yes, spending money like water. I'm amazed her part-time job is paying so well, but good luck to her.'

She popped the kettle on and sat in the chair, suddenly tired and cheesed-off.

'Elaine's off to the doctor's later. She's got a bit of an infection or something going on, she took great delight telling me just after we finished lunch. Yuk! And then they're away Tuesday for their week in Cornwall. Everybody's having a great time, it seems,' she ended lamely.

Her mother rubbed her shoulder, 'What's the matter?'

'Oh, nothing, I suppose. I just feel a little weary. It

159

would be nice for *us* to have a few days away, maybe. A wee bus tour or something. We could leave the lads in charge for a couple of days without a problem, I'm sure.'

Isa filled the teapot and sat beside her, 'I think that would do us both the world of good. I'll have a look if you turn your computer on for me, if you're sure I cannae mess up anything. Where were you thinking?'

'Oh, I don't care, maybe see some castles or hop over to the islands on the West Coast? As long as the weather holds and we take our midge-repellent cream, I'm sure we'll be fine.'

'Right, you put your feet up and I'll think of something for a few days. Duncan is feeding the pigs the now, so I'll speak to him and make sure they have nothing on next week.'

The lads agreed to look after the place, with Duncan doing the early and late feeds and the dogs, and Roddy would manage the cider sales and keep an eye on the computer. Isa managed to secure them a late booking of two seats on an island hopping bus trip, leaving from and returning to Oban, leaving that Friday afternoon on the train. Ann-Marie quickly rang Lynda and postponed Sunday lunch, and then telephoned Elaine. The trip to the doctors was inconclusive, and Elaine was a little upset.

'So, was it thrush then?' Ann-Marie asked the curiously reticent Elaine.

'No, it's a wee infection. She's getting more tests done to confirm, and'll phone me whilst I'm away, but I'm on antibiotics now.'

'So, what sort of infection, then? Nothing serious, I

hope?' Ann-Marie was concerned at the uncharacteristic quietness of her friend.

Elaine took a deep breath and tried to bluster, 'Oh, it'll be fine, I'm sure. Just one of those *women's' things* probably. Anyway, you're off to Oban with your mum for a few days. Have a great time, and I'll see you when your home.'

She hung up abruptly, leaving Ann-Marie concerned and bewildered.

***

Tidying up loose ends around the farm was finally completed on Friday lunchtime, and Ann-Marie threw some clothes into a small case, and they were ready to go. It had been years since Ann-Marie had a holiday and she was nervously leaving lists and telephone numbers for the lads, who thought it all quite amusing as she rushed around like a headless chicken.

'Now, Duncan, you need to watch Bracken, she's coming to the end of her season, so don't let her out unless you're with her. And Roddy, can you write down any messages with a name and number and just send me a text if it's important?'

The lads stood and exchanged glances, just like being at home; they both appeared to be thinking. Eventually, Isa; who had been sitting quietly watching the clock, spoke up as the hands hit twelve, 'Right Roddy, can you drive us to Queen's Street station? I think Ann-Marie's done enough panicking for us all now.'

Cases stowed, mobile phone charger retrieved at the last minute, and they were off.

Duncan waved them goodbye and headed to the kitchen to find a packet of biscuits. He was in charge now, and needed some sustenance.

Chapter 17

The train was busy, with a mixture of ages and nationalities, and the women squeezed into seats next to an American couple. They were *doing the highlands* and would change onto the Harry Potter line at Crianlarich. They chatted non-stop in a friendly drawl, and were positively buzzing with excitement as the train neared Crianlarich station. They left noisily, and the clanking of machinery and shuffling of carriages told the women that they'd soon be moving again, and on their way to Oban. Left to themselves in a much quieter carriage, Isa shared the small packed lunch and a flask of coffee between them, and they sat happily watching the highland scenery and lochs roll past their window.

'The weather is to hold for a few more days, then we're in for a week or so of showers, but, for Scotland, it's been a terrific summer.' Isa said contentedly.

'Yes, we'll be okay here I think, but poor Elaine might get the rain down in Cornwall, that'll put another damper on the second honeymoon, together with the infection she's picked up,' she added sadly in response to Isa's quizzical look.

'Och, it'll be thrush for sure! All that nonsense with

her and Malky having a sort of second honeymoon! Nylon knickers'll be the problem. The doctor's probably just running a few tests to reassure her. Anyhow, you'll see her in a week. Look - here's Connel and the bridge! Oh, this was *such* a good idea Ann-Marie, I'm fair enjoying my wee holiday even though it's only just started. Stop fretting about Elaine, she'll be fine!'

They arrived in Oban with the hustle and bustle of the station and ferry terminal, and soon found the tour minibus waiting with their driver, replete in full kilt and jacobite shirt. He was a youngish man, all smiles and full of information as he herded the women and their four companions onto the minibus and to their first hotel in the town. Thoughts of Elaine were whisked away as Ann-Marie was caught up in the excitement of the trip, and she and Isa happily became tourists.

As the weekend passed easily for Ann-Marie and Isa, seeing the sights of Oban, with trips to the islands of Mull and Iona; poor Elaine was left to deal with a bombshell of news from the doctor.

Chlamydia, the doctor announced to Elaine on the phone, and after explaining that it was a sexually transmitted disease, insisted on doing a complete sexual health check on her return, much to her embarrassment and distress. Of course, the doctor wanted to see Malky too, as soon as possible and Elaine agreed to make an appointment, but she didn't tell Malky. She didn't tell Malky *anything*, and sadly faced the fact that her suspicions earlier in the year *must* have been true. She spent the day crying and forced her mind back to try and work out when he'd been out, where he'd been and who with. The doctor couldn't tell her how long ago she'd contracted it, so Elaine spent the long hours poring over her wall calendar and diary, reliving conversations and finally realising that Malky's rekindled interest in her was merely a cover-up.

She refused to confront him that evening, even though she was furious and broken-hearted that not *only* had he cheated on her, but that he'd passed on a sexually transmitted disease.

Malky, oblivious to the sea of emotions going on inside Elaine's head, put it down to excitement of the trip to Cornwall. Only another night and they would be driving down the long road that led to Padstow and the Seafood Restaurant. It would prove an expensive week, but he was delighted that he'd covered his tracks so well, and after Cornwall, he could begin to think about cosying up to Ann-Marie Ross. He'd listened to Elaine chattering on and on about how High Glen Farm was making money hand over fist, and that Ann-Marie was now renovating that old cottage to rent out to summer holidaymakers. She really was an astute business-woman, and he had day-dreamed about how he could take advantage of the now very eligible widow. It was a good few months since Bull's death now, and she *must* be lonely. If he could get in there he could retire and be looked after for life! Her mother might take another stroke and die, or even take a wee fall, he daydreamed gleefully.

As he watched Elaine silently packing her suitcase for the trip, he wondered just how easy it would be to ensure *Elaine* took a wee accident, clearing the way for him to be free to comfort Ann-Marie.

'Got everything you need there, my love?' he asked her absently. She was packing enough for a bloody fortnight, and was still uncharacteristically quiet. God knows what had upset her in the last couple of days, but she was keeping it to herself. She should be *pleased* that he'd booked that expensive trip, and that ridiculous restaurant, when he could be wining and dining some pretty thing from one of the offices in the West End. She'd *even* started to refuse him in bed, for God's sake, and he was now looking forward to returning from Cornwall, returning to some sort of normality, and being able to sniff around some of the West End's classy bars for a suitable and discreet relationship.

Elaine snapped the case shut and turned to him, with a fixed smile.

'Yes, I think so. I put that new outfit in for our special dinner, and some waterproofs too. The weather looks like it might be a bit wet, so best be prepared.'

'Aye, well, the rain'll no bother us much. I'm looking forward to getting away from everything and everybody. The South West Coast Path looks fabulous; sandy beaches, towering cliffs… he smiled broadly, 'I can't wait. It'll be memorable.' Aye, memorable if you were to take a tumble right off one of those cliffs and leave me single, he thought, and with that happy thought he ambled downstairs to watch TV.

Earlier that evening, Elaine had managed to scroll through his phone again, searching yet again for any clue as to who he'd managed to pick up that infection from. Reading on the internet had assured her that you could *not* pick it up from a toilet seat, and she faced the fact that Malky had definitely strayed. *Strayed!* What a phrase! He'd been unfaithful, she thought angrily. The trouble was she wasn't convinced it was a one-off, and if she was right, would he ever change? And, she'd possibly got off light with only catching Chlamydia, as the doctor had tactfully told her she had tested negative for the other possible nasties. How *could* he! She was furious and heartbroken.

But, she *wanted* her trip to Cornwall, *wanted* to eat at The Seafood Restaurant. So she'd keep quiet until they returned, then she'd ask Ann-Marie for advice. After Cornwall, all that second honeymoon nonsense would stop, she told herself. She'd start to put money away and get Ann-Marie to come with her to speak to a lawyer – not that nice Jim Muir; that was a wee bit *too* close to home - a lawyer in Glasgow. All she had to do was get through this week, without killing him.

They set off early the next morning on the long drive, and as Malky drove, Elaine quietly watched the countryside fly past, responding briefly to him, but preoccupied with her own thoughts. They stopped overnight at a bed and breakfast near Bristol, and Malky stretched tiredly.

'Good idea to stop here, that's some drive, and it means we've only a couple of hours in the morning and can arrive mid afternoon in Polzeath at our bed and breakfast.'

'I'm knackered too, and my back's killing me wi' all that sitting in the car for hours. I'm going for a shower', Elaine answered shortly and disappeared into the bathroom.

Christ, she *really* was annoyed at something, he thought crossly, she'd hardly said more than a few words all the way in the car. If her mood didn't lift it was going to be a hard week. He carried the cases inside past the older lady owner, who had enquired if they were staying more than one night.

'Oh, no, we're just breaking the journey here tonight and going onto Cornwall. I've booked a table at The Seafood Restaurant. We're on a sort of second honeymoon', he smiled to her.

Her eyebrows raised with delighted surprise, and wished that *her* husband could make such romantic gestures.

***

Preparing her own overnight case for a hastily arranged evening working trip in London was Lynda. Ian Walker had only informed her that morning, and after a slight difference of opinion with David, she managed to persuade him that the money would be good as a deposit on a holiday for them all. He sighed, but agreed and she was soon in a taxi on her way to the airport. She was flustered, a little annoyed and had a bit of a headache too, but was looking forward to the easy evening's work, a good meal in a nice restaurant, and sitting close to her handsome, but as yet unattainable boss.

They met in the airport bar, and she sensibly followed his lead and had a soda water and lime. He seemed more abrupt than usual this evening, and stalked off to take a phone call on his mobile, leaving her sitting alone at the table.

'Slight change of plan', he announced grimly on his return. My first client, who is new, has had to reschedule to later tonight, so it'll be a late night. It's a pain, but he's very influential and he's not the kind of man you say no to.'

Lynda thought he looked angry, but he controlled it well, and they spent the next ten minutes going over his appointments in Glasgow for the next few days. She finished her drink quickly, feeling warm and out of sorts, and excused herself to powder her nose. In the toilets, she rummaged round her handbag for her painkillers and swallowed two. The last thing she needed now was to come down with something, but she was feeling increasingly unwell.

They slowly boarded the almost full plane, and whilst he read a newspaper, she closed her eyes and willed her headache away.

They had two meetings scheduled, at opposite ends of London, and the first one confirmed in her mind that Ian Walker's private work was some sort of money laundering scheme. Not that she cared, she observed; the cash payment of a thousand pounds nightly was very nice thank you, and she didn't care what the tax man didn't know. The second meeting proved to be a completely different experience from any of the others she had attended, and whilst she normally felt apprehensive, this time Lynda felt terrified. Whilst none of Ian Walker's private clients resembled the public ones who attended his Glasgow office, *Baz;* the new client was a tattooed and unshaven giant of a man, with a broken nose and a distinct whiff of eau-de-sweat. The location seemed to be some sort of industrial shed with an area boxed off as a sort of rudimentary, windowless office. She was directed to a hard wooden kitchen chair, whilst Baz and Ian Walker sat on two old brown two-seaters with a rickety coffee table between them. The heated discussion between him and Ian Walker wasn't going well, and Ian Walker's face was tight with tension. Another interesting character stood sentry at the door, and Lynda found herself unable to stop staring at the tattooed spider web on his neck. She knew a couple of thugs when she saw them, and was praying for the meeting to end before something violent happened. After an hour of animated and bad-humoured conversation, Ian Walker stood up, clearly unhappy about how the meeting had gone. He gestured with his head to her that they were leaving, and she followed him thankfully, glad to escape.

He flung himself into the car crossly, 'Well that didn't go as planned, but I'm pleased to say that we won't be keeping *Baz* as a client. Most of the London solicitors wont touch his stuff, but if he doesn't want to pay my price, well…his loss.' He turned to stare at her when she didn't respond, noting for the first time that evening her white face.

'I think I'm coming down with something, sorry,' she managed to smile.

They returned to their accommodation and to their separate rooms, neither keen on conversation. 'I'll see you in the lobby at seven,' he said curtly, 'and I hope you feel better by the morning.'

Chapter 18

Lynda arrived back at her apartment just as David was getting the boys ready for school. He was appalled at her white face and after making her a coffee, sent her to bed. Lynda swallowed more painkillers and agreed to call the doctor later, as she changed into her pyjamas and crawled into bed.

'I'll call you later,' David said, putting his head round the bedroom door, but she was already asleep.

Meanwhile, Elaine and Malky ate their full English breakfast, whilst looking at maps of Cornwall. They couldn't book into their bed and breakfast in Polzeath until four, so Malky had suggested a leisurely drive down, and Elaine sat quietly as he made eyes at the pretty landlady who was suggesting places of interest along the journey.

She suddenly understood that the way he spoke to other women; that she'd previously regarded as friendliness, was actually flirting. She recalled the same behaviour as she looked back at the Golf Club dances, the Ladies Nights at the Lodge, and even recalled him flirting with Ann-Marie. He was always the same, probably always had been. A Ladies Man. As she buttered her toast, she watched him watching the landlady clearing the next breakfast table. Had she been so blind all these years, that she'd never really seen it? Or was it really that she'd seen it, but that her love for him had blinded her to the evidence of her own eyes- that he always seemed to be on the make? Of all the women whom he made eyes at, how many had taken the bait? How many *other women* had there been?

She suddenly felt like a fool. A foolish old woman, who was kidding herself that her marriage was having a new lease of life. She'd seen enough movies, read enough books and known enough other women who'd been duped, as *she* now knew she had been. She'd always trusted her instincts before and they'd never let her down, and she felt a strange mixture of sadness and anger. She wondered how this little holiday, this *charade* was going to play out, and the part she played in it.

He refilled her coffee cup for her with a smile, 'You seem to be a little better this morning, my love.'

'Yes, I'm feeling better, thanks. I'm looking forward to my wee holiday,' she said brightly, 'Shall we get going?'

Soon, they'd thanked and left their host, and were heading West along sunny country lanes, and Elaine fixed a smile on her face as the busy A39 finally left Devon and they joined the snaking traffic entering Cornwall and began to see signs for Padstow.

***

Back on the farm, Duncan had become complacent. With Isa and Ann-Marie out the way, he'd been burning the candle at both ends, trying to get the chores done

172

and get away from the farm early to meet his friends at the pub in Houston. Shona Keenan had been there every night, and he was sure she'd say yes if he asked her to go with him to the cinema, but every night, he failed to summon the courage. The late nights meant he slept late in the morning, and his mother was furious at him. Roddy was giving him the afternoon off today, so this morning he was cleaning out the pigs and having the dogs out at the same time. The radio was blaring, so he didn't immediately hear the car draw in, and it wasn't until a man banged on the horn that he turned the radio off and went to investigate.

The man grinned and strode forward, 'Hello, I'm Bob Anderson. I was here last week for some cider and thought I'd come back and get some more. Is... eh...Isa here?' he smiled sheepishly.

'Oh, she's away for a couple of days, sorry. I've got the key, hang on and I'll open up for you,' Duncan rummaged in his pocket.

'Thank you. She's a fine woman, that Isa,' Bob said, making conversation, 'Could I have six bottles of the medium sparkling please?'

Duncan put the bottles in a box for him and carried them out to his car, whilst the man looked around the yard.

'My dog,' he explained to Duncan, 'He must be around *somewhere*. Probably gone for a pee,' he smiled to Duncan,

'Archie!' he called.

Duncan suddenly remembered Bracken and Bramble were still outside and called them too. Bramble appeared immediately, wagging her tail, but of Archie and Bracken there was no sign. Duncan darted in and out of the sheds, looking for any sign of them, 'They can't be far,' he said uneasily. 'The yard is fenced.'

And then they found them, around the side of the pig barn, locked together in what could only be politely described as a *loving embrace*.

'Ah.' said Bob, whilst Duncan was horrified. Ann-Marie's last order to him was to watch out for Bracken as she was at the end of her season.

'What'll I *do*?' he turned in anguish to Bob Anderson.

'Well, until they've finished doing what *they're* doing, you can't do anything, but I think you need to speak to your vet.'

The two men stood looking at the two conjoined dogs, whilst Roddy drove in with the pickup. He took in the scene immediately and leaped from the cab.

'What the...?' he exploded.

Duncan had the grace to stammer, 'I'm sorry, I was busy, and didnae see them!'

'How long have they been like *that*?' Roddy demanded, turning from one to the other.

'Hi, I'm Bob. Archie's my dog. We just found them a few minutes ago, so it looks like maybe they'll be tied for ten minutes or so. I'm afraid I think the damage is done.'

Roddy was furious, and glared at Duncan. The dogs were well and truly mated and it took a few more minutes before they managed to detach themselves. Bracken looked thoroughly pleased with herself, and Archie was wagging his tail as happily as only a sexually satisfied dog could.

The very embarrassed Bob Anderson ordered him into his car, and handed Roddy a scrap of paper with a number on it. 'Look, that's my number. Can you get Isa to give me a phone and I'll explain about…this.'

He drove off leaving Duncan to face the music. Roddy was furious, 'I'll need to tell them Duncan!'

'I'm *sorry*! The car came in and I didn't hear it, and I didn't know he had a dog with him!'

Bracken and Bramble sat at their feet, looking up at them as if butter wouldn't melt in their mouths.

'At least it was another Cocker,' Duncan added sheepishly.

'Take *them* inside. And put the kettle on, I need to think about what to say when I phone them.'

Duncan called the dogs inside and filled the kettle. Roddy ran a harassed hand over his eyes, 'I don't even know if I'll get Ann-Marie on the phone. They're on their way back today and the mobile signal has been patchy. I've to collect them at the station at 6pm, so maybe I should wait till then? Although, why I'm asking you, *Mr Responsible*, I don't know!'

Duncan pushed the mug of coffee towards him silently, knowing it was best if he didn't say anything more.

'Christ Duncan, you're a right clown!'

***

Ann-Marie and Isa were blissfully unaware of the drama on the farm, enjoying a blustery seal watching trip as their final treat to themselves. The small boat took them around Seal Island and they watched many seals gazing

175

back at them with huge limpid eyes. The captain cut the engine, allowing them to quietly drift past, enjoying the chance to get close to the resting animals. The return to the harbour wasn't an anti-climax either, with a small group of dolphins playing just ahead of the boat. Picking up speed, the boat bounced along the waves, and the two women shrieked with laughter as the waves sprinkled them with cold, salty water. They'd had a fantastic time, the other companions on the minibus were great fun and they'd relaxed and chatted like old times. In a few hours they would be back on the train, travelling back home from a well deserved and very enjoyable short break. They agreed that the holiday had been a resounding success and that they must do it again soon; after all, the lads had obviously managed to run the farm perfectly well without them.

***

Lynda surfaced from her bed after lunchtime and managed to book an emergency doctors appointment for later that afternoon. She took the opportunity to do some laundry and tidied the apartment before she left, and then spent an uncomfortable wait in the surgery waiting room.

The doctor went through the usual questions before handing her a sample jar and sent her to the toilet to fill the jar. The doctor was efficient and thorough and after dispensing with the used sample and washing his hands, he sat and turned to her.

'It's Chlamydia', he said without preamble, 'these new instant tests are really accurate, but I'll confirm it with a sample sent to the lab.'

Lynda was stunned and silent.

'Treatable with a course of antibiotics, but you'll also need to contact any partners you've had within the last six months or so. Sometimes, these infections can sit around unseen until you get a cold or your body resistance is lowered. Your file says you're married, so I'll need to see your husband also.'

Noting Lynda's complete shock to the diagnosis, the doctor leaned forward and took off his glasses, 'I'm assuming that this is a surprise to you, and that you might want some sort of marriage counselling, but to help you understand, and maybe your husband too; it can *only* be passed via vaginal, oral or anal sex and that you will need to refrain from *any* sexual contact until you've completed the antibiotics. Then we'll do another test to ensure you're clear of it.'

'But I've only been with my husband...' Lynda stammered then stopped. She knew it hadn't been David, and therefore, *therefore*, she'd caught it from Malky.

The doctor continued briskly, 'You'll need to get him to come and be tested as soon as possible then.'

The appointment over, Lynda left the surgery clutching the prescription. Instead of going to the usual chemist, where her friend worked, she got in the car and drove to one she never used in the centre of Paisley. Then she had to go and collect the boys from school and work out what on earth she was going to tell David. For the first time, since she'd been married, she suddenly realised how thin the ice was that she was now walking on. If she told him the truth she risked not only his anger and a possible divorce, but also that the family would know, and that she might be in danger of losing her children too. But, she'd *have* to tell him, there was no getting round that. She texted Ian Walker that she had been to the doctors and regrettably wouldn't be in work for the next day or so, and took the boys home. Quickly, she phoned a friend and managed to persuade her to take the boys for a few hours, and then sat down, took a deep breath and phoned David, asking him to come home, that it was an emergency.

Alone and waiting, she went over and over the damning news. Whilst it was shocking enough to tell David that whilst they'd been separated she'd unfortunately contracted an STI, there was no way she could admit that she'd caught it from Malky. The furore *that* would cause between her mother, Elaine and Malky would be never-ending! She'd have to invent someone. Someone who didn't exist; couldn't be traced and that would simply disappear from their lives once everything had settled down. If it could *ever* return to normal, she worried.

She wrung her hands until David burst through the door, his face full of concern and panic.

'The kids?' he asked breathlessly, noting the apartment was empty.

'The kids are fine – they're at a friend's, and staying for tea. Sit down David; I need to tell you something.'

Chapter 19

Whilst she cried and tried to tell him, David sat stony-faced, white and increasingly angry. Eventually, she stopped talking and said, 'Say something.'

'Where are the kids?' he said quietly, his jaw a knot of twitching muscles.

'At Sally's. Look, the first thing we need to do is get you to the doctors…'

'What a piece of work you are,' he raged. 'A dirty cow who's caught Chlamydia and has to tell her husband! You certainly wouldn't have told me otherwise, would you? All those lies and deception from before Christmas. I *knew* you were seeing someone, and you denied it at every turn! What a total mug I've been. Has this *even* been the first time Lynda? Do I *even* know if the kids are actually mine?'

She was horrified at his outburst, 'Of *course* they're yours! What d'you take me for?'

'Well, I *take* you for the slut you so obviously are!' he spat.

'It was a one-off,' she said quietly, dismayed at the direction the conversation was going in, and unable to minimise the damage.

'Well, I don't know that. I certainly don't *believe* it! In fact, it could all still be going on now, couldn't it? Your new job, with your evenings away, what's *that* all about? And me sittin' at home like an eejit, minding the kids whilst you go on overnighters wi' your new boss?' his voice was louder and his anger filled every word he spat out.

Lynda's mouth fell open in shock, but David had the bit between his teeth now, 'And the *money*, Lynda! Is he *actually* paying you for sex? Is that where all this cash for the new telly, for the dishwasher – is that where it's all coming from?'

'No! You've got it all *wrong*! There's nothing going on between me and Ian Walker, I swear!'

'As if I'd believe anything coming out of your dirty little mouth now', he said, striding into the bedroom.

'What are you doing?' she cried, tears running down her ashen face, following him to the bedroom and watching as he yanked a suitcase from the wardrobe.

'I'm *leaving* you, Lynda. I'm going to see a doctor, *then*, I'm going to see my lawyer. I'll be at my mother's if you need to get in touch, but frankly, I think we've run out of things to say to each other.'

He threw clothes randomly into the case, and walked out, leaving her crying on the bedroom floor.

***

In Polzeath, after checking in to their pretty bed and breakfast on the seafront, Elaine stood and looked out of the window. They were scheduled to do a few miles of the Coastal Path today and she had laced her walking boots and pushed a cagoule into her day sack, and was waiting for Malky to finish in the bathroom.

Tomorrow was their big night out, and the Seafood Restaurant had been booked for seven. She was so looking forward to it, even now, after waiting all those months she was excited, but this afternoon, they'd complete this first walk from Polzeath towards Daymer Bay, passing Trebetherick, and then back via St Enodoc church to Polzeath. It was a shortish, circular walk, and there was even a pub on the way, where they could get a meal in the evening. After so many hours in the car, she was looking forward to getting some fresh air, even though she'd have to endure being in such a beautiful location with her slut of a husband. She took a deep breath, determined to make the best of it and tucked her camera into her small rucksack, waiting impatiently.

Eventually, they set off, and headed west along the beach and turned onto the road at Dunders Hill, passing the Oystercatcher pub. Elaine was disappointed, thinking the pub would be somewhere at the end of the walk, but made the point of stating to Malky, rather pointedly, that she fancied eating here that evening.

'It looks a bit expensive,' he commented, looking at the well-dressed holidaymakers sitting outside with drinks admiring the view.

'Oh, and there was me thinking I was worth it, too!' Elaine snapped back.

Malky looked over at her, 'Of *course* you are, my sweet, I just thought…'

'*No*. I want to eat *here* tonight.' she said decisively, 'After all, it's more than just a holiday, isn't it Malky?

We're only going to come all this way once, and I want this to be a holiday to remember, *alright?*'

There was something in her voice, a new hardness; that disconcerted him. Something had happened last week that she wasn't telling him, and he felt he was losing control of the situation. Well, they had to eat somewhere, he thought crossly, but after tomorrow, and that *ludicrously* expensive dinner at the posh restaurant, it would be fish and chips and she'd have to just lump it. He had to stop spending the money that he'd squirreled away into his special account; the account that Elaine didn't know about. The account that paid for illicit dinners and motel stayovers with his female friends, that he'd need again when this ridiculous holiday was over and he'd returned to Glasgow.

Elaine strode on, oblivious, enjoying the warm westerly breeze and the fantastic views out towards the Atlantic. There were many people on the Coastal Path, passing them with cheery hellos and smiles, and she chose to stop at Greenaway beach to take some photos. She sat down, feeling the heat, and Malky joined her.

'It's so beautiful, she said, and I can see why it's so popular. The weather is just fantastic for a British seaside holiday.'

'I'm just going for a pee behind this wall', he said briefly.

'I thought you went just before we left the B and B?' she asked.

'Well, now I need to go *again!*' he said, exasperated, creeping behind the wall.

She smiled to herself, 'That's because you're getting

old', she giggled out loud, but in her head she was delighted, *And because you've got Chlamydia, you dirty old lecher.*

He returned shortly, 'I'm not old', he said crossly.

'Probably, your prostate playing up, you're at that age', she baited sweetly. Oh, it was nice to needle him.

What *was* her problem? he wondered crossly, sitting heavily down beside her again. He was in fine form, a man in his prime; except for this peeing all the time and the burning, and he was cross as she wouldn't let him *rest*, but got up and started walking on, 'Come *on* Malky. You really are like an old man today!'

He muttered under his breath and stood up, following her a few yards behind. She was really catty today, and he was increasingly annoyed and unsettled by it. They came to an unfenced area of narrow path and she skipped ahead, looking back at him. He'd taken his sweater off and it was tied round his waist, and his cheeks were two red angry spots. She waited just long enough for him to catch up and then strode on, knowing it would annoy him. Winning these small victories was a joy. She wondered if the regular peeing was one of the symptoms of Chlamydia in men, and smirked to herself, what's good for the goose, she thought…sod you Malky, it's *payback* time!

At Daymer Bay she sat in the shelter of one of the dunes and marvelled at the huge expanse of golden sand in front of her. Whilst Scotland was beautiful, with some of the best beaches in the world, the weather was the let-down. Even Largs, her favourite seaside town couldn't compete with this. She envied the owners of the cottages dotted around the bay, able to just open their doors and walk down to the beautiful beach. Her happy thoughts were interrupted as Malky threw himself down beside her.

'You're setting one hell of a pace, Elaine', he said shortly, 'It's just supposed to be a gentle, short walk today.'

'Oh, I'm making the most of it. The weather is to turn to showers tomorrow, and anyway, you should be *pleased* that I'm enjoying the walking; after all, doing all this was *your* idea to bring us closer together, remember?'

He didn't answer and sat sullenly looking out to sea.

'After all,' she said innocently, 'we wouldn't want you complaining that we had nothing in common, would we? So many couples just drift apart, and then get themselves into *all* sorts of bother.'

She leaned back into the dune and closed her eyes, listening to the gulls screaming and the muted laughter from children on the beach.

Malky was staring hard at her, just what was that supposed to mean? he thought. Was it just an innocent observation or did Elaine have an idea of something. She couldn't *know* anything; she never *knew* anything, stupid, gullible old trout. He'd been really careful and Lynda certainly wouldn't have said anything, and besides, that was all *months* ago. There *was* that one-nighter with that lassie from the estate agents on Byres Road, but that was before he was with Lynda. No, she couldn't know anything; she was just saying one of those *stupid* things women said, because she was just a stupid woman! Anyway, she *loved* him, he reasoned, and lay down beside her, hands behind his neck.

***

Roddy was standing in the concourse at the station, looking for Isa or Ann-Marie. The train had just arrived, and the sea of passengers flowed towards him. As the crowd thinned, he saw them stepping from the train, being helped down with their bags by another passenger. He leapt forward and was greeted with smiles as he grabbed the bags, thinking it best to wait until they were in the car and on their way out of the city centre before he started to explain, even though Ann-Marie was asking the expected questions, which he answered in short one-word answers.

The women settled into the journey home and he took his chance.

'Everything is absolutely fine. Just one *wee* thing. A man came by to buy cider; apparently you've met him Isa. He has a wee Cocker called Archie?'

Isa nodded, smiling.

'Well, anyway, Duncan was cleaning out the pigs and didn't hear him drive in, and Bramble and Bracken were out in the yard….and well, Archie jumped out of Bob's car and …well, Bracken and Archie….' his voice trailed off into silence.

'*Please* don't tell me that Bracken has been mated?' Ann-Marie said eventually.

Roddy nodded, keeping his eyes firmly on the road ahead.

'When did *this* happen?' she asked angrily.

'This morning. I phoned the vet, and he said you can get some sort of morning-after pill for a dog, but…well, I spoke to Bob, Archie's owner and Archie is a pedigree

Cocker, and well…it would be shame not to have puppies. Its no' as if they'll be mongrels.'

Ann-Marie sat tight-lipped in the pickup. Roddy and Isa exchanged concerned glances in the rear-view mirror, but Ann-Marie was giving nothing away. They arrived home and, of course both dogs ran out to meet them, followed by a very sheepish Duncan.

'I'm so sorry,' he said immediately, 'I'll understand if you want to fire me. It was a stupid mistake.'

'Go home, you idiot,' Ann-Marie snapped at him, 'I'm not firing you! I should *leather* you for being a fool, but well, it's happened and nobody died! Leave me to phone this man, and I'll decide what's to be done!'

Duncan shot Roddy a grateful look and disappeared. Ann-Marie took the scrap of paper with Bob Anderson's phone number and disappeared into the office. Roddy carried the bags upstairs, and when he returned Isa had put the kettle on and placed three cups on the table, 'Stay and have a cuppa. I'll talk to her and we'll see what we can do.'

Ann-Marie returned from the office. 'I've just spoken to that Bob Anderson. He's going to pop over now, *without* Archie, so we can have a chat. I've asked him to bring all of Archie's' paperwork.'

Isa blushed, and pushed the kitchen chair back with a scrape on the floor, before suddenly rushing out of the room and hurrying upstairs.

'Mum?' Ann-Marie called after her, 'you alright?'

'I'm just going to change!' came the breathless answer.

Ann-Marie ran a harassed hand over her forehead,

'Christ, one coming *out* of season, and one, who should know better at her age, apparently coming *into* season!'

Chapter 20

Bob Anderson arrived at High Glen Farm armed with a sheaf of paperwork and was welcomed by a twittering Isa with tea and a hastily made plate of shortbread. Ann-Marie felt like a gooseberry as she sat between the two octogenarians and tried to keep the conversation focussed on the problem of Bracken's possible pregnancy, whilst her mother and the dapper Bob kept chattering about their respective single status and how life was a little lonely.

She looked at Archie's impressive pedigree and noted that he also came with a clear health status, which; as an experienced farmer, she understood was essential if Bracken was to indeed produce a litter of healthy and saleable puppies. Isa refilled Bob's coffee and took the momentary lapse in conversation to mention that whilst she was happy enough at the farm with her daughter and the lads for company, and of course had her own female friends; it was a *shame* not to be able to have a little male company from time to time.

Bob's eyes lit up, and he agreed that since he'd become a widower some five years previously, he too missed the chance to visit his favourite restaurants and the cinema.

Ann-Marie rolled her eyes. It was like a blind date, with her feeling very much in the way, and she decided it was time for her to make a decision and guide the conversation back to Bracken.

'Well, Archie's paperwork is impressive, Bob, I have to say. Although Bracken is a bit elderly at five years old, I'll take her to the vet for a check up, but I don't see any reason not to let her continue a pregnancy, if she is indeed pregnant. We won't know until she's had a scan, which I can arrange for about a month's time. You're black and white boy, and Bracken's blue roan colouring means we could have black and white, blue roan and possibly some orange and white pups, which should make it easy to find appropriate homes when the time comes. It's not something I would have *planned* for her, but well; it's happened now and I think we need to let nature take its course. Can I photocopy the paperwork to take with me to the vets, and for when the time comes, if, of course, she is pregnant? Any buyer will want to see their background?'

Bob agreed enthusiastically, 'He's a great wee dog with a lovely character. I'm sure any pups of such a union will have nice temperaments. And of course, if we stay in touch, I'll do my best to spread the word and find homes for the puppies too. It's all quite exciting really. I'd love to keep up with the expectant mother's progress and see the puppies, if I may?'

Isa nodded enthusiastically, and Ann-Marie wondered if her mother could make it any more obvious that she was more than keen for Bob Anderson to stay in touch.

'Well, now that's all sorted, I need to catch up with

Roddy to ensure that nothing else has happened whilst we've been away,' Ann-Marie said, expecting them both to say their goodbyes, but as she stood up, she realised that she'd be the only one leaving the table, and left them both to chat and finish their coffee together.

Roddy was mooching around outside, waiting for the outcome, and Ann-Marie beckoned him to the cider shed.

'Love's young dream!' she said, shaking her head, and rolling her eyes, 'Come on, let's have a look at what's going on in here,' she said, pushing the door open, with Roddy at her heels, keen to hear about the future of his beloved Bracken.

'No more talk about dogs until we get Bracken scanned in a month. Meantime, we've a business to run, so lets see how much cider we have left to sell this summer.'

The rest of the day was spent doing a quick inventory, and Roddy suggested confirmed that they would have stalls at two of the local agricultural shows in the next month, and of course, their new monthly stall in Glasgow near the West End. Sales had been steadily increasing with the summer weather, but they knew that the weather was on the turn, with some squalls and wet weather expected anytime.

'I think we'll try and get the summer done and start on this building project before harvest comes. Duncan can do the stalls for the next month, and you can split your time between farm work and starting the groundwork on that bothy. I'll speak to the architect tomorrow and see what the state of play is with the council, so if you can just feed the animals tonight, I'll go back and split up those two cooing doves.'

Roddy crossed the yard to the pig shed, whilst Ann-Marie returned to the house in time to see Bob Anderson finally taking his leave of Isa.

'I'll be in touch Bob, and thank you for the information about Archie,' she said, trying to signal the end of their meeting.

'I hope you wont be too hard on that young lad', Bob said as he left the house, 'it was obviously love at first sight for the dogs, and poor Duncan; well, it wasn't his fault really.'

'Well, it really was, as he'd been told to keep an eye on her, but it's not the end of the world. It's fine – he's going to be doing all the stalls and markets for a month as a punishment, but that'll suit him as he'll attract all the young lassies in his kilt, whilst on the stall.'

Isa followed her out to wave goodbye, and sighed as he drove out of the gate.

'I think you can go and change out of your finery now, mother,' Ann-Marie said pointedly, 'I think he knows you're interested, and I'm sure he'll be back soon to see you.'

***

The next morning Lynda arrived in her car, and Ann-Marie immediately realised something was very wrong. Dressed in black leggings and a sweater she looked deathly white, and Ann-Marie noticed with alarm, was devoid of a trace of make-up.

She refused a coffee and sat uncomfortably on the

sofa. With her mother and grandmother nervously waiting for her to speak, she started to cry.

Isa and Ann-Marie exchanged concerned looks and Isa moved to sit next to her grand-daughter, putting her arm round her shoulder, 'Whatever it is, we can't help until you tell us,' she said kindly.

'I've been so *stupid*,' Lynda blubbered.

Ah, so it's trouble with David again,' Ann-Marie thought immediately. But she wasn't prepared for the full, unvarnished confession that then spilled by drips and drabs from a clearly heart-broken Lynda.

To give Lynda her due, she made a full and frank, if hesitant confession to her audience, and both Ann-Marie and Isa were stunned at the revelation that Lynda and Malky had been lovers, even though Lynda had insisted that their relationship had been very brief. Their main concern was Lynda's now obviously doomed marriage and the children, but both were very upset and appalled. Ann-Marie recalled her conversations with Elaine who, it turned out had rightly suspected her husband. But Lynda hadn't finished. Lynda finally also told them about the Chlamydia, and that it could only have been passed to her from Malky. Ann-Marie had the unenviable task of explaining briefly to her mother what Chlamydia was to her mother's disgust and horror. Isa left the table to return a few moments later with three glasses and the now almost empty bottle of malt.

The three of them sat in silence, each lost in their own dark thoughts.

'I honestly don't know what to say Lynda.' her mother said eventually, 'I'm not even going to imagine how bad your marriage was that you felt you had to have an *affair*, but an old man like that? And what about poor Elaine? Did you even think at any time, about the repercussions?'

Lynda shook her head.

But it was Isa, level-headed Isa that had realised that *poor Elaine* now had to be told that Malky had Chlamydia, 'That poor woman, on a second honeymoon with that…that…dirty, no-good…'

'And now, she must have it too!' Ann-Marie realised with horror.

Lynda nodded sadly, through her tears, 'I just realised that this morning, that's one of the reasons I had to tell you. You'll need to call her, tell her…'

'Oh no, my girl!' snapped Ann-Marie, 'This is *your* doing Lynda. Malky is a low-down snake of the largest degree, but I'm no' telling *my* best friend that her husband and my daughter have been lovers! Jesus, what a mess.'

'She'll have to be told,' Isa said quietly, 'we owe her that, but I think that can wait till she comes back home; after all, the damage is done, and she has no-one there with her right now, except *him*. But Lynda has to be our *first* concern,' she said, looking at her grand-daughter grimly.

More silence.

'David is going to divorce me,' she said quietly, 'and I'm so worried he'll want custody of the boys…'

'He can't work *and* look after two boys,' Isa said shortly, 'but, be under no illusions Lynda, this is a *helluva* mess you've got yourself into. If he does divorce you, the flat'll have to be sold, so you'll need to think about how you're going to live, *and* if you're going to keep this cash-cow of a job, although, I don't think you'll be able to continue your nights away from home, even if I thought that was *ever* a good idea!'

Lynda stared at the floor, 'I'll need to give the job up, I see that, and some of the clients were probably criminals and it was quite scary sometimes', she admitted.

Ann-Marie stood up and paced round the small room, 'look, I think we all need a wee break. Lynda, you look like hell; why don't you go upstairs and have a shower, and mum and I will have a talk amongst ourselves.'

Lynda nodded and walked slowly out the room to the stair. At the bottom she turned, 'I'm so *sorry* mum. You must be *so* ashamed of me; I'm ashamed of myself.'

They waited till they heard the shower running and Isa turned to Ann-Marie, 'Well, what do we do?'

'God knows! I knew *something* was going on around Christmas time, and Elaine did tell me she suspected Malky, but *Lynda and Malky*? That's a bolt from the blue. What a mess!'

'She could move in here…'

'*No*, mum, she can't! Not with two boys. There's no room here, and besides, I don't really want her moving in here. I don't think I could cope with that.'

The memory of Bull's death hung unspoken between them and Ann-Marie cursed him; still affecting her even after all this time. She downed her malt and again, her thoughts were with Elaine.

'That poor woman,' she whispered, whilst Isa nodded sadly.

'Aye, that'll be another hellish conversation. I still can't believe it.'

They sat quietly together, trying to let the information sink in.

'She'll need to speak to a solicitor,' Isa said eventually. 'Jim does matrimonial work, doesn't he?'

'Yes, and when it all comes out and the tongues start wagging, *which they will*, mum, her name and her reputation'll be mud. It'll be some conversation she'll have to have with Jim, but yes, I suppose you're right. She needs to get herself sorted if possible, but I'm not getting involved. I'm sorry, but poor David is the wronged party here, and I feel *so* sorry for him, and the boys. She's a grown woman and needs to deal with her mess herself.'

Her mother looked at her crossly, 'Since when did you become so hard, Ann-Marie? This is your *daughter!*'

Ann-Marie looked Isa square in the eye, 'Since I heard her siding with Bobby and Liz trying to persuade me to sell the farm,' she answered harshly, and calling the dogs brusquely, took them out for a much needed walk.

***

Elaine and Malky had just reached the top of The Cheesewring; a fabulous natural outcrop on the heights of Bodmin Moor, and Elaine was happily marching along, with Malky lagging behind, feeling uncomfortable and increasingly unwell. The medication was obviously clearing her infection, and Elaine was quietly elated that whilst she was feeling better and better, Malky was suffering, *poor soul*. Tonight was her big night and she was looking forward more and more to the delights of the famous restaurant, and wanted nothing to spoil that.

He'd had the *temerity* that morning to suggest he see a local GP, and she'd scoffed and refused, worried that this would turn into an excuse to cancel the long-awaited dinner engagement, and was having none of it. He could go to a doctor tomorrow, she'd said, enjoying his discomfort and also more than a little reluctant to face the showdown that would inevitably happen when he was diagnosed. Like a dish best served cold, her revenge could wait.

Chapter 21

Elaine was sitting on a bar stood in the small bar of the guest house drinking a large glass of white wine and was chatting to some other guests who were staying. She'd been waiting for Malky for about twenty minutes and his pint of beer had gone flat.

He took a sip and with a nod to the barmaid, asked her to put a head on it, which she did.

'I wonder if you have the phone number for a local doctor?' he asked her as she passed the pint back to him. Elaine turned to listen and he smiled palely to her, 'I'm still feeling out of sorts', he explained moodily.

'Oh, that's a real *shame*,' she added, 'and today too.' She turned to the couple who she'd been chatting to, 'We're booked at the Seafood Restaurant tonight, so Malky'll need to be at death's door if we were *ever* going to miss that!' she explained with a smile, 'It's been booked for months.'

The barmaid handed him a number and Malky walked over to the window to make the phone call. He returned a couple of minutes later, 'I can get seen today, if I go and wait', he said and looked at Elaine's glass of wine.

She took the unsubtle hint and finished the crisp, cold

contents and waving goodbye to the couple, following him out to the car.

Traffic in Padstow was difficult, but they eventually found the surgery, and went in to speak to the receptionist who indicated the waiting area and told them that the doctor would see Malky at the end of his lists. They might have to wait around forty minutes, she explained.

'Oh, I'll go for a walk down to the harbour, 'Elaine said brightly, 'You don't need me to go in with you; you're *not* a child.' She grinned, 'I'll meet you down at the café at the harbour and we can get your prescription at the chemist down there, if they give you one,' and with that she pecked him lightly on the cheek and walked out.

Malky was furious. Leaving him there whilst she swanned off? He didn't know what the hell Elaine was playing at this week, but he had no choice but to sit there and wait.

The doctor eventually called him in apologetically, and Malky explained his peeing, the pain, and the temperature he had. A quick examination followed and the doctor asked him to give a sample at the reception desk,

'I don't have access to your notes, obviously, but you've got some sort of infection. I'll give you a broad spectrum antibiotic, and the results'll be back in a few days, so if you phone the receptionist here, we'll take it from there. No alcohol, I'm afraid', he finished with a wry smile. Great, just great, Malky thought as he took the prescription and headed down the narrow street back to the harbour.

Elaine was sitting with an ice-cream watching the boats, and he sat beside her.

'The chemist is just over there, dear,' she pointed. 'He gave you some antibiotics, then? Best to start the course right now and then maybe you'll feel better by tonight.'

He grunted and headed to the chemist, and Elaine took a deep cleansing breath and closed her eyes in the sun.

A few minutes later, he'd returned and popped two pills and a painkiller in his mouth, 'the doctor'll send a urine test for analysis and I can get the results in a couple of days,' he said sullenly, 'No drink.'

'Oh, that's a *shame*! Well, I'll just have a *glass* of wine tonight at the restaurant, there's no point in having a bottle if you can't join me,' she pressed his hand affectionately.

'I feel really awful,' he confided, looking for a little more sympathy, but she laughed, 'probably a wee waterworks infection, honey. You should be a woman – we have to endure *all* sorts of infections!'

Oh you just *wait*, she thought maliciously, you just wait! When you get those results, the chickens'll come home to roost, and then you're for the high jump!

The clouds thickened that afternoon, and they returned to the guest house to rest and then to get ready for their dinner date. Elaine had a leisurely bath, and as she started to change, she remarked on the worsening weather.

'Looks like a storm brewing', she said looking out of the window to sea. 'Just look at that wind!'

Malky was half-listening as he sat reading the tourist information he'd picked up in Padstow, 'Mmm, it says here the weather can change dramatically because

Cornwall is a peninsula. We'd best take raincoats tonight, just in case.'

***

The car park outside the restaurant had emptied somewhat as evening approached, and they managed to park close to the door as the first large raindrops began to fall. Inside, Elaine gasped as she admired the décor. This really *was* a high class place, she noted, admiring the waiters and waitresses in their crisp black and white uniforms. They were escorted immediately to their table in the centre of the restaurant, and Elaine was glad she had made an effort tonight, with her cream button-through dress and matching sandals and shoulder bag. Her new hairdo even made her look *a little* like Joanna Lumley, she thought as she caught her reflection in one of the mirrors as they walked to their table. The Maitre welcomed them and introduced their waitress for the evening, wished them *bon appetit* and left them with a smile. Elaine felt like she'd died and gone to heaven. She spent some time looking at the menu, and asked her waitress one or two little questions regarding specific items, 'I've never dined in a place like this before,' she said confidentially, 'and I'm a wee bit out of my depth,'

The waitress smiled, and explained the menu without snootiness or distain, putting Elaine immediately at her ease. She accepted the suggested glass of red wine, noting with barely concealed glee that Malky was sticking to iced water. He raised his glass to her, forcing himself out of his mood and tried to match her excitement, 'To us!' he exclaimed.

She held her glass back for a fraction of a second, 'to the future', she smiled broadly.

After a starter of grilled scallops, Elaine chose the turbot in a hollandaise sauce, whilst Malky chose the pan-fried Dover sole. They managed to pass the evening discussing the meal and the restaurant, with Elaine catching the waitress's eye after the main course, and asking for another glass of the delicious red wine.

'That's over eleven quid a glass!' Malky hissed at her. She smiled sweetly at him and replied, 'Well, you only live once Malky.'

He glowered at her, simmering with anger because he couldn't have a glass himself, because she seemed to be *gloating* at him, and well, because it was just bloody unfair!

Rather than rub his face in it, Elaine politely refused the offer of a dessert, and asked the waitress to bring their bill. Malky was relieved – at almost a tenner each, dessert he could live without, although his face fell when the waitress brought them a small dish of petit fours alongside the bill. She smiled and whispered, 'It's okay, they're free.'

As they left, the rain was thundering down and the wind blew them across the road towards their car. Finally, they managed to get in, with Elaine a little giggly with the wine, 'Oh that was wonderful! Just *wonderful*! I haven't enjoyed myself so much in *years*!'

'Over two hundred quid! And did ye see that they included a massive service charge too? Bloody cheek!'

'Don't be so mean, Malky! How often would you go for dinner in a place like that?' Elaine snapped crossly, as they pulled out from the car park and drove slowly back to their guest house. She smiled as she relived the whole experience over and over in her mind, whilst Malky sat seething, peering through the rain spattered windscreen.

***

The next morning was cloudy and breezy and the sea was wild, churning and dashing itself along the cliffs. He'd fallen asleep almost immediately last night, after taking the tablets and some more painkillers and felt slightly better this morning at breakfast. Elaine had chattered on and on at breakfast about the superb meal they had enjoyed, whilst he ate as much as he could, cheekily asking the breakfast waitress for some more bacon.

'If we eat well now, we can skip lunch,' he said in a whisper to her.

'Grudging me this wee trip, Malky?' she asked sweetly.

'You've got a right bee in your bonnet Elaine. D'ye want to just come out with whatever's bothering you, because *something* is!' he snapped.

'I'm just enjoying this holiday. We've no' been away for years and suddenly, it's been a weekend here and a weekend there and now this trip out of the blue. If I was a suspicious woman, I'd say you were feeling guilty about something!' she hissed back, collecting her handbag and leaving a stunned Malky sitting at the table.

At ten, with a lull in the wind, they left Polzeath and drove west along the coast to do a short walk to see the Bedruthan Steps. They donned their waterproofs in the car park, which was almost empty, and chatted to the warden who was sensibly keeping warm in the small shop, who warned them to watch out for the swells and to look for the peregrine falcons that frequented the area.

Malky was determined not to be left behind today and he strode out confidently down the path, with Elaine happily following in his wake.

When she caught up with him he confronted her angrily, 'What did you mean by that comment at breakfast? I've *nothing* to feel guilty about!'

There was no-one around and she decided it was time to tell her husband some home truths. 'Alright Malky, you've asked for it! A week ago *I* started to feel unwell, just like you are now…well, I went to the doctors and she did a urine test, and *guess what?* I've got Chlamydia. Don't know what that is, eh? Well, it's a sexually transmitted disease, and Ah know for a *fact* Malky, that *Ah've* no been the one playing away. So, *you*, ya dirty womanising pig are the one that gave it to me!'

She stopped to catch her breath, all the anger and hurt and disappointment overwhelming her,

'Ah don't know *who* ye've been with and, d'you know what? I don't *care*, because now I've had my holiday and my lovely meal in a posh restaurant, and when we get back, I'm *divorcing* you! I *loved* you Malky! Loved you since we met and you betrayed me! Infecting me wi' a horrible disease! How *could* ye? How could ye do that to me?' she stumbled on, determined not to let him see her crying.

Malky was stunned and trying to think quickly, caught her up, 'Elaine, darlin', I'm sorry! It was a mistake! A one-off! Please stop and let's talk. I love you', he cried trying to grab her arm, but she dragged herself backwards.

'You're a LIAR! A *liar*! All those years watching you making eyes at every woman you ever met. How many, Malky? *How many*? And who *are* they? Where are you meeting these women that find you so irresistible? At work? I don't think so!' she cried, her mascara running down her face as she cried with her heart breaking.

The wind whipped her hood off and her hair caught and blew in her eyes, but she didn't care. Now that she'd started, she couldn't stop, 'You *even* made eyes at Ann-Marie Ross, for God's sake! Ma *best* friend! What wis the idea? Cosy up to Ann-Marie and move into the farm? Did ye really think a woman like that would be interested in a dirty beggar like you? You disgust me! I want nothing more to do wi' ye! Whaddy'ye think Calum'll say when I tell'im you've been putting it aboot?'

Malky grabbed her shoulders and angrily pulled her face close to his in the rising wind, 'It's *your* fault! I'm a man in my prime and I've got needs, and you're...*old*. Don't blame me that you're past it! Yer a ball and chain!'

Her eyes opened wild with disbelief, 'Past it? *Past it*? So yer wee floozy is some *young* bit of skirt? You don't *know* any younger women Malky! And what younger woman would fancy an old has-been like you? Don't flatter yersel'!'

And then it just spilled out of him before he could stop himself he was so angry, 'Well, I was good enough for Lynda Bell, she couldnae get enough of me! Gaggin'for it! And Ann-Marie could do a lot worse than me.'

Elaine stared at him in horror, '*Lynda*? Ann-Marie's daughter? You were having it away with my best friend's

204

daughter? You're old enough to be her *faither*, for God's sake! Did ye give *her* Chlamydia too?'

He recovered himself almost immediately, panting hard with anger, 'No, I *told* ye, it was a one-off...'

'Couldn't get enough of ye, ye jist said!' she accused, turning to walk back to the car, 'See ye in court Malky!'

He spun her around again to face him, 'Ye cannae *leave me*, Elaine, I'll be ruined!'

'I don't *care* Malky, you should've thought of that before you started dipping yer wick! I'm going home. You can stay here or do whatever the hell you want, but *I'm* going home and I'll be seeing a lawyer as soon as I get there!'

She angrily pulled away, her foot slipping on the uneven rocks and she put out her hand to grab him and steadily herself, and suddenly Malky *knew* what to do. If she was to *fall*, there'd be no divorce. He'd be free to pursue Ann-Marie. *No-one* would know. No scandal, no selling the house. He looked around quickly, no-one was walking; it was wild, and no-one was around. No witnesses. In desperation and anger, his common sense deserted him as he shoved her hard, and her feet slipped again on the crumbling path. His eyes blazing with anger, he shoved her again, harder, back towards the edge of the path, where the rocks had already fallen away after the heavy rain in the previous night's storm. She cried out, and tried to grab his jacket, but he held her at arms-length, pushing her further and further to the edge with her feet failing to find purchase on the sliding path.

'Yer finished, Elaine, and there'll be *no* divorce! I want

it all!' he snarled and gave her a final brutal shove.

She teetered backwards as the wind sucked her downwards, grabbing and pulling at his legs as she fell.

Chapter 22

Bob had become a regular visitor to High Glen Farm in the following month, and was taking a keen interest in Bracken's wellbeing. The little spaniel had fattened out since her brief romance with Archie, and like expectant parents he and Isa had both taken her for the scan at the vets, and retuned with jubilant news. The pregnancy was confirmed with a photo-shoot for the website, and Isa and Bob discussed the Big Event over what were becoming regular lunch dates.

After Lynda's devastating news, Ann-Marie had quietly spoken to Jim Muir in his office before arranging for him to come and chat to Lynda about what a divorce would entail. Even after a month to calm down, David was adamant that he wanted a divorce, but had agreed to joint custody of the boys, and Lynda sadly accepted that her marriage was over and agreed to the apartment being put up for sale. Ann-Marie ensured that Lynda kept Malky's name out of the whole divorce talks, trying to limit any possible damage and repercussions.

Jim and Ann-Marie walked with Bramble over to the bothy. Piles of earth surrounded it, and the septic tank was now in place and foundations laid for the small extension to the building.

'Rome wasn't built in a day,' Jim sighed, 'and autumn's almost here.'

Ann-Marie was more positive, 'The bones are there though, and Roddy says the walls'll be up and the place watertight before winter.'

They walked back through the orchard towards the house, enjoying the warmth of the sun, whilst acknowledging that summer was all but finished.

'It's been some year,' he said, helping her over a stile.

'Aye, one I'll be glad to see the back of,' she agreed, and sat on the stone wall.

'Life's a funny thing, you know? It trundles on for years without any surprises and then suddenly…'

'Like buses?' he smiled.

She nodded, 'David's accepted an offer on the apartment, and Lynda knows she's on a countdown now, maybe a new start is what she needs. She's resigned from that job and is looking to get another a bit closer to home. I think she's had enough of the bright lights and a fast life, thank God. I've seen a nice wee semi-detached house in the village that might suit her, and once they've sold that apartment and split the money, I'll help her to buy that. Maybe she's ready to grow up a little now. Sad, but, well these things happen.'

'You're being very broad minded,' Jim said, shoving her over to sit next to her.

'Well, I'm her mother, what can I do? Just because they grow up and leave, doesn't mean you stop caring or stop worrying. I was very angry with her for a while around the time Billy died. I really was; but I think a lot of that stems from Bobby and Liz interfering and having a bad influence on her. Anyway, I'm trying to put that behind me. The marriage breaking up is a bitter pill, but they are trying to behave well for the boys. She's been very silly, but hopefully they might be able to at least talk to each other in the future. Thank you for agreeing to handle her divorce.'

'Yes, she'll be fine. I'm more concerned with that terrible business with Elaine and Malky. The newspapers have moved onto other stories and finally left her alone, and the post mortem's confirmed that the cause of death was the fall. Hard to believe it's been a whole month since it happened.'

She hopped down from the wall, 'Today's news is tomorrow's fish wrappers, but I think there will be stuff in the 'papers about it again when the inquest happens. I've been through all that remember. Even though she can have a funeral, it'll no' be over for a long time.' she said as they walked shoulder to shoulder back to the farmhouse. Chubby and bored Bracken greeted them enthusiastically, and Ann-Marie went through the routine of putting the kettle on. Sadie's old car lurched into the yard, and she bounded into the house as usual without knocking, 'It's only me!' she cried.

'She's not here,' Ann-Marie answered, 'she's out with her boyfriend.'

'*Again?*' cried Sadie, 'This is getting serious! I'll have to start thinking of buying a new hat!'

Ann-Marie laughed. Sadie bought a new hat for every wedding she'd been invited to and her collection was famous.

'Do you want tea?' she offered, as Jim opened the cupboard to search for the biscuits.

Sadie shook her head, 'No, ta. Tell her highness, I'll catch up with her soon. Bye-bye.'

And she was gone.

'What about you?' Jim said passing her the biscuits.

'I'm over Billy's death, if that's what you mean. People; outsiders I mean, never really see what goes on between couples, and I have to admit, its nice to have my independence and freedom back. I've been able to develop the business here the way I wanted, which I was never allowed to do whilst he was alive.' She looked at Jim sideways, wanting him to understand, but holding back the necessary damning details.

'You'll always be a dear friend, but I'm afraid, that's all I want from you, Jim. I know you're nothing like Billy, but I don't want a new relationship and don't want to lose my independence again.'

'Well, to quote a phrase, the problems of two little people don't amount to a hill of beans, and anyway… we'll always have Largs.' He sighed, but was smiling at her.

'You're such a melodramatic idiot, Jim Muir,' she snorted.

'Casablanca. My favourite movie,' he said unapologetically as he stuffed a whole hobnob into his mouth.

'Anyhow, are we good for the movies tonight?' she said, 'Isa's out again, and well, we did say that the new release was on the cards?'

'Yes, indeed, I'll pick you up at six thirty. Tomorrow,

I've got a busy day with two sets of conveyancing and some other loose ends to tie up. What are you up to?'

'Mum and I are finally going to see Elaine,' she said quietly.

***

They arrived at four, and found Elaine putting washing into the dryer. The house, usually immaculate, was a little untidy and Elaine had been obviously having a clear-out. She stopped immediately and offered the women a gin and tonic, which they accepted as they sat in the lounge of Elaine's bright terraced sandstone villa, surrounded by half-filled cardboard boxes.

Expecting to find her still upset, they noticed some house brochures on the table, and Ann-Marie picked one up curiously, 'Thinking of moving?' she asked gently, briefly showing it to her mother.

'Yes!' Elaine announced a little breathlessly.

'D'you not think it's a bit *quick* Elaine?' Isa ventured, 'After all, it's only really been a month since the accident, and I think you might be making a mistake, trying to move on too quickly. You need time to recover from all the shock.'

Elaine downed her gin and tonic in one, and slammed the empty glass onto the table.

'The shock? Ha! Well, let me tell you the *full* story, and then you judge whether I'm in shock or not.'

Elaine then explained the whole story about Malky's infidelity. Ann-Marie confirmed sadly that Lynda and Malky had indeed had a brief affair, but stressed the fact that she was very repentant. Elaine's eyebrows furrowed, and it was obvious that she wasn't impressed by that. She shocked her audience by revealing that after admitting his fling with Lynda, they'd had a massive argument and then at the end, knowing he was beaten, he'd tried to push her off the cliff. 'I didn't tell the police that, or Calum. It would be just *too* complicated and horrible. But he just came over like a mad-man, shoving and shoving. And the *hate* in his eyes – I'll never forget that. I was lucky. It all just happened so *fast* – one minute he was shoving and I was slipping, then I fell and he went right over. *Right* over.'

She got up quickly and went to the sideboard and poured herself another large gin with a splash of tonic, and sat back down.

'My hands were all scratched and bleeding, and I must have looked a *right* state, soaking and bawling my head off, but I managed to get back to the warden's hut and he called the police and the Coastguard. I sat in that wee hut wi' that man staring at me for what felt like hours. Then a nice policewoman came and took me back to the police station an' a doctor came and looked at my hands and cleaned them up, and saw my jacket sleeve was pulled almost out of the shoulder. He told me I was very lucky, not to have fallen too! All I did was cry. Calum arrived the next day.'

Ann-Marie could hardly believe what her friend was telling her, 'He *pushed* you?'

'Aye. Called me *old* and a ball and chain, said I was holding him back. Even said he wanted me out o' the way so he could make a move on *you* to get the farm! Can you believe it? He wisnae gonnae lose everything in

212

a divorce, was what he said. *So* angry! You should have seen the look in his *face*. I've never seen him like that – like a man possessed wi' a face of pure evil. Of course, I couldnae tell *Calum* that, or tell the police the *real* story. So - he lost his balance and slipped and I tried to grab him and he fell. *That's* the story,' she finished firmly, looking them both in the eyes.

Isa took both her and Ann-Marie's glasses and refilled them and sat back down.

Elaine trembled and cried as she relived the whole incident and the three of them sat quietly, not knowing quite how to continue the conversation.

Eventually Elaine gave herself a little shake, and smiled hesitantly, 'It was lovely in Cornwall, really lovely. I thought we were on a second honeymoon, and now, when I look back and try and put all the pieces together, I think he'd planned it all along. All the walking, and the bait to go to that restaurant. He *hated* the restaurant, you know? All he could think about was the cost! So *why* plan that trip? He *must* have been planning it the whole time.'

Tears fell from her eyes, and Ann-Marie leaped forward to comfort her friend, but Elaine pushed her back, '*No*. I'm *glad* he's dead. Glad. Don't feel sorry for me. Now I'm *free*. Free of a man who despised me for years. I see it now, always chatting up women at any opportunity. I'm sure Lynda wasnae the first, or the last…' she spat.

Isa cleared her throat and indicated the boxes, 'So, what's all this then?'

'His stuff. I'm boxing it all. Calum can come and look

through it, if he wants, but I want it all gone. Actually, I want to move. Too many memories here. I liked being at the coast so much that I'm going to look for a wee house in Largs. I always wanted to live there, d'you remember me sayin' that Ann-Marie? I thought we could retire there, but I see now why Malky wanted to stay here – closer to Glasgow and all the *women*. I'm going to retire to Largs and get a cat.'

An uneasy silence fell on the room. Isa sighed and shook her head, 'He was a fool, Elaine, there's no denying it. Look at what he ruined; but, you need to be careful. Careful what you *do* and careful what you *say*. If you want my advice, get the funeral over before you start clearing Malky from the house. By all means, tell Calum that you can't face living here – that there are too many memories, but *wait* a while.'

'Oh, the funeral'll be in ten days,' Elaine remembered suddenly. 'There's a backlog apparently, the woman at the registrar's told me. She was very apologetic. Didn't know what to say to me, really. Isn't it funny how word gets about? Calum's arranged the funeral, I couldn't.'

They stayed an hour, watching Elaine getting drunker, until Isa went and made her a sandwich, 'Eat,' she said pushing the plate into her hands, 'and lay off the drink, for God's sake.'

'Can I come and stay wi' you for a day or two?' Elaine asked in a small voice, 'I jist don't trust masel' right now…'

Isa sat back down, 'Go and pack a bag; you can sleep in the spare room.'

Elaine disappeared upstairs and left Isa and Ann-Marie sitting in the lounge, surrounded by family photographs, 'I don't know what to say,' Ann-Marie began, 'I know he was always making eyes at every woman he met, but I never expected this.'

'I'm sure we'll hear even more about him in the next few days,' her mother said, shaking her head. 'I'll phone Lynda when we get back and warn her not to come over for a while, I don't think it would be a good idea if they met.'

Chapter 23

Elaine took her things up to the spare bedroom at High Glen Farm. It wasn't what she was used to; the wallpaper with the small pink rosebuds was unfashionable and the patchwork quilt homely, but she was with friends and felt a burden lift from her shoulders as she returned to the living room where Isa sat quietly and pulled her knitting from a bag. She began the final sleeve of the cardigan she was knitting for Ann-Marie, and waited till Elaine settled on the opposite sofa.

'Sadie's coming over later,' she remarked, 'I hope that'll be alright. She's been a bit lonely since Mark died and I've been busy with Bob, so it was already arranged. It'll take your mind off things maybe,' she finished. It would be a house full of widows this evening, and they'd all have to try and avoid talking about dead husbands, but that was the way the dice had fallen. Isa tried to lighten the conversation, 'Are you serious about moving to Largs? D'you have any friends there?'

'No, but it's a busy wee place and I think it would be lovely, living by the sea. Before the accident happened, I have to say that I was really enjoyed the wee fishing villages and harbours in Cornwall, there was always something going on and something to see. Largs is a bit like that, and not too far away. I've got my car, and can still pop over to see Ann-Marie, and there's a station to take me to Glasgow, when I need to. I realise now that I've almost been living my own life until recently, with Malky and me drifting apart, but I have to say that I'm actually enjoying the walking now. Maybe I could join a ramblers group or something. I'm only sixty. I've got probably another twenty five years left, so time to do all those things I've never done. I don't want to sit in that house in the suburbs being a curtain-twitcher and living a grey life. Maybe I'll travel. Cornwall opened my eyes a bit to another world. You and Ann-Marie went on a wee bus tour – I could do that too. And then again, maybe I'll even meet someone else. You and this Bob Anderson, that's a wee romance now, isn't it? And you're older than me.'

'I'll take that as a compliment,' Isa said with a grin, 'and yes, why not? You and Sadie both are far too young to spend the rest of your lives being alone. They say sixty is the new fifty, and you've no money worries, so you're a bit of a catch now Elaine.' she ended positively, bringing a smile to Elaine's face.

Ann-Marie returned from the kitchen triumphantly, 'Lamb chops and potato salad and an apple crumble for dessert', she announced, 'It'll be ready in about twenty minutes.' She sat down next to her mother, squeezing gently in next to Bracken.

'We're going to be starting the harvest soon Elaine, and the boys'll be busy until December, so I wondered if you were at a loose end if you would be interested in doing some part time shifts in the shop here. It'll be afternoons, as they are so busy and if you weren't doing anything…'

Elaine's face lit up, 'Really? That would be fab. I'd been wondering what to do all day on my own. After all,' she laughed, 'I can only clean the house so much! Yes, please.'

Isa smiled at her daughter affectionately, 'It would be company too. Then, in a wee while, we could maybe come with you house hunting. *After* harvest is done.'

Ann-Marie was impressed. Her mother had cleverly managed to gently steer Elaine away from a hasty move without any fuss.

'Right, I'll take Bracken out for a wee waddle round the yard and then we'll have dinner,' she said, getting up and leaving the others chatting quietly.

***

Whilst Bramble ran happily outside, Ann-Marie kept alongside Bracken's slower pace. With only four weeks to go, she was looking forward to the chaos and noise and mess that a litter of puppies would entail, and perhaps less looking forward to the inevitable heartache when most of the puppies would be leaving to go to their forever homes. Bittersweet. A bit like life really, she mused. She heard the sound of fence-posts being struck home, and realised Roddy was still working on fencing off the bothy. He'd bought post and rail fencing, insisting that it looked prettier than the conventional post and stock fencing. After ushering the dogs back inside, she followed the noise and was pleased to see him shouting to Duncan to hold the posts straight, before he manoeuvred the tractor's post basher to hammer the post home. His assessment had proved correct and the fenced off area around the still raw-looking building would by next summer actually look like a garden.

Such big changes since she'd taken over the running of the farm, and all positive. In the long term it had proved the correct decision to terminate Bull's association with the farm, if that was the right phrase, she thought, and she had no regrets. Now, the cider and juice business was revitalised and increasingly profitable, she'd provided jobs for three people, if she included Elaine as her newest recruit, and of course, she had no more personal abuse or fear to face. Had it all been worth it? She smiled grimly to herself. If she believed in heaven and hell then, yes, she'd have to face a reckoning in the end, but after the years of domestic abuse, she didn't care, and hopefully, she'd have as many good years watching the farm go from strength to strength and even provide a living for her grandsons. She waved from the edge of the orchard and then returned to the house. Now that she'd thrown a lifeline to Elaine, perhaps she could pick up the threads of her life and realise that she too could have a future where she felt valued and useful. Even her mother was settling into what appeared to be a budding romance with the dapper Bob Anderson in her golden years. There was always hope.

After they cleared the table and had some coffee, Sadie arrived with her usual, 'It's only me,' bursting with news.

'I've landed a job!' she exclaimed excitedly, then realising that Elaine was there, she immediately restrained herself apologetically, 'Oh hello Elaine! I'm *so* sorry to hear about Malky.' She sat, somewhat abashed next to Ann-Marie, who patted her hand, sympathetically, 'Elaine's landed a job too, but let's hear your news first.'

'The old college in Paisley has offered me a term-time job as a library assistant!' she grinned, 'They'll even let me do a qualification, too!' she said, her eyes shining.

Elaine smiled at her, 'I'm so pleased for you. Ann-Marie's offered me a wee part-time job too, here selling cider in the shop.'

Sadie pulled a bottle of champagne from behind her back, 'Well then, *this* is really suitable, then!'

Isa did the honours and they all had a glass of the sparkling wine and chattered happily for a few minutes, recalling their first jobs, years previously.

'When I got my first job, I had to give my mother all my pay, and she gave me a weekly allowance,' Isa recalled, 'the first thing I bought was some very unsuitable high heels. I thought I was a real Bobby Dazzler, but my God, they were the most uncomfortable shoes I ever had!'

The buoyant atmosphere continued and when the champagne was finished, the women switched to gin and tonics, and cider with some ice. Ann-Marie wrinkled her nose at the thought of ice in her beloved cider, but it was hot, and Elaine was a guest. They moved outside to sit at the picnic tables set up in the taproom garden and enjoyed the late summer sun.

Bracken waddled around, wondering if anyone had any titbits, but was disappointed and threw herself down beside the table in apparent exhaustion.

Sadie looked at her affectionately, 'How long now to

the big day?' she asked Isa.

'Just under three weeks now. We can't know exactly, but we're keeping an eye on her.'

Sadie leaned back, enjoying the sun, 'If it hadn't been an accident, you'd swear it was *planned* to fit in with the harvest, but you'll be awfy busy this year with pressing *and* puppies around the place,' she mused.

'It's been years since Bracken and Bramble were puppies, but I remember the noise, and the mess,' Ann-Marie agreed.

'*Especially* the mess,' Isa laughed.

The lads suddenly returned to the yard, sweaty and tired, and Ann-Marie beckoned them over with offers of cider.

There was no room for them to sit, so Roddy and Duncan pulled another picnic bench over to join theirs, and sat gulping cider thirstily.

'We can't stop ladies', Roddy said, wiping his mouth with the back of his hand, '*Duncan* has a big date tonight!'

The women whooped with delight, much to Duncan's acute embarrassment.

'The famous Shona, is it Duncan?' Isa said, her eyes twinkling.

He nodded with a cough, 'We're going to an Italian restaurant in Greenock. She *finally* agreed, when I told her about the puppies. Turns out that puppies are a real babe magnet,' he grinned.

'*Babe magnet*', Elaine laughed, 'I've no' heard that expression for years!'

'Is that Shona Keenan, then?' Sadie asked, 'Her dad's got a nice place over near Brookfield. You keep in there son, that family has *money*!'

The lads made their excuses and left, leaving the women to sit quietly, each lost in their own thoughts.

'Money's no everything, is it?' Isa said eventually, 'We had nothing when we started out, and were as happy as we could be.'

'Well, my new job'll certainly help me put a wee nest egg away,' Sadie grinned.

Ann-Marie looked up and met Elaine's eyes, troubled and clouding over.

'You okay?' she asked gently.

'I thought that money'd make us comfortable, and we'd be able to spend our retirement together', she said with tears in her eyes, 'but… well, now I know that we'd been on different wavelengths for years and when Malky eventually retired, he'd have been bored and it would have all come to a head anyway. Money's *not* everything.'

Sadie smiled gently at her, 'I felt like that when Mark died, but now I see he was destructive. Didn't *care* that he was gambling and drinking away our future. The way things have turned out, I've had a second chance at life; that's how I'm looking at it.'

Isa gathered the empty glasses together and then sat down again, 'It's been a watershed year for us *all* ladies. I've recovered from a stroke, Ann-Marie, Sadie and now you Elaine have lost a husband, but look at the positives – none of us is ill, we're all lucky to have good friends around, and the future, if we look hard, is rosy. Let's try and keep positive. The road hasn't ended here; we've all got other destinations ahead and need to just keep on keeping on. Now, *less* of this maudlin talk. It's getting chilly and I'm going inside to open that very special bottle of twenty year old Talisker and have a few drams. Sadie – you're driving, but I'll let you sniff the glass, before you leave. Help me take these glasses in', she said with a smirk to Sadie.

They collected the glasses and wandered towards the house, Sadie remonstrating that she was *perfectly* capable of driving home after a wee dram, and didn't want to miss anything. Their voices got quieter as they went inside and the air was again filled with the gentle sounds of bees and birdsong.

Ann-Marie and Elaine remained on the bench, watching the sun slowly dip behind the Campsie hills. It was Elaine who broke the silence first, 'You know, sunsets in Cornwall are lovely, but they are incredibly short. It must be because they are further south than here; the sun just seems to *drop* under the sea really quickly. Here, the sunsets are much longer. Thank you for the job, it's the new start I need,' she finished brusquely, brushing the tears away, 'Now let's go in and share that bottle, before Isa and Sadie drink the lion's share of that nice malt!'

Chapter 24

Isa and Ann-Marie sat with Elaine, watching her drink more and more malt, and as the alcohol loosened her tongue, and listened to her veer from feeling sorry for herself, to angrily recalling her discovery of her husband's infidelity and the few eventful days in Cornwall. They let her talk herself hoarse and cry herself dry, shocked not only by the twists and turns of the story, but by Elaine's growing assertiveness as she confronted Malky and fought for her life on the cliffs.

Isa was exhausted and taking the advantage of Elaine visiting the toilet, told Ann-Marie to her to give her a sleeping pill or none of them would get any sleep. 'I'm exhausted,'she admitted and left Ann-Marie to take care of Elaine, 'Goodnight love,' she said mounting the stairs, 'Let's try *not* to have too early a start tomorrow, eh?'

Ann-Marie nodded and let the dogs out for a last toilet visit, and put the empty bottle of malt in the bin. When Elaine reappeared, Ann-Marie called it a night and they both headed for bed.

Elaine spent a difficult night, tossing and turning in a strange bed, and cried herself to sleep, and it was three bleary-eyed women who appeared in the kitchen in the morning, unwilling or unable to discuss the drunken conversation of the night before.

As Ann-Marie filled the kettle the phone began to ring.

'It's Calum for you', she said, handing the phone to Elaine.

A brief conversation took place of which Ann-Marie could hear Elaine apologise for not telling him where she was. He'd obviously been worried all night as she could hear his raised voice at the other end. Elaine soothed him and told him she was fine and would be staying for a few days, and then rang off.

'You should be glad he cares,' Ann-Marie said quietly.

'Och, he's a good lad, but he's taken it very hard. When he came down to Cornwall to collect the car and me and drive back up the road, we hardly spoke. I think we were both in shock, but obviously in different ways. Hopefully, he'll get over it in time. I just find it awkward to be with him right now, because he wants to talk about Malky and I don't. I can hardly tell him his father was a womaniser who tried to push his mother off a cliff, and it kind of leaves us with nothing I really *can* talk about. Maybe that'll change with time, I don't know. Do you talk much about Bull...er Billy?'

Ann-Marie hadn't been expecting that turn in the conversation. Isa and Ann-Marie never talked about Billy, or that dreadful day. She'd found it hard enough to remove all thoughts of him, and of what she had been forced to do from her mind, and talking about Bull to Isa or Elaine, or *anyone* was not something she was comfortable with.

'Not really. Lynda was too preoccupied at the start, and that time has passed I think. Mum and I just avoid talking about him.' She knew they had to talk about Lynda, and decided that sometime soon they'd need to discuss that; after all Lynda was bound to visit soon and if Elaine was going to do shifts in the taproom shop, Ann-Marie would rather get any unpleasantness out of the way earlier and not in front of the public.

She made more tea and started to make some rounds of toast for them all.

Roddy and Duncan appeared, made themselves coffee and bacon rolls and sat at the table. They weren't used to so many women in the way first thing in the morning, and Ann-Marie shooed Elaine and Isa through to the living room, whilst they discussed the day's work. The last batch of pigs to be processed before harvest were going to the abattoir this morning, and then the delivery of new roof slates for the bothy was arriving in the afternoon. The lads were to juggle the animals, customers and anything else between them, Ann-Marie explained.

'Oh Jim Muir is going to drop by with the architect later, he said he told you?' Roddy mentioned.

Ann-Marie groaned, 'Oh, I'd *forgotten* about that! Well, let's hope they don't all arrive at the same time,' she pouted. Breakfast was short and sweet and Ann-Marie managed to have a covert conversation with her mother whilst Elaine went back upstairs to change.

'Can you take her out with you today to give me some space? It's going to be a busy day.'

'But Bob is taking me out for lunch!' Isa whined.

'Well, I'm sure *Bob* won't mind meeting one of

your friends.'

'Well, technically, she's *your* friend, but alright. I'll send him a text and warn him,' Isa harrumphed and switched on the television to catch the news.

Roddy hitched up the trailer to the pickup and was manoeuvring it next to the pig shed, and she went out to help him and Duncan persuade three pigs into the back of the trailer. Once that was completed, she and Duncan cleaned and hosed out the empty pens.

Bob Anderson then arrived to collect his charges, and he and Ann-Marie exchanged hellos before he headed into the house. She took the opportunity to have a mid morning cuppa with them all before they left and then rounded up the dogs for a walk down to the bothy. The new roof trusses were in place and the waterproof roof membrane was awaiting the slates. Clouds were rolling in and she hoped the rain would hold off for a few days to allow the building to be made watertight. Roddy was itching to move in, but she thought it would be a month or so before he could give his landlord in Erskine notice, he could hardly call it home, when there were no internal walls, or services inside. Her phone crackled into life as Duncan called to announce that Jim had arrived, and she returned to the yard, conscious that she was still in her working duds. She smiled at the architect and was briefly introduced to the case officer from building control, and they both began to walk down towards the bothy, leaving Jim to talk briefly to Ann-Marie.

'We'll do the site visit and then I need to have a chat with you about Lynda and Elaine. I've had some news I need to tell you about,' he said mysteriously, and hurried to join the others.

After she had changed, she began to make a pot of coffee and Bramble's tail began to thump rhythmically on the floor, announcing Jim's return.

'That went well,' he said, 'project all on track and the drains and work so far signed off. Now, what do you want first – the news that Lynda' ex-boss has been arrested for money-laundering and that she might be called as a witness, or the news that Malky had recently taken a life-insurance policy out on Elaine?'

If she thought today was going to be another run-of-the-mill average day on the farm, she was sorely mistaken, and she felt her heart quicken at the thought of bad news.

He poured them both a coffee and matter-of-factly began to explain firstly about the news he'd heard through the legal grapevine about Ian Walker.

'I got a call last night from a colleague in our Glasgow office to tell me Ian Walker was arrested yesterday morning at his office. His computers and phone and everything have all been taken away by the Fraud Squad who're working with H.M. Revenue and Customs. Now, the only bit of this that concerns Lynda is that she was employed by him for a very short time. She *could* get called as a witness. I've heard of him, of course, but I try and stay clear of his kind of work and I don't really know him, but this could roll-on for months and I'm going to suggest she speaks to another colleague of mine to prepare a statement.'

He stopped talking to ensure she had understood what he'd just told her, and registered her shock. He pushed the biscuits towards her, but she shook her head.

'I *knew* that job sounded too good to be true!' she exclaimed, 'Did you know he was paying her cash for evening meetings in London for his private clients?'

Jim put his hands melodramatically over his ears, 'I'm not listening! *Don't* tell me anything. Look, *she's* not done anything wrong; the tax man wants to nail *him*, she's just unfortunate to be involved on the periphery, but at least she was only there a matter of weeks. I'll talk to her later today, don't worry. Now, for the *really* juicy news!'

He took a deep breath, as if weighing up the best way to deliver the bombshell,

'Were you aware that Malky had taken out life insurance policies on both himself and Elaine?'

Ann-Marie shook her head, 'It never occurred to me to ask her,' she admitted.

'As I'm trying to tie up the mortgage and stuff on the house, I've been dealing with all the paperwork. The endowment policy'll pay off the mortgage, that's all fine; *but* I came across a life insurance policy that he'd only taken out in January this year. Oh it covers both him and Elaine, and if one dies the other benefits, but it's the *timing*? Now; Elaine's *your* friend, not mine, and you know her well, so I need to ask, Ann-Marie – it's helluva suspicious that he only took it out a few months before he fell to his death in Cornwall, don't you think?. It *was* definitely an accident?'

Ann-Marie's head was reeling. She pushed the chair back noisily and hugged her arms around herself. Could Malky *really* have planned this? She recalled Elaine's off the cuff comment the previous day that she thought

Malky had planned to kill her, but surely, *surely*, that was just anger. She couldn't believe it. She looked at Jim, who was waiting for her to say something, but what could she *say*? She couldn't tell him that. Couldn't tell him that Elaine suspected, no; was *sure* that Malky had planned to kill her.

'I honestly don't know Jim', she said truthfully. 'She certainly hasn't said anything to *me*. I *can't* believe that!'

'Well, I'll need to speak to her. If the police ask me, I'll have to give them some sort of answer. In fact, if I speak to her and she has *any* knowledge of it, I'll have to make a statement to that effect. The thing is Ann-Marie; and *understand* this – if there was *anything* dodgy about this, any *hint* of foul play, then they might refuse to pay out.'

'I'll bring her round tomorrow morning,' Ann-Marie volunteered, smoothly. At least she'd have time to ask Elaine herself tonight. Poor Elaine was in for more revelations regarding Malky's behaviour, and she and Isa would have to coach her before she had to go and see Jim.

Jim downed his coffee and got up, 'Look, I need to go, I've got clients coming in soon, and I'm already late. I know she's your friend, but, *I* never told you this, alright?'

She nodded and impulsively hugged him, 'You're a good friend. I'm sure there's nothing in this, but I'll bring her over at nine tomorrow, and you can talk to her yourself.'

He grinned, 'I must try and give you bad news every day, if you're going to give me hugs. But seriously, don't fret too much, I'm probably over-thinking it, but I'd rather deal with these things and make sure everyone understands the accepted story. *If* you know what I mean,'

Ann-Marie understood exactly what he was inferring and smiled. He kissed her briefly on the lips, and stood back, 'I *really* have to go,' he apologised, 'Try not to worry.'

She washed up the breakfast dishes and when Roddy returned, they went to the pressing shed to start the annual clean down of the press, the cloths and the barrels. That would keep her occupied until Bob Anderson returned with the ladies of leisure, and she could have a chat with her mother and then Elaine.

The morning continued with some semblance of normality, and Duncan chattered happily about his big date with Shona Keenan, keeping Roddy and Ann-Marie entertained until the end of their lunch break, when Bob Anderson returned the ladies from their outing.

Ann-Marie asked Roddy to deal with the slate delivery, saying she needed to have a private chat with Elaine and Isa and that she didn't want to be interrupted, and then after they all waved goodbye to Bob, she ushered them inside, dreading the impact that the news would have, and hoping that Elaine wouldn't have any more revelations to make. The day had been stressful enough already.

Chapter 25

The next morning they awoke to a monsoon with heavy rain and a westerly wind whipping leaves and twigs from the trees. The forecast on the morning news said it would probably blow itself out by lunchtime, with lighter showers in the afternoon. The boys were working in the shed and the yard, cleaning and sterilising cider equipment, and readying themselves for the end of the month and the first picking of the dessert apples that wouldn't keep for very long.

Isa was to stay at home whilst Ann-Marie took Elaine to visit Jim, and then she would drop Elaine back at the farm and go to see Lynda. Another stressful day beckoned and lots of strong coffee was drunk before they set out.

The night before, Elaine had recalled that Malky had indeed set up new life insurance policies for them both at the start of the year, the reason being that because the endowment was soon to mature and pay off the mortgage, they'd need some sort of cover, just in case. Thankfully, this made sense, and Ann-Marie was sure Jim, and the insurers would accept this reasoning and see that the new policy was just a sensible precaution, and not some sinister plan. She was pleased that Elaine hadn't over-reacted to her news, although the look on Isa's face told her that once Elaine had gone back to her own house, the subject would surface again for discussion.

***

The meeting went smoothly and Ann-Marie dropped Elaine back at the farm, before driving to Lynda's apartment. The boys were at school and Lynda was sitting with her laptop applying for jobs, when her mother arrived.

'Tea?' she asked cheerfully, switching the machine off.

'No, I've had too much caffeine already', her mother answered, 'Lynda, I need to tell you something,' she said, patting the sofa beside her.

As she recounted the information Jim had told her, Lynda's face paled.

'But, I haven't done anything, why do they need to speak to *me*?' she asked nervously.

'Jim wants you to be sure you have your story straight, just in case you're called as a witness against him, because you were an employee. The thing is Lynda, he was paying you cash in hand, and if there are *any* records of this, they'll want to ask questions. They're trying to make fraud charges stick, so they'll be looking at every single thing to try and get him.'

She nodded, 'There was nothing. I wrote the receipts out for his clients, but nothing was officially recorded anywhere. He even kept a mobile phone; a pay as you go phone, just for those clients.'

'I want you to get a sheet of paper and write down

everything you *want* them to know, and Lynda; *less is more*. The less they have to dig up, the less chance of you being involved. Don't volunteer *any* information unless you have to. I'm sure it'll come to nothing, but be prepared, and you need to stick to your story, so get it right first time.'

'Yes, mum, I understand. I'll do it after I've thought it through, thank you,' she hugged her mother.

'I need to talk to you about something else too,' Ann-Marie said, taking the opportunity to talk about Malky and Elaine.

'Without me going into details which don't concern you, let's just say that Elaine is still understandably very angry at you and Malky.'

Lynda had the grace to blush, but sat quietly.

'Now, she's *very* sensitive at the moment, and needs a lot of support. She's actually been staying with us a couple of nights, but she said she's going back to her own house today, but anyway; I've offered her a part-time job working at the shop on the farm until harvest is over, because I need the men to help me with the pressing and your grandma is busy with her new friend Bob. Bracken is due to have puppies in a couple of weeks and having someone else there is useful right now. So, I'm just telling you that she'll be around for a while, and I really don't want any unpleasantness.' She looked at Lynda, who was listening intently.

'Do you want me to talk to her; to explain?'

'No, I want you to apologise again, and to tell her that the affair was all his idea. I know that sounds a bit strange, but well; things have come out now that I can't

234

tell you about, but let's just say, he's not exactly been honest with anyone, and that's the line I think you should take with her. It's not going to make *any* difference to your situation between you and David, but would be the right thing to do as regards Elaine. You're my daughter, and she's my best friend, and you're bound to meet up, but let's try and keep it civilised, yes?'

Lynda nodded.

'Now, make me a coffee now, and tell me about how you and the boys are, and what jobs you're applying for,' she said relieved at how the conversation had gone, and determined to end on a positive note.

Lynda made the coffee and gave her mother some paintings of the farm that the boys had made for her, which delighted her mother.

'I'm applying for a non-teaching assistant job in the local primary school. It'd be term-time only and school hours so would be good if I got it. I went and spoke to someone in HR at Renfrewshire Council and they gave me a print out of suitable jobs. She said with my qualifications and experience, they'd look at my applications favourably,' she smiled, 'Very different from my last job, but I've learned my lesson.'

'I'm sure you'll be fabulous.' Ann-Marie hesitated to mention David, but Lynda brought it up first.

'David has been taking the boys twice during the week and on a Sunday. I spoke to his mother the other day; she's still a bit frosty, but we had a chat and we've agreed that this is probably best for everyone. She said he'll never trust me again and is adamant about the divorce, so I have to accept that, I think.'

Ann-Marie hugged her daughter sadly, 'I'm so sorry, love,' she said quietly.

'Mum, I know I'm to blame. I'm *not* proud, and I think we both wanted different things and I had delusions of what marriage should be. Well, I've come down to earth with a bump and learned a hard lesson. I just hope that with time, we can talk and be good parents to the boys.'

'That was very honest, and a hard lesson to learn from. Now, remember where I am. I know we've got harvest soon, but you'll make sure I don't work too hard if you and the boys come regularly to see me and your grandma', she finished and gave Lynda a fierce hug.

When she arrived back at the farm, she fastened the paintings onto the kitchen wall and picked up the note on the table.

YOUR DINNER IS IN THE DOG it announced in capitals; but underneath her mother had written that her lunch was in the fridge and that she'd be back soon after she'd dropped Elaine off at home.

Relieved to have the house to herself, Ann-Marie flopped onto the sofa and closed her eyes, allowing the softly falling rain to lull her to sleep.

Bracken woke her an hour later, wanting to go out, and Ann-Marie got into her boots and Barbour jacket and took them out into the drizzle.

Roddy and Duncan had cleaned and stacked all the equipment and were now talking about topping the grass in the orchards before the harvest started. She indicated she'd be back shortly and went around the small sheep paddock with the dogs, before returning them to the house.

In the barn, Roddy was on his phone checking the weather. 'We only have two dry days this week, so we need to top the grass to ensure the machine can collect the apples cleanly.' The machine was her father's old Tuthill Temperley, a giant orange-liveried mechanical apple harvester, which made short work of the fruit to be collected for cider making. Apples destined for apple juice, still had to be picked by hand, and the first pickers were arriving the following week to camp in the orchard.

'Well, you can organise the grass cutting between yourselves. We're ready to start whenever the apples are ripe - I'll do some sugar testing on the apples tomorrow to see what we're picking first.'

Duncan, in his quest to redeem himself after allowing Bracken to become pregnant had updated the farm website's blog with a progress report and short video of Bracken, and photos of the orchard groaning with ripening fruit, and the timely publicity ensured that customers flocked to the taproom and farm shop.

Although the rain had persisted and hampered the re-roofing of the bothy, Roddy had managed to cover half of the building, and was planning a complicated schedule to start the harvest and continue to make the building watertight. Duncan's romance with Shona was going from strength to strength, and he mentioned that her visit to his parents had gone well, with his mother and Shona having the same sense of humour and attitude to farming. Ann-Marie was pleased to hear that Shona and some of her Young Farmer friends were planning to come for a day to help with the hand-picking in the middle of the season when the farm would be particularly busy.

The following week, the Agricultural College students arrived and pitched their tents, relived that the forecast was for cloudy but dry weather, and one of the curriculum managers wanted to meet with Roddy to discuss some on-going courses to be based at the farm. Ann-Marie looked to the near future when she could hand more and more of the running of the business over to Roddy, in the hopes that she could help Lynda if and when she managed to find a suitable job. It all seemed to be going well.

***

Malky's funeral came and went. Elaine sat next to Calum and his family, and Ann-Marie, Isa and Jim went along to support her. She was silent throughout, only crying when Calum read the eulogy. Many of Malky's work colleagues and men from the Lodge attended too, alongside a couple of lone women, which Elaine studiously ignored. Ann-Marie noted them sitting at the back of the Crematorium, and wondered if they were some of Malky's *special* friends. Elaine was the picture of widowhood, in her funeral black outfit and maintained a quiet dignity, and Ann-Marie admired her faultless performance. That evening the two friends relaxed alone at Elaine's house with some chilled white wine, whilst flicking through the European city breaks brochure that Elaine had requested.

August arrived with Bracken looking fit to burst, bringing out Roddy's parental instincts. She was no longer allowed to jump onto or off the sofa, and he was acting as her hoist. Whenever the house was empty he hung around the yard or house, inventing reasons to stay near there, and one evening, just as he was about to go home, he saw her nesting on a pile of hay in the pig shed. She'd dug a hole in the soft, sweet-smelling hay and had managed to drag one of Ann-Marie's discarded sweatshirts to lie on, and was panting quietly. He walked over to pick her up and she warned him away with a soft growl. Surprised, he attempted again to move her and then saw that she was having contractions.

In a bit of a panic he ran to the house and found Ann-Marie in the office, 'It's starting!'

'What's...?'

'The *puppies*! The *puppies* are coming! She's having them in the pig barn!' he cried and ran back to the shed, leaving Ann-Marie to switch the computer off and grab the cardboard box with the whelping kit in it, which had been moved to next to the front door.

Back in the pig shed, a small crowd had gathered. Duncan had heard the commotion and come to see, and sensibly kept the agricultural students well back to allow the expectant mother some privacy and quiet. Ann-Marie spread out the kit and had the old, well-laundered towels ready and the multicoloured collar strips which would make identification easy. To keep Roddy busy, she gave him the pre-printed arrival sheet, where he had to mark down the order of arrival, record the birth weights and any other stuff, and they watched with bated breath as first-time mum Bracken endured the growing contractions.

With a cry of pain, the first pup arrived; a soft, fat, wet black and white bundle and Bracken turned to inspect and lick it clean. After petting Bracken quietly, Ann-Marie picked up and examined the tiny bundle. A boy; and breathing happily. She passed him to Roddy, who with tears streaming down his face, weighed and then cradled the little bundle, before Ann-Marie took him back to return to Bracken. In less than twenty minutes, Bracken had produced another two healthy little bundles, and then, things slowed down.

After twenty minutes of Bracken pushing but nothing emerging, Ann-Marie decided to intervene. It was just like lambing, she told herself, only a smaller animal. She managed to help Bracken deliver a small, but perfectly formed orange and white pup, but sadly, on inspection, he didn't seem to be breathing. Roddy was distraught, and took the bundle in a soft towel, cradling it to his face.

'It happens,' Ann-Marie said sadly, and noted that Bracken was pushing out another puppy. She concentrated on ensuring that this one was alive and healthy, and then heard Roddy's whoop of joy. He'd been gently rubbing his still little bundle and somehow managed to kick-start the breathing. He handed him back to Ann-Marie, who placed him under Bracken's nose. With her mothering instincts in full flow, she licked and nuzzled the little bundle and nosed him towards the others to keep warm.

Bracken then announced to everyone that she'd finished by unceremoniously getting up and walking outside where she had a long pee. The students were delighted and moved back to allow her to return to her squirming family.

Ann-Marie turned to Roddy gratefully, squeezing his hand, 'That was well done. We could have lost that wee boy. You did really well.'

'Troy – his name's Troy,' Roddy said still crying.

Duncan emerged from his vantage point beside the students jubilant, 'I've got it all on video, and these guys have taken some great photos!'

Ann-Marie let Bracken clean up the mess that always happens when any animal gives birth, and then suggested that they take her and her puppies inside the house to the whelping box, where they could ensure they didn't get cold and Bracken could have peace and quiet to feed them. Roddy picked up Troy and another pup, Ann-Marie another two and Bracken picked up the smallest one of the litter, and slowly they carried them all inside to the awaiting whelping box in Ann-Marie's office.

Bracken settled down and began to nurse them, all five easily finding her milk, and the small room was filled with a gentle mewing and snuffling.

Ann-Marie pushed Roddy out into the kitchen and put the kettle on.

'I'll make the tea, you go and wash your face, *dad*,' she laughed.

Chapter 26

To give him his due, Duncan had been very proactive. He'd edited and posted puppy photographs and the birthing video on the website and even sent a message to the local newspaper, who were keen to come and photograph the new arrivals, because the public needed feel-good stories.

Isa sung his praises to anyone who would listen, especially as the customers surged in numbers, buying meat, cider and keen to see the little bundles of joy. A Daily Bulletin was printed off and put on the taproom door, and a discreet camera fitted in Ann-Marie's office relayed a live video to a laptop set up in the taproom for visitors to watch the puppies. It would be three weeks before their public debut, but Roddy started to make a puppy play pen, which would soon be housed in the taproom, away from the sales area.

Meantime, he hovered around the farmhouse, citing any and every excuse to catch a glimpse of his beloved Troy. Eventually Ann-Marie chased him and Duncan to go and finish reproofing the bothy and asked Elaine to start that afternoon in the shop.

Unfortunately, this coincided with Lynda arriving

after school with the boys, and a tense few minutes ensued, until Isa left her place in the kitchen and took the boys to see the puppies in the office, after suggesting Lynda and Elaine go and put the kettle on.

Tea, after all, cures every problem there is; and after finding Ann-Marie a few minutes later, sent her to see if everything was calm or if a first-aider was required.

Ann-Marie hesitantly opened the door into the kitchen and found Elaine and Lynda both in tears, but hugging. She was unsure what had occurred, but Elaine was dabbing at Lynda's mascara with a tissue.

'Thought I'd have a cup of tea,' she said, interrupting.

Lynda turned and smiled, 'It's alright mum, we're not killing each other,' she sniffed, and Elaine nodded. 'We've had a chat. I think we're okay going forward from here. It's not *all* her fault, after all. I've found a wee black book he'd hidden in his stuff, so I know Lynda wasn't the first, so we need some perspective, and realise he was just a no-good rat.'

She ran a hand through her hair, and met Ann-Marie's eyes, 'There's none as blind as those who won't see what's right in front of them,' she said sadly.

Ann-Marie hugged them both, glad that the first moves of reconciliation had been made, 'Now, if you're not having tea, Elaine needs to get back to the shop and Lynda, *you* need to come and make sure that Neil and Alex haven't chosen a puppy for themselves.'

Sure enough the boys were sitting in Ann-Marie's office watching the puppies and Roddy was supervising them. Ann-Marie shot him a look, and he groaned. 'Alright, I'm going, I'm going!' he laughed and left them to it.

Ann-Marie explained to Lynda, 'He's taken a real shine to that wee fat orange and white one with the pink collar. He brought him back from the dead when he wasn't breathing, and has bonded with him. Of course we can't keep all five, but I think *Troy*,' she raised her eyebrows at the unusual name, 'has found his forever home with Roddy.'

'You'll keep one of the girls?' Lynda asked.

'Yes, there's a nice blue roan girl. It *has* to be a girl with Bracken and Bramble, after all, we don't want a repeat performance, with boys and girls in the same house,' she smiled.

With the boys' intent on the puppies, Ann-Marie took the opportunity to squeeze Lynda's hand, 'Everything alright between you and Elaine?' she asked.

'Oh, she did her nut for about a minute, then started crying. She blames Malky for breaking up me and David. I tried to explain that most of the blame is mine, but she was adamant. I know there must be more to this story of him falling off that cliff, but I don't *want* to know mum.' she said quietly.

'Good girl,' Ann-Marie said, and turned back to the boys, 'Now, choose a puppy for a photograph Neil, *not* to take home. You can come and see them anytime, but they need to stay here with Bracken.'

She took some snaps with her mobile phone, and then went to join Elaine, who was busy at the shop, wrapping some lamb joints for a customer.

'Busy?'

'Aww, it's *great*. I get to chat about all sorts of things, but everyone loves the shop, and Duncan's weird signs everywhere.'

'Yes, I'll need to speak to him about those,' Ann-Marie laughed, 'I thought having silly posters with sheep on Wanted posters, and posters with pigs saying Eat Like A Pig would put people off, but they seem to like it.'

'I think it's a real winner, this shop. People love that everything is local, and being able to see the animals happy in the fields. Thanks so much for letting me join in. And thanks Ann-Marie, for talking to Lynda. I think we'll be okay now.'

Ann-Marie was pleased. She left Elaine explaining to a customer how to slow-roast a joint of pork with cider, and headed outside.

Crates and crates of apples were stacked in the yard leading to the press-room door. Duncan was colour marking the crates to differentiate between apples for juice and apples for cider, and he waved happily.

She left him to it, and went out to the bothy to find Roddy on the roof.

'Come down here, you,' she cried, 'We need to talk about that puppy.'

Roddy gingerly climbed down the scaffolding to face her, 'I love him and he loves me. I'll pay you whatever the going rate is, but please don't sell him to anyone else, please,' he begged.

'Roddy, you're living in rented accommodation, then you're intent on living here until this place is finished; that's no life for a puppy. I don't doubt you'd make a good owner and I *know* you love him, I can see that, but...'

'Well, he'll be with Bracken for eight weeks, then I'll

have the roof done by then. The electrics and the water just have to be connected, everything is just about there. Let me talk to you about it again in eight weeks, *please.*'

'Alright. *Eight weeks,* but you need to stop mooning about and get on with the harvest and the bothy. No more playing with Troy, understand?' she tried to sound severe.

'I promise,' he said, and climbed back up the scaffolding to prove he meant it.

She walked back through the orchard, watching the pickers' intent on their job. The students were happy, laughing and smiling as they filled crates, and then at the yard, she noted that Isa was now directing Duncan to place all the picnic benches together.

'I've made them a big dinner with some cold roast pork, bread and potato salad,' Isa announced, 'There's some sponge cake on its way too.' She was in her element, the matriarch in charge. What a change in her since she'd recovered from the stroke, Ann-Marie thought, hoping she wasn't overdoing it.

Tonight, they'd have some quiet time together. Isa had put off Bob, claiming fatigue and she and Ann-Marie were looking forward to a quiet night in.

The shop was closed, Elaine drove home and the lads cleaned down the pressing equipment and locked up. They were taking some of the pickers to the local pub and headed off sharp, leaving Isa to lock the gate.

Ann-Marie had a quick check on Bracken, and then went for a bath. When she returned, dinner was on the table and Isa had poured them some elderflower cordial.

'I have to say, even though Elaine is my friend, it's nice

to have the house back to ourselves', Ann-Marie said, 'I've had enough excitement this week, and I'm looking forward to falling asleep in front of the telly tonight.'.

'I know it's a bit soon to ask, but Bob asked me to stay over at his this weekend,' she began a little quietly and blushing more than a little. 'Would you feel safe being here on your own?'

Ann-Marie burst out laughing, '*Staying over*? You make it sound like a sleepover!' she rolled her eyes at her mother, 'Are you asking my permission, mum?'

'I wasn't really sure how you'd react, to be honest,' Isa admitted, 'I know we've only known each other two months, but when you get to our age, every second counts.'

Ann-Marie smiled and patted her hand, 'I don't mind in the slightest mum. I'm happy for you. Just make sure you take precautions; five babies in the house is more than enough for me to cope with, thank you!'

The next morning, after feeding the animals and cleaning out the maternity ward, Ann-Marie determined to spend an hour in the office, catching up on emails and paperwork. An email from a prestigious national newspaper begged for a photo shoot and a story for their weekender lifestyle section. This was an opportunity not to be missed and she replied suggesting the following Tuesday. She wrote the date on the idiot board above her desk, and began the laborious monthly accounts.

An hour later, she was aware of Bracken staring fixedly at her, and sighed.

'Come on then, I could do with a walk too', she said and took her out. They walked down past the busy and noisy pressing shed and into the home orchard. The sheep had been moved to another field to allow the pickers to get on and Roddy was working the mechanical harvester back and forth between the lines of trees. A trailer stood full of apples and even in the still warm air, she could smell the scent of ripe and overripe apples. Instantly, she was transported back to her youth, and working the trees with her father. He'd have been proud of her, a woman working in what had until very recently been a man's world, and making a success of the farm. A thought occurred to her to maybe ask her mother to look out some of the old farm photographs to be copied and displayed in the taproom. It would be a fitting tribute to the man who planted all these trees and started the business, which was viewed as a frivolity in the local farming community many years ago.

She returned Bracken to the office and her snuffling, wriggling pups, all doubled in size and unfortunately mess. After all, what went in at one end, quickly came out the other. She tidied the soiled newspaper lining of the whelping box and went out to the pressing shed.

They worked till lunchtime, pressing the early varieties of apples, first for juice and then for cider. She explained the reasons to the students, and let them taste the sweet, fresh juice as it came out of the press. The summer had been good, and the sugar content high, and she predicted that the resulting cider would finish around 6% ABV, which was pleasingly high for Scotland.

Duncan was marking up the record sheet and concentrating hard. His earlier mistake with allowing Bracken to be mated was forgotten, and his romance with the very sensible Shona Keenan appeared to have matured him slightly. At lunchtime, she returned to the house to help carry out the lunch to the workers. Today's menu was ham and cheese quiche, with salad and boiled new potatoes. Isa was a little flushed, and Ann-Marie ordered her to go and rest.

'You *can't* keep working all the time like this,' she barked. 'You're nearly eighty! You need to let the staff do the lifting. Go and watch telly and put your feet up.'

Isa scowled but did as she was told, taking Bramble with her, 'Come on Bramble, we'll watch that women's programme and maybe have a bo-bo's,' she said to the dog.

Ann-Marie returned to the pressing shed, and mentioned the workload to Duncan.

'Well, good luck to you! I've tried and she won't have it. She's got a tongue like a sacking needle, your mother!' he snorted, 'If you can persuade her to take it easy, you'll do better than me!'

Ann-Marie had to smile; she'd been on the end of her mother's sharp tongue many times, and knew exactly what he meant, 'I think we'll need to get Bob to take her off the farm even more than he is at the moment, then we'll be able to get on without her. Elaine is doing the shop in the afternoon now, so maybe I should organise the lunches?'

He nodded and then scurried back to the press to remove the spent pomace, 'Roddy's going to feed this to the pigs, but we're going to have a lot left over. I can't keep feeding them this or they'll have the squirts. D'you want me to ask dad to bring his trailer over? The cows'll eat it; it'll be a wee treat for them.'

'Great idea, we need to move it or the wasps and hornets'll be hanging around and bothering the customers.' she agreed, turning to see Jim Muir's car pull into the yard.

Chapter 27

'I've come to see these new arrivals,' he said with a smile, 'and I have good news for Elaine, if she's here.'

Ann-Marie wiped her hands down her jeans, 'I wish you'd give me notice, Jim. Look at me! I've got bits of apple in my hair and my hands are as orange as an Ooompaloompa!'

'And you smell gorgeous!' he laughed inhaling, 'Intoxicating even!'

She led him inside the farmhouse and washed her hands, before quietly opening the door to the office. Bracken was nursing, and the puppies paddled her sides in a frantic effort to get more milk.

Jim was spellbound, and knelt on the floor beside the whelping box, stroking Bracken's head, 'Aren't you a clever girl?' he praised.

In the box, two puppies were curled up sleeping, with pink fat bellies, whilst the others were still guzzling milkily. He tickled one of them gently with a finger, and looked up at Ann-Marie with such joy that she felt her heart surge with pleasure.

'Aren't they up on their feet yet?' he asked curiously.

'Maybe next week. Then the week after they'll start

solids.' she answered.

'Still keen for a puppy?' she slid him a sideways glance, 'We're going to keep this little blue roan girl, and Roddy has earmarked this one for himself,' she indicated the orange and white boy.

'I don't know if I'm ready', he said, 'I've never had a dog. Ever.'

'Really?' Ann-Marie was surprised.

'Oh, Jill was never really interested in animals, and well, with no kids, there was never really any need. I do *like* dogs, but I don't know if it is really practical for me, on my own.'

'Then, you can dog-share with us,' she offered impulsively, 'You can come and enjoy all this puppyness, and then help me train this wee girl. I'll need to think of a name soon, so maybe…maybe we can talk about it over a glass of wine, sometime,' she finished with a little hint of a blush.

'Why, Ann-Marie Ross, are you suggesting we go out on a *date*?' he laughed.

'Well, I'm sorry I mentioned it!' she snapped, angrily.

'Oh no!' he answered, 'No changing your mind, woman! You asked! No going back now,' he ended gently and kissed her gently on the lips, 'If I find you *this* irresistible with your working clothes, apple in your hair and orange hands, I'm definitely up for a puppy-naming date!'

She pushed him away slowly, 'My *mother* is in the living room, you fool. Behave yourself.'

Her mother answered loudly, 'I'm asleep. Never heard a thing. Totally oblivious!'

Jim grabbed her hand, 'Come on, let's go for a walk round this beautiful farm of yours and let Isa have a rest.'

They walked towards the burn running slowly around the edge of the orchard where the bothy, now actually resembling a little cottage, showed off its new slate roof, shining in the sun. The post and rail fence had been finished and a new wooden gate led up a gravel path to the doorway where, very soon a new door would hang. The exterior certainly looked impressive, although they both knew that the time-consuming work was just beginning inside. The old orchard wall beckoned to them, and they sat, comfortable with each other and yet full of anticipation of the future.

'Before I kiss you properly, I need to tell you my news', he teased.

'Elaine *will* inherit the insurance, and can go ahead and sell her house if she wants. I've had a chat with the Cornish police officer dealing with Malky's sudden death. They've taken statements from the staff at the restaurant and the bed and breakfast they were staying at and are satisfied that it was just a tragic accident, and the post mortem as you know agreed that death was from trauma caused by the fall. So, although there will still be an inquest that she'll have to attend, it looks like that'll be fairly straightforward.'

Ann-Marie was pleased, but with her vast experience lately with so many untimely deaths, she realised she was getting rather blasé about it all, and still needed to mind her tongue. 'Poor Elaine,' she said. 'She'd been so looking forward to going to Cornwall. She's always loved the seaside, and dreamt that she and Malky would someday retire to Largs. Now, she's in that big house on the south side of Glasgow on her own, and hates being reminded of him…I mean, that he's no longer *there*,' she corrected herself quickly, 'She's serving in the shop, if you want to go and tell her. I know she'll be relieved.'

He closed his eyes and inhaled deeply, in no hurry to move. 'I don't really take enough time off, you know. This is just the most perfect spot to sit and just…*be*. I'm not in a hurry; let's just enjoy the peace.'

With his eyes closed, she sat and looked at him. So different from Billy. Quieter, and steady, she thought, but, she really didn't know him at all.

'Jim,' she asked.

'Hmm?'

'What do you do for fun; when you're not working?'

He laughed and turned his face to her, 'Well, I used to play golf once a week, but I stopped going about a year ago. I was in the same club as Malky, and between you and me, he wasn't a very nice person, deep down. Far too keen on the ladies, if you know what I mean. I think Elaine *might* have had an inkling, but I'd rather you didn't tell her.'

Ann-Marie was shocked to hear this, and Jim took her hand, 'I'm not *completely* blind, you know. In my job, I see it all. Oh, I could tell you stories, but, well, you learn to keep a lot of secrets. Shame really, I miss the golf – it was a good excuse for a decent walk in nice surroundings,' he finished, having turned the subject neatly back to golf.

'What about you? When you *actually* have time off here, and you're not ferrying your mother around, what do you do for fun? Cinema? Opera? Collect stamps?'

He was teasing again, and she ignored the stamp collecting comment, 'Well, cinema yes, but not gory films or horror. I've never been to an opera, so I don't know if I'd like that. I've never really had the time until now, but with the boys here, I'm starting to pull back a bit. Mum's in cahoots with her new beau, Bob Anderson, and I think it's getting serious, so maybe I'd better start finding new things to enjoy.'

'Maybe, we could have a *regular* day or evening date to find out what we'd both like?' he suggested with a smile.

'You're manoeuvring me again,' she smiled.

'I'm a solicitor, I manoeuvre everybody,' he said, and taking her unawares, kissed her softly on the lips. Her heart did a little flip; a feeling she hadn't had since she was a girl. When she opened her eyes, he was smiling at her, his china blue eyes focussing on hers.

'There. That wasn't so bad, was it? But you're out of practice, and I think you need to be kissed at least once or twice a day to get up to speed,' he laughed.

'And you're the best teacher, I suppose,' she laughed.

'Of course! Although, I'm a bit out of practice myself, so we could help each other.'

'You've got an answer for everything,' she answered.

'Solicitor,' he repeated with a grin.

They walked back to the taproom and shop, and Jim discreetly took Elaine for a stroll to the orchard, whilst Ann-Marie went to check on the house-full of sleepers. Bracken and the pups were awake and feeding, whilst Isa was awake and preparing dinner for the students.

Tonight, they were having spaghetti bolognaise and tons and tons of garlic bread. A huge pot of sauce was ready, and the garlic bread all foiled up, ready to go into the oven. Ann-Marie's eyes were watering at the smell of so much garlic and onions, 'Should I hang a sign up warning any passing vampires?' she asked, opening the kitchen window.

'An army marches on its stomach, my dear, and *we* have an army of pickers. You just need to take a look at Duncan to realise that food is the most important thing in his life! Although that Shona Keenan seems to have stolen his heart. Anyway, it's all ready, bar the spaghetti.'

'Dessert?' Ann-Marie asked.

'Apple crumble,' her mother replied, 'already in the oven, and a scoop of ice-cream on the side. Doddle.'

Ann-Marie was impressed, easy to make, satisfying, and not too much effort for her mother. She spied Jim returning with Elaine, who was trying her best to contain her delight. Ann-Marie caught her eye, and shook her head ever so slightly to warn her to behave, and she sobered up immediately. Jim politely refused to stay for dinner and said his goodbyes, telling Ann-Marie with a smile that he'd call her later.

As he left, Isa and Elaine turned expectantly to her grinning.

'*What?*' she answered hotly, 'He's just a friend!'

'Yeah, and I'm the Pope,' Elaine laughed. They watched him drive off impatiently, and walked back to the farmhouse.

'Right, tell us the news', Isa demanded of Elaine, once they were alone.

'I'll get the insurance cheque in the next week or so. A wee bungalow in Largs will *definitely* be happening, *and* I can sell the house too!' Elaine almost danced on the spot she was so full of glee, and whilst her friends were delighted for her, they needed to bring her back down to earth.

'*Calm*. You need to keep a lid on it Elaine; remember poor Calum has lost his dad, whatever *we* all thought of the sleekit git. Careless talk and all that,' Isa warned.

Elaine took a deep breath and pulled herself together with a nod. With shining eyes, she returned to the shop, as if all the cares in the world had been lifted off her shoulders.

'We'll need to keep an eye on her,' Isa warned, and Ann-Marie nodded, 'It would be a shame if she blew it now,' she agreed. 'Although Jim seems pretty certain that the Inquest will find that he fell and broke his neck; that it was a tragic accident. Very neat and tidy,' she said with a knowing stare at her mother.

'Goodness me, who'd think knocking people off was so easy? With our perfect track record, maybe we should set up a business?' Isa smiled merrily.

'I think *not*, mother.'

Roddy burst through the door, his face flushed.

'Some…*woman* is here from a newspaper. She wants me to take my top off for a photograph! She *says* you're expecting her!'

Isa and Ann-Marie looked at each other in consternation, then Ann-Marie clapped her hand to her mouth, 'Oh! The journalist from The Scotsman! I'd forgotten!' she rushed outside to meet the smart young lady standing next to a sleek estate car.

'Hi, I'm Jen Soutar, you *are* expecting me? It's just your terribly dashing highlander here seems to have come over all shy and retiring,' she laughed.

'I'm so sorry', Ann-Marie began, 'I completely forgot you were coming,'

Jen touched her hand to her head, 'You know, I seem to have that effect on people. I can't think why? Maybe I need to dye my hair pink or something?' she laughed.

Ann-Marie smiled, liking her immediately, 'Come in for a quick cuppa and tell me what you're after,'

'I don't suppose this hunk of a man would like a cuppa too?' she said, grinning at the scowling Roddy.

'No! I'm working!' he said stomping off to the barn.

Over tea, Jen explained that the weekend section was a relaxed affair, inviting readers to explore via travel, culture, food and all sorts of other stuff that folk wanted to do on a weekend. It was also a great opportunity for businesses, she said, but there had to be a balance, not just an outright advert. She suggested a tour, and to take photographs as they went, then a short recap before she returned to the office.

'I've had a look at your great website, and wondered if your staff would pose for some shots in their highland gear?' she smiled, 'Although, that titian-haired one I just met seems a bit grumpy.'

'Roddy's a bit shy round pretty young ladies, but he's my farm manager now, and brilliant. Duncan does the website and the advertising. How about I get him to show you round, and I'll organise the staff for some photos?'

258

'Great!'

The next hour was spent with Jen roaming the farm and orchards, talking to staff and customers and taking photographs apparently randomly. Roddy was in the pressing shed, trying to keep out of the way, but Ann-Marie had ordered him into his kilt and told him *not* to take off his polo shirt, 'It's a feature and we're advertising, so keep it on, even if she does flutter her eyelashes at you!'

She pushed him towards the house to change, and caught up with Jen Soutar at the pressing shed, where the staff were being directed for yet another photo. Roddy appeared a few minutes later, to stand next to Duncan in front of the towering boxes of apples. Jen smiled briefly at him and asked him and Duncan to pose in front of the apples, then at the press itself which was pouring forth some more juice.

Finally, she appeared satisfied, 'It's a shame that he doesn't smile much,' she remarked to Duncan.

'Oh that's *easy*; just ask him to bring Troy out for a photo,' Duncan blabbed, and turned to Roddy, 'Go and get Troy for a photo,' he said grinning.

Roddy returned a few minutes later cradling the fat little bundle, and Jen enthusiastically posed them both sitting on a straw bale next to the display in the shop.

A few minutes later, she announced she was done, and returned to the farmhouse with Ann-Marie.

'I've got loads of photos, and possibly enough material, I just need to fact-check a few things with you before I go', she said, whipping out her notebook.

Ann-Marie sat, waiting for the predictable questions, but was taken aback when the first question Jen asked was about Billy's death,

'So, it's been a few months since your husband died in that tragic accident here on the farm; how has it been, moving on without him?'

'Well, obviously, it's been difficult', she began carefully, 'but the farm has to go on. It's a lifestyle more than a business; all farmers will tell you that, but my family has been producing apples here for many years, and...Billy's death; tragic though it was meant that we obviously had to look at staffing and work practices.'

She hoped that would be sufficient, but the journalist wanted more, 'So, the revamp of the cider and the farm so soon after his death would have happened anyway?' she probed.

Ann-Marie swallowed, 'Well, some of the plans had already been in the pipeline.' She didn't like the direction the questions were going in, and decided to take more control, banking on the fact that the reporter was a woman and would like a woman's angle in the story, 'Whilst farming may have traditionally been a man's world, there's nothing here that a woman can't do, and in fact we employ women of all ages to harvest, press and work in the shop. It's a changing world and we need to constantly ensure that small farms like this continue to be part of our future.'

'So the family have been right behind you in the changes from more traditional farming to developing the food and drink side of the business?' Jen pressed.

'My mother is the real owner of High Glen Farm, and a great business-woman. We've all had to move on from various tragedies over the years – my father's death, Foot and Mouth, mum's stroke at the turn of the year and then my husband's death; but like all families we sit down and talk and decide how to move forward. Fortunately, we have a great team here now – a sort of extended family, and together we're moving forward to ensure a bright future for High Glen Farm.'

Jen stared at her for a moment, and Ann-Marie recognised that the journalist knew she wasn't going to find any skeletons in the family cupboard to use as a story. She gathered herself together, and prepared to leave, 'I've got enough for a nice article, which should be out possibly next weekend,' she smiled.

'I'd really prefer to check the article and the photographs *before* publication please, just to ensure all the facts are correct,' Ann-Marie smiled benignly back.

'Of course, no problem,' Jen said, shaking her hand.

Chapter 28

Jen emailed the article and the photographs that she intended to use a few days later. Ann-Marie had a small meeting in the kitchen to discuss it with the staff.

'*Red Hot Highlander?*' Roddy spluttered, as he read the article which Ann-Marie had printed out.

'Actually, I'm cross she didn't mention me much', Duncan replied, stuffing lemon drizzle cake into his ever hungry mouth.

'Let's look at the positives first, before we all go off on one please,' Isa suggested. 'There's a great photo of the product in the shop, which looks attractive and well-stocked, and Elaine looking friendly and helpful', she smiled to Elaine, who was pleased.

'And a nice photo of the lads working the press and the cider coming out', she said, smiling at the photo which concentrated more on Roddy and Duncan, than the actual pressing process.

'Eye candy,' Elaine sniggered helpfully.

'And this nice photo of the staff in the front of the new taproom; so that's all good. Very positive!' Isa finished.

'The actual article is pretty good, a wee bit on the history of the farm, what we do, how many acres and the shop, and a nice bit on the rise in popularity of cider in Scotland, and the other things we do. Who told her about the bothy?' Ann-Marie looked round the table.

'It was me,' Roddy said, 'she was asking where I lived...' he blushed ferociously, causing Duncan to splutter cake crumbs all over the table, 'So I told her I was living here at the bothy, whilst we did it up as a future holiday let.'

He kicked Duncan under the table, 'I wasnae going to tell her where I lived!'

Ann-Marie slapped his arm, 'Stop it, you pair! Well, she *also* sent me a charming portrait of you with Troy, Roddy, which I know you'll like,' she said pushing a sheet of paper towards him, 'I'll get Duncan to print off a couple on photographic paper – one for you and one for the shop.'

Roddy pored over the picture silently, 'Maybe she wasn't so bad after all,' he smiled.

Ann-Marie drew the meeting to a close, 'So, nothing awful in there, and a nice article. We'd better ensure we have the shop stocked up, *and* check there's enough cider in the taproom for next weekend, it looks like we might be busy.'

Meeting over, they returned to the pressing shed. With the main glut of the harvest sitting waiting, there was no time to lose, and the schedule was increased to add an extra two hours in the evening. Ann-Marie and Duncan agreed to share this between them, as Roddy continued in the evening to work on the bothy, as agreed.

And so the days passed, scented with slightly sickly smell of over-ripe apples and spent pomace, being collected by the local farmers to add to the animal feed.

The article duly appeared in the newspaper and was also picked up by the agricultural college, some of the larger cider associations and the surge of visitors to the shop was noticeable.

Jen Soutar made an unexpected appearance on the Sunday afternoon, and offered to help with the pressing. Isa sent her to the pressing shed with a smile.

'You need *old* clothes,' Roddy explained looking at the pristine blue chinos.

'These *are* old!' she retorted.

'Whatever,' he said, handing her a rubber apron, 'This'll protect you a wee bit, but you'll have orange hands and stains everywhere.'

'You could *actually* be glad I came to help,' she smiled sweetly.

'You're on the pulper then,' he said handing her a pack of ear defenders, 'not too many apples in at a time or it'll jam, and I'll tap you when to stop.'

She took her place and switched on the machine. As the apples passed through, the noise was deafening, and conversation was almost impossible, she realised. After ten minutes he tapped her shoulder, and she switched the machine off.

'Now what?'

'Now we make up the cheeses and press the juice,' he said.

She watched him place a cheesecloth inside a former and when it was full of pulpy, wet chopped apples, the former was removed, the cloth neatly folded over and a pressboard separated it from the next layer. Once the tower of cheeses and boards had reached six, he placed a

264

final board on top and started the hydraulic press.

Almost immediately, sweet, golden juice started to fill the tray and down the pipe into the large container underneath.

He handed her a cup full, which she tasted a little gingerly, 'It's lovely!' she squeaked, and so sweet!'

'Fresh from the press and no additives,' he smiled. He really did have a lovely smile, she thought. But Roddy was already removing the spent cheeses and tipping the pomace into the large blue skip which would feed the pigs and sheep that evening.

They spent an hour or so quietly pressing, and gradually the smiles became more frequent, as Jen become more and more orange. When the batch of apples had been pressed, Roddy finally switched on the pump to move the juice into a settling container.

'I have to clean everything down or the acid'll eat into the metal,' he said, 'if you want to go.'

She shook her head with a laugh, 'I'm already filthy and wet, so I can help, if you tell me what to do.'

'Well, I'll dismantle the machine, but if you could take the empty apple crates outside and hose them down, they'll be ready to go back to the orchard for the harvesters tomorrow. There's a hose just outside.'

She happily began moving the dirty crates outside, and began to hose them out. By the time, she'd finished, he had cleaned down the machine and was hosing out the shed. Ann-Marie appeared with the pickers, who had finished for the day and looking forward to their dinner.

'Stay, if you have time. Mum's cooked roast pork, and

there's baked apple for dessert. You er…might want to go and clean up,' she said, noting bits of apple in her hair, 'go use the bathroom in the house.'

Jen happily went for a quick wash, and returned shortly afterwards. The customers gone for the day, the picnic tables had been pushed together for the ten or so pickers to sit and eat their dinner. She sat at the end of the bench, next to Barrie and his wife Sandra, a couple who were staying in their caravan whilst helping for a week, just as they had done for the last two summers. Roddy sat opposite her and watched her eat hungrily. The chatter at the table turned to discussing the meteor shower the previous night, and Jen happily sat and listened to the students and staff, feeling like part of the team, until with a glance at her watch, she reluctantly felt that she really had to make a move to leave.

'Need to go?' Roddy asked, taking her empty plate from her.

She nodded, 'I've had a great afternoon,'

'Come and see us again soon,' he said with a grin.

Isa elbowed Elaine at the table, and whispered to her, 'Wee romance starting there,' she said conspirationally. Elaine giggled, 'Aye, she seems *very* taken with her *Red Hot Highlander*.'

Roddy walked her to her car, and handed her a black bin liner to sit on,

'You might want to protect the car seat. Next time; *if* you visit again, bring a change of clothes.' He smiled and held the car door open for her, 'And *thank you* for the photograph of me and Troy.'

She drove away and he returned to the table aware

that everyone was watching him and smiling. He sat next to Duncan, and flipped the top off a bottle of sparkling cider, 'Can't resist me,' he bragged.

'Not that you put up much of a fight,' Duncan noted and got a friendly shove in reply.

***

The puppies grew in size, mess and noise levels and during the day were banished to the play pen in the taproom. Bracken had decided enough was enough and had stopped feeding them, leaving Ann-Marie or Isa to do a bottle feed of diluted goat milk at night. As the puppy-cam that Duncan had set up became more and more popular, enquiries flooded in by phone and email for future homes for the puppies. Jim and Ann-Marie had decided that the new addition to High Glen Farm's Cocker population was to be called Willow, and they began basic toilet training, much to Isa's amusement. Whilst Ann-Marie obviously had years of experience with dogs, Jim was completely out of his depth, and becoming frustrated at the apparent lack of progress.

The looming decision about Troy's future was being avoided by everyone. With some setbacks at the bothy, and a budding romance between Roddy and Jen, Roddy was still living in his rental in Erskine. As Ann-Marie wrote an initial advert for the local paper to advertise the puppies, she hesitated more than once before sending the email.

The weekly team meeting that morning was tense, and after the sales, schedules and events briefing, Roddy stayed behind, to Ann-Marie's annoyance.

'I'm not talking to you about that dog,' she warned, 'It's all we've talked about for the last two weeks!'

'Please!' he pleaded, 'I'm almost there now. The insulation's in *and* a combi-boiler. The radiators are going in next week. I just need a bit more *time*. They'll not leave for another fortnight, and I should be in by then.'

'One more week Roddy, that's it; and I *don't* want to be having this conversation again this week.' She closed the office door behind her and waited till she heard him leave. The last thing she wanted was to be cruel, but the welfare of the pups had to come first. He had a week to sort himself out or Troy would be sold alongside the other three pups, and she already had dozens of keen puppy owners waiting to be contacted.

She had written a short document that she could email to all the prospective buyers, in which she wrote the price, asking them to confirm family make-up and age and if any one was at home during the day, and the fact that home checks would be required, then she emailed it to them all.

Pushing this task finally away, she called Lynda.

The boys were fine, and she had received a negative reply to one of her job applications, the primary school in Glasgow. She was a little down, Ann-Marie could hear, and rather than ask her if she'd heard from David, she simply said, 'Why don't you come over on Friday after school with the boys?'

'Thanks mum, I'd like that,' she replied and rang off.

Ann-Marie sighed. Today had been difficult so far and she needed a walk to blow all that negativity out of her head. She called Bracken and Bramble and off they went, past the orchard, past the burn, and out to the edge of the farm, where the meadow turned into moorland.

The heather was blooming and the purple and mauve sheen covered the hillside. In the far distance, past the patchwork of fields, she could see the sea, but today the wind was blowing in from the South, and some clouds were already building on the horizon. It looked like rain was moving in and she hoped that it was just a brief day or so, as they had the rugby club's barbeque and ceilidh looming. It was to be the last big event of the harvest season, and then the farm was on the slow down till Christmas arrived. Roddy had asked Jen, and Duncan was bringing Shona and some Young Farmer friends. The students, who were returning to the college, all promised to come; both to help and to enjoy themselves, and a traditional ceilidh band had been booked. She returned to the farm to find Bob and Isa waiting for her, with some news of their own that would further dampen her spirits.

Chapter 29

'You're moving in together?' she repeated, almost falling into the chair in the living room.

'We thought we'd give it a go and see how we get on, love,' her mother said gently. 'Bob's house isn't too far from here, and I can still come and help out, but I'm getting a bit old for all this Ann-Marie and I'd like to rest more,' her mother said with a smile.

'Are you feeling ill?' she asked quickly, feeling guilty at all the work her mother had to deal with on a daily basis with the food preparation for the pickers.

'No, I feel *fine*,' her mother reassured her, patting her hand, 'I'd just like to spend a bit more time with Bob. Life doesn't always give you second chances, and we've talked about it, and maybe it's time for me to move out, and start this new chapter in my life.'

'I don't know what to say mum,' Ann-Marie mumbled. Poor Bob stood looking very sheepish, not really knowing what to say himself, and looking a tad guilty; and Ann-Marie caught his eye, 'Oh its not *you* Bob. I'm happy for you both; it's just that I never ever thought the day would come when mum *left* me.'

'Well, it's not immediate. We thought we'd give you

time to get used to the idea, and of course, I'll stay until the pickers have all gone, but I do want to give it a try, love. Now, Bob and I are off to book our French evening class. We thought we might take a wee weekend trip to Paris in the spring, so we want to learn some French before we go. I'll see you later this evening.'

Her mother patted her hand again, and hand in hand, she and Bob left a rather stunned Ann-Marie sitting in the chair feeling more than a little overwhelmed by the events of the day.

Before she could even think over the startling news that her mother was now leaving at the age of eighty two, to go and shack up and live *over the brush* with dapper Bob, the phone rang.

It was Jim and he was in a serious mood, 'Sit down, right now. Are you alone?'

'Yes, I'm alone. What's the matter? You sound very mysterious.' she smiled, waiting for the joke or the punch-line that he usually came out with.

'I've just had the police on the phone, Ann-Marie. Some journalist is asking questions about Billy's death. I think I'd better come over and tell you what I've heard.'

The world just stopped and she sat there with the receiver in her cold, clammy hands, until Jim finally took it from her hand and replaced it.

'Good grief woman, have you been sitting there like that since I phoned?' he asked needlessly as he took in the pale, shrunken woman beside him.

'Ann-Marie! Ann-Marie!' He shook her shoulders to try and free her from the stiffness that had imprisoned her body. Exasperated, he left her for a second or two and returned with a tumbler and some whisky and pushed it into her hand.

'Drink,' he commanded and watched whilst she tipped the half a glass into her mouth.

'I'm sorry!' he said, chafing her cold hands to restore some life, 'I should have been more tactful on the phone.'

She raised her empty eyes to him, waiting. *Waiting for the axe to fall?*

'Okay, I've had a phone call from the officer in Case Management who was dealing with Billy's Fatal Accident Enquiry and his report. She tipped me off today, that a journalist, some *Ms Soutar* has been making enquiries regarding Billy's death for a story she wants to write.'

Ann-Marie was horrified, but instantly recognising the name, sobered her up immediately, '*Jen* Soutar?'

'Has she been in touch?' Jim asked with surprise, 'I thought I was here to warn you, but if you already...'

'It was her who came to do the weekender article. She was lovely, *seemed* lovely, came back to help us do a pressing. I think Roddy and her are dating...'

'You mean she's using *Roddy* to get information for a story?' Jim said crossly.

'She *was* asking me questions when she came to do the original weekender article. I remember feeling very uncomfortable', Ann-Marie said in a whisper, 'Asking me how things were going after he died, and if the family were behind me in all the changes – that sort of thing.'

She realised even as she spoke, that Jim was weighing up the possible angles that the journalist would be looking for; something sensational to make a big splash in the newspaper. She herself was panicking. How much had she *researched*, what did she *know*? *Who* had she spoken too? She knew that she wouldn't have gotten much from Roddy, but she was obviously still digging.

Jim sat on the sofa beside her, 'I think we need to speak to Roddy, but I'm afraid that this'll be difficult for him *and* you. We need to know what she's been asking him, and what, if anything he's told her. But before we get him in here Ann-Marie, I need to know – have you told me *everything*?'

The silence between them was uncomfortable, and Ann-Marie was afraid.

'Is there anything you need to tell me?' he repeated.

She *couldn't* tell him. Not *him*. The only people who knew anything were her, her mother and Elaine. Her mother was too sharp to divulge anything, she was sure of that. If Jen Soutar has asked her anything about Billy, she'd have been the first to mention it to Ann-Marie. Elaine? *No.* Okay; she wasn't the smartest of woman, but she'd be able to smell a rat pretty fast and besides, she'd *never* say anything. And besides, if the police had never found anything to incriminate her, even the slightest doubt at all, there would have been so many more questions and investigations; so officially, she was in no danger from that quarter.

No, Roddy was the only possible weak link, and Jim was right; they'd have to question him, which would put their working relationship on the rocks.

'No, I can't tell you anything more than you already know. We'll need to speak to Roddy. I can't think he'd say anything to... give her any information for a story – after all, he wasn't employed here until *after* Billy's death, but we need to ask him.'

Jim sat besides her, and held her hand.

'Well, I hate to say it, but we need to *know* and stop anything before any story gets any momentum or gains ground. Will you go and call him in?'

She nodded, and got up, moving quickly to the door.

Roddy was standing in the yard, talking to Duncan about the setting up of the marquee for the barbeque. He turned and saw her face and walked straight over, 'What's wrong?'

'Can you come in for a while? We need to talk,' she said quietly.

In the living room, Jim asked Roddy to sit, and Roddy looked from one to the other, realising something was very wrong.

'Has someone died?' he finally asked, as neither of them seemed keen to broach the subject, whatever it was.

'Jen Soutar is apparently researching an article,' Jim began.

'Yes?'

'About Billy Ross's death.'

'*What?*' Roddy was stricken.

'I've had a tip off from the police that Ms Soutar has called and has been asking questions about Billy's death here at the farm. Ann-Marie's just told me that you and this woman have started going out, dating.' Jim asked.

Roddy nodded dumbfounded and wide-eyed.

'We need to know Roddy, what she asked you and what you've told her. If there *is* a story, it'll be sensational, and neither Ann-Marie nor Isa need that sort of publicity; neither does the business. Now take your time, and just try and remember what she asked you about the farm, or the family.'

Roddy sat confused, 'Nothing! The only thing she asked…well, the only thing she said was that it must be nice for the family that after such a tragedy, everything was going well.'

'That's all? Try to think…'

Roddy sat hunched, twisting his hands. Jen Soutar! He couldn't believe what he was hearing! His mind sped over the few conversations they'd had on the few dates they'd had. He'd been so wrapped up with the pressing and the work on the bothy that he'd only seen her a couple of times over a drink.

'Well, she *did* ask if Billy's side of the family were involved at all in the business, but that was all. She didn't ask *anything* else about the accident.'

'*Billy's* side of the family?' Ann-Marie repeated, horrified.

'Aye, she'd read his obituary in the paper, and saw that Bobby Ross and his wife had been at the funeral.'

Jim and Ann-Marie looked at each other. Bobby.

Roddy was protesting his innocence, 'Ann-Marie, I *swear* I never said anything! I'd *never* say anything about you or Billy. *She* never said she was writing another article!'

He was reliving the conversations in his mind, Ann-Marie could see, trying to see if he'd said anything to fuel a story. Then he sat very still, 'She was using me, wasn't she? *Using* me to get a story? That was the only reason she went out with me,' he spat angrily.

Ann-Marie put her arm round his shoulders, 'You're

not the first, and won't be the last. Sadly, there are quite a few people like that in the world.'

'I even invited her to the barbeque!' he stood up, pacing in the small room, filling it with rage and power, 'I feel like a fool!'

'Sit *down* Roddy,' Ann-Marie ordered, 'A man your size in a bad mood in this wee room is like trying to contain a storm!'

He did as he was told, stroking Bramble's head. She didn't like the raised voices one bit and was trying to placate her friend.

'I think Ann-Marie and I need to speak alone. I'd prefer you *not* to mention this outside this room Roddy, and especially to avoid any contact with Ms Soutar for the time being.'

'What about the barbeque?'

'Just don't call her at all for the time being, and don't answer any calls from her till we figure this out, please.' Jim said.

Roddy rubbed his sweaty hands down his jeans, 'Can I go and work on the bothy the now?' he asked, keen to try and redeem himself.

Ann-Marie nodded and she and Jim were alone again.

'Well, *that* went well,' she began. 'So, this reporter has probably been in touch with Bobby and Liz, who have an axe to grind regarding the farm, Roddy has now found out he's been taken for a fool, and I have to deal with a possible newspaper article. This has been the climax to a fantastic day.'

Jim loosened his tie and sat down.

'Glass of wine?' she asked, 'I've got a nice cold bottle

of Chardonnay in the fridge.

'Please.'

Ann-Marie took a long gulp, and looked hard at him, 'So; which snake do we deal with first? My charming brother-in-law or the dirt-digging journalist?'

'Unfortunately, I think I need to speak to Bobby. I think I'll leave that till the morning. I need to figure out the angle to take with him. It may be that he's totally innocent, and she's just been fishing, but I won't know until I speak to him.'

He took a long sip of the wine and smiled at her, 'You know, I really could just give it all up, some days. I don't need the money and my house is paid for. I sometimes just ask myself if I only do it to fill my days. But, a day like this, I don't need. I was *so angry* when that officer called today. A muck-racking journalist. Surprising for a quality broadsheet – I wonder if her editor knows what she's working on, and how she's getting her information?'

Chapter 30

That night Ann-Marie had the night terrors again. Absent for many months, Billy's bloated and now rotten face danced before her in the dark, laughing. At four she gave up any idea of sleep and crept quietly downstairs to make coffee. A few minutes later her mother joined her, looking equally bleary-eyed.

They sat in the kitchen, each rocked to the core over the news that threatened everything. The previous evening when Isa had returned she knew immediately that something had happened and her daughter quietly explained the news. They had talked till after midnight, going over everything from the day of the accident, the funeral, the Enquiry, everything; looking for any sign, any possible indicator that could throw the lid open and expose the murder.

'We'll need to talk to Lynda,' Isa finally said. 'She's the only one who really had anything to do with them after Billy's death.

Ann-Marie unhappily acknowledged this, although she didn't want to involve Lynda at all. Didn't want the possibility of Lynda starting to doubt the events that had been previously accepted about Billy's tragic accident. The delicate relationship that she and Lynda were building together since the marriage break-up had pulled them closer together, and she didn't want anything to jeopardise that.

'But, we'll need to be very careful what's *said*', she stressed.

'I'll call her in the morning; I mean *later* in the morning,' Isa said looking at the clock, 'Maybe she can call in on her way back from dropping the boys at school? We can't waste any time, just in case.'

Ann-Marie nodded, 'I'll send her a text at eight,' she said with a yawn.

***

Lynda mobilised quickly, dropping the boys off a whole ten minutes early at school and had arrived with a screech at the farm before nine. After assuring herself that they were both well, if looking haggard, she made herself a coffee and sat down.

'So, what's up?' she asked, ever direct and to the point.

Isa took charge, explaining that the solicitor had been told that a journalist was trying to put together some sensational story about her father's death, and that some of the information she had gained might have come from Uncle Bobby.

Lynda's eyebrows raised in amazement, '*Really?* Uncle Bobby? What would he know? He wasn't here.'

'Well, no, he wasn't, but you know how journalists are, taking one and one and making five just to sell a sensational story,' Isa said. 'You were with them a lot at that time, so we wondered if Bobby had said anything that would shed some light on this. Obviously, we don't want the whole tragedy brought up again, for everyone's sake. Did he say anything to you, at the funeral or he Inquest, or after?'

Lynda remembered the uncomfortable journey in the car to the Inquest. Bobby had been insistent on going, but all she could remember was his pressure on her to persuade them to sell the farm. He'd even said that on the morning of the funeral, *and* when they scattered his ashes.

'Oh!' she gasped, 'In the car on the way to the Inquest, they were arguing, and I'd said I was going to leave early if it went on and on, *sorry mum*; but *this* is the important bit – I got cross and said something like how I didn't understand why they were there, it wasn't as if they were going to *gain anything* from it. He kept on and on about persuading you both to sell the farm.'

Isa and Ann-Marie looked at each other. On more than one occasion Bobby had been pressurising them to sell up, it was true. Could that be enough motivation, if indeed he'd told the journalist anything at all?

Lynda was still confused, 'I don't really understand how the papers would be trying to cover some sort of story about dad's death now? Why *now?* And what sort of story? It was an accident.'

Ann-Marie leaned forward, 'Lynda, newspapers need to make money, and a sensational story sells well, you know that. Muck-raking is what they do, trying to find some tiny detail that might be truthful or not. Bobby might have seen the latest big article in the newpaper and got a bit jealous, felt a bit hard-done to, and just be mouthing off to anyone who would listen. Now, this journalist can see some mileage in that, and is trying to make this a big story. Jim told me he'd got wind that she'd been trying to find out more from the officers who came here when the accident happened.'

Lynda understood all too well. Bobby had used her to persuade her mother and grandmother to sell up, and his friends in the housing trade would have given him a tidy bung. If a story *did* materialise, she might be named; after all she'd sided with them to try and force a sale. Not only would her father's accident come back into the spotlight, with nasty comments about how her mother might have benefited, but she'd look like a scheming gold-digger, and that wouldn't help her divorce or her chances of getting a job. 'I wouldn't put *anything* past Uncle Bobby,' she said firmly.

Ann-Marie picked up her mobile and phoned Jim,

'We think we've worked it out,' she said grimly and repeated what Lynda had told her.

The atmosphere on the farm was muted and brooding, with Roddy avoiding the women and the women waiting for Jim to report back. Lynda rolled her sleeves up and helped with the day's pressing until it was time to collect the boys and she washed and changed ready to leave. Impulsively, she hugged her mother, 'It'll be alright,' she said. 'Don't worry. Call me the minute you hear from Jim. I'm sorry I have to go, but I'll come back tomorrow to help, if you like; after all, what else am I doing?'

Ann-Marie brushed her hair back from her face with a tender gesture, 'I appreciate that, love. We all need to stick together, right now.'

When she had driven off, Ann-Marie took the puppies, together with Bracken and Bramble out onto the lawn outside the taproom. The Red Devil tree was growing strongly, and she grimly recalled that although Billy wasn't actually there underneath it, his presence had returned to haunt the farm. Would she ever be free of him and his malign influence?

The next day Jim arrived in person in time for morning coffee. As his car pulled in, Roddy, who was starting to press the next batch of apples looked up.

'Come inside,' Jim commanded, walking into the house. Lynda, Isa and Ann-Marie were waiting, and without any ceremony he smiled and announced that the story had been stopped in its tracks.

'She's been fired and the story is dead in the water; *you*,' he motioned to Ann-Marie, 'will get a letter of apology from the newspaper, and Bobby has had a stern warning from me.'

Lynda placed a mug of coffee in front of him.

'Bobby had his nose out of joint when he read the weekender story, so *he* contacted her, moaning and causing trouble. He couldn't accept that Billy's death had been an accident, mainly because the business quickly started to recover, and alleged that there must have been some foul play,' Jim shot a knowing look at Ann-Marie and smoothly continued, 'I've been assured by the pathologist *and* the police that they have no intention of reopening the case, and the editor of the newspaper, who is known to me, was horrified that his paper narrowly avoided being involved in a libel case. So, *I* think I deserve something a bit more substantial than a biscuit.

Any chance of some cake, preferably lemon drizzle?' he finished with his usual smiling countenance.

Ann-Marie started to cry, and he got up to hug her. Isa tactfully shooed Roddy and Lynda out of the house, 'Back to work, you two', she ordered, 'there's apples to press and nothing to be seen here.'

***

The week of the barbeque was also the week the puppies were leaving with their new owners. One after the other, families or couples came to collect their little bundles of joy, promising to keep in touch with their progress. Roddy was desolate; the bothy still wasn't habitable as the plumbers had yet again let him down, and the radiators lay stacked against one wall, with the kitchen sink unconnected. He'd failed to deliver, and had to remain in his rented apartment for at least another month.

Lynda's apartment had now been sold, and as a temporary measure, she and the boys had moved into High Glen Farm, as soon as Isa had moved into Bob's house. The boys had been delighted, and were getting underfoot and filling the house with excited chatter and noise, forcing Ann-Marie into a better acquaintance of long division, '*Not* how they used to do it when I was at school,' being her new favourite phrase.

The barbeque had been a resounding success, with the rugby club harvesting and processing all but the very last of the harvest, and dancing the night away to the sound of the Scottish fiddles, drums and keyboard.

Elaine and Sadie spent the night dancing, drinking cocktails and screaming with laughter, encouraging the rugby lads to dance faster and faster, and wilder and wilder. Duncan was keen to join in, but Shona was ensuring that he didn't make a fool of himself, much to his mother's delight; although she had her own hands full with Ewan, who had drunk a *wee* bit too much and was loudly telling anyone who'd listen that he was on a promise tonight.

Roddy deleted Jen Soutar's number from his mobile and blocked her from calling him, his embarrassment at being duped rivalling his embarrassment at the near disaster for his employer. Feeling out of sorts with life generally, he volunteered to puppy-sit the night of the ceilidh, and spent a precious few hours with Troy.

***

Lynda began collecting the rubbish early the next morning, filling the pickup with bottles, and bags full of rubbish to take to the recycling centre. She made coffee for everyone, and then rounded the boys up for school. She rolled her eyes at her mother as she picked up her car keys, 'Roddy has a real case of the blues and a face likes he's been sooking sour plums! You need to put him out o' his misery about that puppy!' she said, striding towards the door.

Ann-Marie sighed, knowing that with just Troy and Willow left in the play-pen she had to make a decision, and so she called Roddy to her office.

He'd been bracing himself for her decision, and stood quietly, determined to accept that for the second time in a week, his heart would be broken.

'When d'you think the plumbers'll finish that central

heating?' she asked him with a sigh.

'They've promised it'll be done and all commissioned by next Monday,' he said quietly, then it's just a case of fitting the kitchen units and the wood-burner. After that it's just decorating. I've been working as hard as I can.'

She looked at him, aware that it had been a hard week for him as well as the family. She recalled something she'd said to Jen Soutar; that the staff were now *extended family*, and that was true. Roddy, Duncan, and Elaine were part of her family now, and Lynda, it appeared had returned to the fold too.

The decision regarding Troy was made, but would Roddy accept it?

'He'll need to be castrated so we don't have any nonsense with the female dogs, of course, and you'll have to train him properly, Roddy. But; he can stay with us until you finish the bothy and move in – with Troy. Troy can stay.'

His eyes shining and unable to say a word, he nodded, gulping down the tears and quickly ran back to the taproom, where he scooped up Troy, who licked his face dry and beat his tiny tail as quickly as Roddy's beating heart.

***

If you have enjoyed Mum's the Word please tell your friends. Book reviews make a huge difference to independent authors like myself, so if you've bought online please DO leave a review - and thank you!

Printed in Great Britain
by Amazon

66614773R00170